Book One of The
by award-winnin

'Here is a rarity –
colour and more t
enthrallingly rea

There is revolution in old Bagdad! When the Government decides to hang the famous Moderate Man the radicals of the Ripe Fruit Party rise up and murder the Caliph – and anarchy ensues.

As parrots fly shrieking through the halls of the great palace, and the shadowy 'That Which Is Within' emerges, the medieval world of *The Arabian Nights* undergoes a violent and vivid mutation.

'Those who have been captivated by the magical tales of *The Thousand and One Nights* will find *Bagdad* irresistible' *Toronto Star*

'Dennis's story of a corrupt fictional kingdom, with its fawning potentates and colourful street life has a ribald humour and modern flavour all its own.'
Macleans

Book Two:
THE PRINCE OF STARS

Born in Kingston, Canada in 1952, Ian Dennis studied English at the University of Toronto where he was the editor of various student literary magazines. He graduated with an MA in 1976 and was awarded the Epstein Literary Award in the same year.

Since then, Ian Dennis has travelled the world and currently works for the Government of Ontario while continuing to write in his spare time.

Ian Dennis is a musician, hockey player and birder. He also enjoys opera.

BAGDAD

◆ IAN DENNIS ◆

UNWIN PAPERBACKS
London   Sydney

First published by Allen & Unwin, 1986
First published by Unwin ®Paperbacks, an imprint of
Unwin Hyman Limited 1987.

© Ian Dennis, 1985

UNWIN HYMAN LIMITED
Denmark House
37–39 Queen Elizabeth Street
London SE1 2QB
and
40 Museum Street, London WC1A 1LU

Allen & Unwin Australia Pty Ltd
8 Napier Street, North Sydney, NSW 2060, Australia

Unwin Paperbacks with Port Nicholson Press
60 Cambridge Terrace, Wellington, New Zealand

British Library Cataloguing in Publication Data

Dennis, Ian
  Bagdad.—(The prince of stars in the
  cavern of time; bk. 1).
I. Title   II. Series
813'.54[F]   PR9199.3.D445
ISBN 0-04-823307-2

Printed in Great Britain by
Cox & Wyman Ltd, Reading.

Contents

1 O Zardin al-Adigrab!

'*That Which is Within must come forth*!' exclaimed Zardin al-Adigrab, leader of the Ripe Fruit Party.

'That Which is Within *shall* come forth!' cried out the Party as one, so that the sound echoed on the garden walls and along the still surface of the waters.

'Let them die who must!' added a single voice.

'Let them live who *will*!' cried the whole Party together again.

'That Which is Within,' said Zardin al-Adigrab, 'lies deep in the heart of the palace. The palace is comely and deceptive, and shimmers with light. That Which is Within is dark and hidden and strong. It is like the interior of a woman. It is like the burning centre of the earth. It strains to be free!'

'It *shall* be free!'

'It moves, it trembles, as before its very birth!' went on the leader. 'It shall break forth from its confines and breathe! Its people shall have it amongst them and shall taste it and touch it even with their mouths and fingers, far and wide! It shall melt the chains of eternity from their minds! It shall power them upward with its relentless fire! That Which is Within shall come forth, and all shall acknowledge it, and love it, and hide from it no longer, but live peacefully and joyously by its rule!'

The leader smiled at his breathless and attentive followers.

'Now let us drink sherbet,' he added.

Everyone reached eagerly for the crystal sherbet glasses that stood before them.

'O sherbet!' cried one. 'Cold, sweet, wet!' There was a sound of drinking.

'O sherbet, tasting of lemons and limes!'

'O sherbet, that makes us go cold behind the eyes, that makes us shiver delightfully!'

'O delightful shivering!' cried several voices.

The Ripe Fruit Party was meeting in a secluded garden on

the outskirts of Bagdad, in the quarter called Rusafah, across the river Tigris from the round city and the palace. The garden was enclosed by a stone wall, just beyond which ran one of the city's many canals, upon whose still waters lay leaves and petals and small branches blown down from the orange trees in the garden by a recent wind. Everything was shady and delicious, cool in the late afternoon sun, scented with orange blossoms and other flowers, and resonant with the trickling and slapping of several fountains. The earth was tiled in porcelain painted with green and orange patterns of leaf and fruit, and all the brightly clad young people sat on ceramic benches, or on mossy stones, and their voices rang musically in the soft air.

'*Zardin al-Adigrab*!' said one of the Party, which was composed equally of youthful men and women. 'Is That Which is Within *love* itself?' The young women were all unveiled.

'Of course,' he answered. 'But it is not *only* that. It is all things, love and hatred and all passions together.'

'All together? All at once?'

Zardin al-Adigrab laughed. He was a man of the most remarkable appearance. You did not know quite how to look at him, because all of him seemed equally alive and expressive and demanding of your attention. You could not simply fix upon his eye, because of the intense beauty of, say, the gleaming white row of toes protruding from his sandal. Only gradually could it be ascertained that his features were clear and perfect, his beard intensely black; that of figure he was slightly below average height, but strong and well formed, and his skin glowed with the warmth of the blood beneath. At the question, as at every passing occurrence, his expression subtly altered from turband to toe-nail, transforming him utterly, and swaying the mood of his audience as well. 'As it *is* truly,' he said, 'so shall it finally become!'

'When That Which is Within comes forth,' asked a young man sitting beside Zardin, 'will all love as I do, and as does my beloved?' His hand was linked to that of the comely young woman who sat next to him. Both wore shirts of white, trimmed in red and gold, and their pale skins were smooth and unmarked. She smiled when he spoke and looked at Zardin al-Adigrab.

'As it *is* truly!' cried he, laughing again. 'For it is not as if That Which is Within is far away, in some other place. I am not a prophet – no man needs a prophet. It is within the palace at our very door, and its stories are the hidden stories that are ever told by women and men. Only soon it will come forth resplendent, and breathe free air!'

The young woman put her arm around the young man's shoulder. 'Is this not resplendent?' she asked in a challenging voice, and pride shone in her eyes.

'As it truly *is*!' replied Zardin al-Adigrab. 'When That Which is Within comes forth, I shall remind you of your question and you shall answer it yourself!'

'Zardin al-Adigrab,' asked someone from the other side of the circle, 'what is the best way of love, and what is the best way of revenge? When That Which is Within comes forth, will all discover them in bliss and joy?'

'I cannot tell you such things!' cried Zardin al-Adigrab. 'For That Which is Within is not a choice of better or best, but merely *is*. There is but what it is – or it denied.'

'What of husbands and wives, and kings and caliphs and rulers, and men and eunuchs?' came another voice. 'What of all these when That Which is Within emerges?'

'That you shall see,' answered Zardin al-Adigrab. 'But I can tell you that What Might Be is always with us, did we only know, were it only to come forth.'

'*O Zardin al-Adigrab!*' cried a dozen voices at once. 'What *is* it? What *is* That Which is Within?'

However, now Zardin al-Adigrab replied nothing, but only profoundly smiled. A very small and almost withered young man who had been dancing restlessly on the verges of the circle, a very small and ill-shaped young man, with colourless eyes and an open mouth, now rushed forward.

'O Zardin al-Adigrab! O Zardin al-Adigrab!' he pleaded. 'There is a *tale* that could be told! And in the tale there is a lie! And in the lie there is a truth! And in the truth there is an answer!'

Zardin al-Adigrab regarded him.

'When That Which is Within emerges,' he said, 'there shall be no more tales.'

'O Zardin al-Adigrab!' cried the whole Party. 'No tales!'

'Nor anything which is not a tale,' concluded the leader.

'O Zardin al-*Adigrab*!' cried the small young man again, terribly agitated, jumping from foot to foot.

'No more lies!' Zardin gaily declared. 'No more truths!'

'Let him tell it, though!' suggested several fresh-faced members.

'He does not *need* to tell it!' Zardin al-Adigrab now spun and angrily admonished them, 'It shall tell *itself*!'

And, even as the words escaped the Ripe Fruit champion's lips, everyone was startled by a sudden desperate hammering at the outer garden door. A voice could be heard, hailing out to him: 'O Zardin al-Adigrab! The storm is breaking! The river is brimming! All is upon us!'

Zardin al-Adigrab sprang to his feet with fiery eyes and commanded the gate be opened. In burst a group of cloaked messengers who cried out tumultuously as follows:

'O Zardin al-Adigrab, we have come from the round city and the palace, where the great square has filled with people! The event is one of the largest import, and most utterly untoward, and it is this: the famous Moderate Man, Salim bin Haubut, has been *hung*, and he swings even now for all to see!'

'*The Moderate Man, hung*!' cried out the Ripe Fruit Party as they crowded about the messengers. 'But this is intolerable and unthinkable! Truly, the Caliph has gone too far in his will!'

Zardin al-Adigrab leapt boldly upon a porcelain bench and there was silence.

'It is as it *is*!' cried he. 'The Moderate Man *was not*, truly, and now is no more! The Caliph's mad usurping realm is laid bare – and he may reign no longer, now we are face to face! Veils of confusion are falling everywhere, falling as from the faces of women, falling like waterfalls – I can see them, I can *feel* them! Veils of light are falling from the sky, bearing the darkness beneath! Falling! Falling! That Which is Within must come forth! That Which is Within *shall* come forth!'

'O Zardin al-Adigrab! O Zardin al-Adigrab!' shouted the Party, dancing about him now in ecstasy.

With a surprising movement Zardin bounded from the bench and soared to the top of the garden wall.

'At dawn tomorrow you shall hear my call!' he exclaimed. 'Come to me in the round city, in the courtyard of the populace, in the very palace itself! Come to me at the rending of the gates, and you yourselves shall see That Which is Within come forth! For in that very hour it shall feel the sun once more!'

Then amidst the wild cheers and cries of his followers, the leader jumped down from the wall into a small boat and was poled rapidly away along the canal by two young men who scrambled hurriedly after him. So quickly did he vanish, that when the main body of the Party had rushed to the wall and clambered up to look over, all they found were several little circles of orange petal spinning on the dusky surface of the water.

As they climbed slowly back down into the garden an uncertain silence fell upon them.

'But how can this be about the Moderate Man, and tell us of his end,' asked someone presently of the messengers.

2 Concerning the Last Hours of Salim bin Haubut

There came to the door of the Moderate Man a certain person richly dressed in purple silk and diamonds, girded up with jewelled chains, and wearing a turband ornamented by an enormous sapphire.

Bowing courteously and giving greetings, he informed him that the Caliph desired his presence upon the instant to discuss matters of national importance.

Just as they stood speaking the small daughter and small son of the Moderate Man came running and clattering into the foyer.

'Father!' they cried. 'Where are all the people from the streets? Have they gone to a meeting again?'

'Yes, so I imagine,' said he in a mild voice.

'Do you not know where the people go then, when they go to a meeting?' asked the purple messenger of the children.

'They go to the round city, to the great courtyard of the Caliph's palace,' said the children.

'Do you not know what they do there?'

'They have a meeting,' replied the children.

'Have you never been?' asked the messenger. 'To see for yourself?'

'Father does not allow it,' said they.

'Well, he is a moderate man,' said the messenger.

'So everyone says,' agreed the children. 'And we believe it is true.'

'Now, however,' said the visitor, turning to Salim bin Haubut, 'perhaps we should make our haste, as the Caliph, I am sure, must grow impatient to hear your views.'

'Haste, even towards the Caliph himself,' slowly responded he, 'is perhaps not *always* best.'

'But it is not a judgement which we ourselves have any right to make, I think ...' suggested the messenger delicately.

'Father!' said the children, who had not left. 'We would have a new singing bird, a green one!'

'When I am through at the palace,' said he, 'I shall perhaps be able to get you one. Now, however, I would take a certain water pipe to smoke while I converse with the Caliph. Pray go quickly and get it for me, the smallest yellow one that is in my chest.'

'The moments, the moments, the minutes,' said the messenger softly, as if to himself, 'pass, expire, fly away, so rapidly!'

'Indeed they do!' agreed the Moderate Man, gesturing to his children to hurry and do his bidding. 'Indeed they do. But on the whole, I should say, neither too fast, nor quite fast enough.'

'Faster for some, and slower for others,' observed the purple man. 'I might even suggest, O worthy Moderate Man, slow perhaps for the Caliph, and fast for those that should obey his commands!'

'But for the Caliph, O worthy messenger,' replied he, 'in his exalted existence, may we not hope that they do not move at all? But patience is ever rewarded. Observe, here return my eager servants.' For at that moment his children came running back to him with the pipe.

'Now,' said the Moderate Man, bending to take it and kiss each of them, 'I bid you only to tell your eunuch that the hour and the day and the season are now right to plant my two little flowering trees – those that I received from the King of Java. Tell him to look for high and dry ground for them, plenteous sunlight, and not too many birds. We have discussed the topic, as he will recollect.' Then he turned to the purple messenger, saying, 'And I come, as you see.'

So they went out and the purple man led Salim bin Haubut quickly through unfrequented streets until they came to the walls of Madinat al-Salam, the round city, where they entered through the southern gate. Without pausing he directed him on across the wide expanses of paving to the palace of the Caliph, but swerved from the great entrances of the ambassadors and went in instead at a small door on the western side. Here they passed through a quiet garden, and a marbled porch, and came into a long row of richly furnished rooms. Then, hurrying on, they took such a series of turnings and twistings and climbed and descended such an assortment of staircases, that even the Moderate Man, who had been to the palace so often before, was soon completely confused, and did not know where he was. He saw many sights that were new and strange to him in its cool chambers: lovely foreign women lounging unveiled beside trickling fountains, beautiful statues and images embedded with jewels and star-like designs, unearthly animals and birds drousing in the partial sun of skylights, aged books and jars and rows of weapons sitting untouched in dim forgotten rooms. But he could stop and admire none of them because the man in purple silk continued always to carry him rapidly forward. Somewhere far off, he detected also a sound he had never heard in other parts of the palace, a dull steady pounding that reverberated queerly through the quiet halls.

Finally they arrived in a darkened chamber, at the end of which stood two imposing brass doors. Above them, in glittering golden characters, was written:

> O Mere Mortal Man at This Absolute Door
> Know This Thou Masters and Ask No More!

'How very remarkable!' said the Moderate Man. 'And most fearsome, of course.'

The messenger began to adjust his elegant clothing, and generally neaten himself, so the Moderate Man, following his example, did likewise. 'Am I fit to be presented to the Auspicious Eyes?' asked he then of his host.

'Yes, if in your heart you are properly humble,' said the purple man, surveying him. '*Are* you?'

'Oh yes,' replied the Moderate Man. 'Humble I most certainly am.'

'Then you must go first,' said the other, approaching the portal, and giving two sharp raps. The doors swung open before him and Salim bin Haubut stepped calmly out into the brilliant noonday sun. Two men took him firmly by the arms, while a third dropped a noose over his head and drew it snug.

'Ah,' said the Moderate Man, 'I see.'

The man in purple, who had followed a few steps behind, came forward and smiled and made a slight respectful bow. Then he turned to the vast assemblage of people which was waiting silently in the courtyard.

'*Salim bin Haubut!*' his solitary voice sang out clearly in the gleaming air. 'Lord Protector of the Orange Trees and Honorary Emir of Abyssinia! The famous *Moderate Man!*'

The stillness was broken by a huge roar of applause which arose like the roar of the sea, and echoed repeatedly from the four surrounding walls of the palace.

The two men at his sides guided Salim bin Haubut a little farther out on to the platform and began to busy themselves undoing his outer garments, while a bare-breasted slave in yellow pants came politely forward to offer him sweetmeats and coffee from a golden tray.

'Thank you,' said the Moderate Man. 'Perhaps later.' The slave sniggered and retired.

The man in purple, after conferring briefly with some of the other personages who were gathered on the long, marbled platform, gestured for quiet.

'O Bagdad,' he began again, when he could be heard, 'I need hardly rehearse for you the long list of achievements, honours, and qualities which ornament the reputation of my guest on our platform today.'

'It is well known that they are all as the dung of a goat, O Purple Man!' shouted a voice from the crowd.

'*We* hate him!' added someone else, approvingly.

'For thirty-five years he has earned fame and the admiration of all here in the Abode of Peace,' went on the Purple Man. 'His voice has been respected everywhere, and his word has ever soothed the waters of strife among us.'

'He never soothed *me*!' objected a member of the audience.

'He was a detestable middleman, a compromiser and a milksop!' shouted a woman.

'They should be hung, obviously!'

'He began his career,' proceeded the Purple Man, all unruffled, 'as a modest merchant of fruits, and as he sold always good wares, and as his debts always were paid, so men came gradually to lay great trust in him.'

'He was probably a thief even then!'

'*I* never trusted him!'

'I recall, he used to sell bad oranges, and cause horrible indigestion among the innocent!'

'He was notorious for that kind of thing!'

'Then,' went on the Purple Man, 'in an hour of our need, the Commander of the Faithful called him forth to supply with oranges the army that went to face the terrible Khazar Khans, and this he did so well, and with so moderate a profit, that the Leader was disposed to appoint him Lord Protector of the Royal Orange Trees, a function which all men agree has been carried out with the most perfect devotion ever since.'

'O come! come! Purple Man!'

'The Khazar Khans weren't even defeated, they were bought off with a huge ransom!'

'I don't agree about the Royal Orange Trees either!'

'They have gone into an obvious decline!'

'He purloins public oranges for his own use, at a fixed rate! We have facts!'

'In the past few decades,' continued the Purple Man, smiling indulgently, 'Salim bin Haubut has steadily risen in the offices of responsibility and esteem, taking successively many important commissions from both the Caliph and the Kazis of the city. In every position he assumed and every task he undertook, his characteristic virtues have shone forth with a proverbial consistency.'

'Name *one*!'

'For every issue and question that arose in our mind, his greatest and most precious function was always that, by a mere taking of his position, he seemed to make all that was said on many sides infinitely more *comprehensible*. Even if he was invariably deemed wrong, every man fell either on one side of him or the other, and all could measure their own opinion by its distance from his veritable Northern-Star of moderation.'

The populace were beside themselves with exasperation at this portrayal of the Moderate Man. '*No! No! No!*' was their largely incoherent chant.

'For this, and a multitude of other signal services,' continued the Purple Man, unmoved, 'the Caliph was pleased graciously to bestow upon him an honorary Emirate in the mystical realm of Abyssinia, as the most appropriate reward for a pragmatism and restraint so unwavering as to be almost otherworldly.'

The gradually increasing clamour of their voices now finally did as it had threatened to do, and burst out into another loud, confused roar, which persisted many minutes. The Purple Man took the opportunity to refresh himself with a swallow of sherbet from a leather bottle handed him by a slave.

Meanwhile, the hangmen had disrobed the Moderate Man, leaving him dressed only in his long shirt, and were bending his arms gently behind his body and binding them there. But as this was being done, instead of listening attentively to what was being said, he appeared to let his mind wander, and gazed thoughtfully about the courtyard.

Filling its grand squareness was a veritable liquid rainbow of people, soft yet bright, a surface that swelled and undulated on the stone floors with the motion of oceanic waters at dawn or dusk, or the tops of trees in the wind, seen from the crest of a high promontory. The day was hot and their intense perfumes rose and mingled with the sound of their voices, the low continuous rushing that reverberated from the many-arched galleries and whispered in the drooping greenery along the white walls, the gorgeous crustings of decoration that everywhere proclaimed the limitless magnificence of Caliph, Court and Populace. Over all, on tall rods the brilliant pennants hung motionless in the wavering golden air.

'How vividly the people smell!' remarked he aloud to himself. 'They rise in your nostrils quite unlike attargul or incense or any other exotic fragrance. But as you try to look at them, they glimmer and flicker, dissolve and reform in patches and patterns in the sunlight. As for this sound, it sounds like the absent sea echoing in a seashell, vaguely roaring like a vacuum in your ears, confusing, indeed, bemusing you as you listen. It is, truly, a most curious sensation, perhaps even worth it after all, to be able to stand here this way.'

He stopped speaking and turned, aware suddenly that the Purple Man, and beyond him the Populace, were looking at him. The Purple Man smiled and winked encouragingly.

The Moderate Man smiled back, and asked, in a low voice, 'Is the Caliph angry with me, do you suppose?'

'Oh *no*,' replied the Purple Man. 'Assuredly he is not! I have it on the best of authorities that he holds no rancour in this or any other matter, but is only pursuing the spiritual health of his realm. In fact, I am not at all sure he is even *aware* of your fate today, although I feel confident it is as he would have wanted it.'

'He always thought me *beneficial* to the health of the realm before,' said the Moderate Man sadly.

'Yes, yes, and perhaps you were, in a temporary way,' agreed the other, 'but he seeks now a more permanent reordering of things. It is possible that he plans to create a *new* moderate man closer to his own position.'

'He will perhaps find that difficult,' whispered back Salim bin Haubut gravely. 'A true moderate man is born and not made. What is more, I am sorely afraid that the Commander of the Faithful misjudges the location of the authentically moderate idea in this era. It is much further from him than he might wish.'

'I believe,' said the Purple Man, 'that the Commander of the Faithful seeks a resolution *beyond* mere politics, or eras!'

'Oh well,' said the Moderate Man, 'that is very good, up to a certain point.'

As the populace was now beginning to grow murmurous, the Purple Man turned back to them and waved his arms imperiously. Quickly a polite silence fell. He gestured to have the prisoner brought forward to a specific point at the edge of the platform, as a long boom, with rope and pulley, was swung out over their heads. He raised and spread his hands. His voice became ceremonious and official:

'*Thou knowest then* this man, Salim bin Haubut, and are assembled here to witness him,' he called out, 'that he may hide himself no longer, but reveal himself as he is truly, for the eyes of the body to see, for the hands of the body to touch! Let all that has been promised now be given! Let all the facts of him come into our possession, to be ours utterly, no more to be denied! Let the firm earth rise solidly beneath our feet, as we remove it justly and naturally out from under his. Let there be no gods among us!'

'*Let what will, come to pass!*' rumbled the people solemnly, as one great voice.

'It is the number! It is the moment!' cried out a cracked and aged tongue. 'It is the day!'

'The man is but a great airy cloud of pretence and mythology!' cried another. 'He has no *real* stature, no *real* achievements! Hang him, *hang* him!'

'Moderation is vanity! Moderation is pride! Moderation is arrogance! Moderation is selfishness! Let moderation take its fall with the rest!'

'Let us have absolutes! This city is everywhere overrun with half-measures! Let the pure live! Let the compromisers hang!'

'Yes, tell us, O Salim bin Haubut, is the *universe* moderate? Is the *world* moderate?'

Suddenly a section of the crowd, swaying together in a kind of dance, and stamping their feet, began to chant in unison:

> They say he is a *Good Man*
> They say he is a *Good Man*
> Let him carry that weight!
> They say he is a *Good Man*
> They say he is a *Good Man*
> We have seen them twist,
> We have seen them try to fly,
> We have seen them cry.
> They say he is a Good Man
> They say he is a Good Man
> Let us see a *Good Man* die!

Let him carry that weight.
Let him carry that weight!
Let us see how *Good Men hang*!

To this sound was added the high whistle of pipes and
flutes, and the twanging of zithers, as various elements of the
crowd began, in an unconcerted manner, to play on the
different instruments they had brought with them.

Numerous voices attempted to make themselves heard.

'He *deserves* to hang! He *deserves* it!'

'Besides, he is not a good man at all! He's vain, conceited,
proud, and has exalted himself above us and at our expense!'

'It is true! It is true! Look at the fussy way he cuts his
beard! Look at his silly turband!'

'That's *not* what we meant!'

Arguments and scuffles occurred here and there. Once a
voice began to howl:

'*Salim bin Haubut was born on the vernal and must die on
the autumnal equinox!*'

'No, no, he should die *now*!'

'Today *is* the autumnal equinox!'

'No it isn't!'

'Yes it is!'

And then, propelled skywards on the shoulders of his
fiercely proud, bustling, elbowing family, a young man
holding a scroll, a scholar, started reciting hurriedly, in a
high, piping voice:

Why I think Salim bin Haubut
should be hanged

I think it is a very interesting and instructive thing to see
any man hang, because of what it can teach about the
human character.

However often we see a hanging, there is always a
surprise. It is never the same. Every man reveals his true
nature in the way that he behaves in a situation like this one
of having a rope around his neck and him about to be
released. Some days a man whom you think would be

brave isn't, but he only calls out and begs for mercy. Some days also a real coward says nothing but just smiles.

Now some people might point out that it is rather a difficult thing for the person who is going to be hanged. What does he get out of it? But however unfortunate it might be for this hanged person, the rest of the populace gets something they enjoy and have a right to see and can profit from. You have to die anyway.

Now there is also the question of this man Salim bin Haubut, who is called 'the moderate man'. But whether or not he is moderate, it has nothing to do with whether or not he is going to hang. When we hang a man for violating women and murdering them, such as we hanged last Tuesday on Murderer's Day, we say he is an unmoderate man. But we hang him anyway, even though we call him, Ulab bin Whoever his father was, the 'unmoderate man'.

Therefore in our conclusions we would just have to say that there is no real good reason why Salim bin Haubut should be hanged. And also hangings can be very instructive and useful as well as protect the city from dangerous criminals. So I think he should hang.

'Incidently,' whispered the Purple Man, leaning over to Salim bin Haubut, 'I do hope you are satisfied with the arrangements we have made today.'

'Well,' replied he, 'I will say that I am glad at least that it was not designated a Veil Day.'

The Purple Man giggled rather loudly and covered his mouth with his hand.

Of all the public hanging days, the Veil Day was the most eagerly awaited, although none had been declared for many years. On this day women only were allowed in the sealed courtyard and, so it was rumoured, were permitted to unclothe themselves, except for their veil, before the hanging man. He too was said to be naked. It was supposed to be a chastisement for crimes of extreme puritanism. Every aspect of the ceremony was much discussed among the populace of Bagdad, for whom such things were the object of the liveliest interest.

'It *was* considered,' murmured the Purple Man, 'but was decided to be a little too . . . "unmoderate".' He giggled once more. 'It might have been held five days from today, but there was *much* impatience.'

'I am flattered,' said the Moderate Man.

'*Or*,' went on the other, 'it might have been held three days *ago*, but that was directly after the hanging of the six underviziers, which would have detracted from its importance.'

'That was considerate.'

'Not at all,' replied the Purple Man. 'I'm sure the Caliph would wish everyone to see his intentions clearly in the matter. This is a Significant or Symbolic Person's Day.'

'We object that Salim bin Haubut was certainly *not* a good man!' a number of voices were continuing to shout.

'We do not like compromises and half-truths!'

'Things are not moving fast enough!'

'Hang him! At once!'

'No! No! Everything is moving too *quickly*, and it is largely his fault! He has not stood steadfast!'

'He should have been hung years ago!'

'He should have been hung as soon as he was born!'

'His mother should have been hung before she bore him!'

Someone began playing tabla drums in a frenzy.

'O Bagdad!' reproved the Purple Man mildly, and smiled and held up his hands for quiet. 'Bagdad, please.'

Only gradually did the sound abate.

'Now, O people, as you know, it is the Caliph and Council's desire that your opinions on every matter be fully heard and considered. I call upon you to produce one official representative to express your feelings on the subject of hanging Salim bin Haubut. These will be duly recorded and read aloud at the next Council meeting.'

A rumble of discussion went through the throng. The rumble then abruptly rose to a roar of recognition and excitement as a strange, lump-like figure lifted itself totteringly above them on long stilts, staggering and leaning for a moment before gaining balance.

'The Burned Man!' exclaimed dozens of voices at once.

He was indeed a very odd-looking personage, with a bizarre and troubling smile. The features that twisted from side to side as he looked swayingly about himself were remarkably disfigured, and the hands that clenched the knobs of the stilts were so swollen and wrinkled as to be nearly unrecognisable as hands. His nose was melted almost all away, and his eyes were hidden within the unnatural folds of a deep scar-tissue that covered his entire face and neck. He was called the Burned Man – though none could say for sure that he had ever been subjected to fire – and arriving in his position of prominence, he but smiled and smiled, turning to the people on all sides of him, biding his moment carefully. The voices continued to rise in anticipation, then slowly fell to a hush. At last, in a loud, harsh voice, much like the growling of a dog, he commenced, saying:

'*Well well*, bin Haubut, *here* you *are*.'

Salim bin Haubut had been gazing abstractedly at a certain flagpole from which a long purple pennant, embroidered with the silver stars of the court party, hung down sparkling in the sun. At these words, however, he too turned and looked curiously at the Burned Man.

'*Well well well*,' repeated the man on the stilts slowly, and then stopped, so that everyone was very eager to hear what he might say next. There was a pause. He continued to smile, swaying slightly, taking little stuttering steps this way and that, to retain his balance.

'Now,' whispered the Purple Man to Salim bin Haubut after a moment, 'is there any matter in which I might be able to oblige you, after . . . *after*?'

'What say you?' responded he. 'Oh, well no, I think not. Though I am grateful, you may be sure.'

'Well, *well*,' said the Burned Man again, even more slowly, and still he smiled. There was another pause.

'Surely there is some small thing I might do,' pressed the Purple Man in an uneasy whisper. 'Some small service I might perform as a means of demonstrating my great respect for an honourable figure such as yourself. I have arranged already for a singing bird, for your children. But as for yourself, come, think on it, I pray you do.'

'Well,' said Salim bin Haubut, and appeared to search his mind.

'Well, well, so it has come to this,' said the Burned Man, and once again stopped his discourse and smiled. The people were breathlessly silent.

'Perhaps there *is* one small thing you might undertake,' said the Moderate Man reflectively, 'if you were of an inclination to do it.'

'O please, my dearest Salim bin Haubut, do but name the thing,' whispered the Purple Man with all possible sincerity. 'It is a point with me to do some small service always.'

'Very well,' said the Moderate Man. 'As I believe you saw, I carried with me today a certain golden pipe. You should still find it among my outer robes. It is a remarkable pipe, this pipe, and it has with it a remarkable story, though there is no leisure for that. But did you carry it to the Caliph for me as a present, and a token of my respect and my emptiness of animosity, I would be most grateful. Tell him that, while I do not believe his hanging of me the *correct* decision, I am sure he did it out of the best possible motives and for the best possible reasons.'

'O Salim bin Haubut!' cried the Purple Man in admiration. 'How moderate this is!'

'Well, well,' growled the Burned Man. 'Now you are going to hang. To hang by your neck from a rope.'

The Purple Man went as he had been instructed to the slave who held the garments of Salim bin Haubut and withdrew the pipe from a small purse. It was, in fact, made of the finest gold, except for the stem and mouthpiece, which appeared to be ebony. Embossed on the sides was a pattern of stars and tree branches of the strangest and most intricate workmanship, and around this were two bands of writing in elegant but enigmatical characters of a sort he had never seen before. This unusual object caused the Purple Man the greatest curiosity, and he returned to his companion and whispered: 'O honoured friend, what *is* this fine pipe, and where does it come from? It is quite unlike any in common usage here in Bagdad. What is the story you spoke of?'

'I suppose,' said Salim bin Haubut in a wistful manner, 'I shall not have the opportunity to tell you that.'

'We must all come to this sooner or later, bin Haubut,' gloated the Burned Man.

'Oh *do* tell me the story,' implored the Purple Man, 'or otherwise, how else shall it ever be known? Tell it as a part of your speech, which I am sure will oblige the populace also, for they are no great lovers of speeches without a tale in them.'

'Well,' said the Moderate Man, 'I suppose I ought to oblige the populace where I can. If as you say, they would like to hear this account, even if it were to delay my hanging a few moments, then perhaps I shall add it to my remarks.'

'Well and generously spoken, O Moderate Man!' said the other, with obvious feeling.

'And here you are. Well well well.' The Burned Man laughed, as a dog barks. 'Well well well.'

'I think we have had enough of *this*,' said the Purple Man, and stepping briskly forward he gestured to a pair of huge slaves, one black and one white, who loitered unobtrusively in the crowd. These at once arose and pushed forcefully through the press until they reached the Burned Man. Each then seized a stilt and wrenched sharply in opposite directions. The Burned Man flipped head over heels in the air, before landing with a thump on the heads of nearby members of the shrieking populace. This done, the slaves retrieved him and knocked him roughly to the ground as he tried (still smiling, and saying 'Well, well,') to rise to his feet, and sat on him, folding their arms and wordlessly defying any attempt to come to his aid.

At such a precipitant action an angry roar of displeasure rose up from the people, and each man looked fiercely and questioningly at his neighbour while an uncertain tension filled the atmosphere.

'Now, Bagdad,' said the Purple Man, ignoring this, 'since there are no more opinions to be expressed, it is only appropriate, as you know, that we hear some words from our guest himself.'

Silence descended slowly on the populace, as they gradually resigned themselves to listening to what Salim bin Haubut would say. The Moderate Man, thus called upon, shuffled forward a little (his rope vibrating lazily above him) and cleared his throat to speak.

'While all of these sentiments have been very interesting and sincere, O Bagdad,' he began in a calm voice, 'we both of us are aware, of course, that they have nothing at all to do with why I am going to be hanged today. This is (as you also know) purely a matter of the Amendment I recently suggested to the Proposal of Zardin al-Adigrab and his Ripe Fruit Party.'

A gasp of surprise escaped the people at this audacity. But Salim bin Haubut did not heed.

'Now,' he continued, 'this Amendment has caused the greatest amount of crying out and concern (and, I may say, criticism and personal contumely) in our city these past weeks, so as almost to threaten our peace and the balance of our minds. However, I would like to take this opportunity to assure you that I believe still, despite the present turn of affairs, that it is a good Amendment, and appropriate, and that I regard it as the most important (if certainly the ultimate) work of my career.'

'*O Salim bin Haubut*,' breathed out great numbers. '*Shame*!'

'Allow me please to make clear certain misconceptions on the subject,' continued he, in mild, reasonable tones. 'I have heard rumours to the effect that I know the nature of That Which is Within, and even, in fact, that I have seen it. This is quite untrue. My Amendment was based upon no understanding of the possible effects of the Proposal, but only upon my continuing belief in *gradual change towards moderate ends* (for which, as I suppose, I am named). I must say, as well, that I do not believe Zardin al-Adigrab knows any more about this object than I do (if it *is* an object), and his now celebrated call for the final and utter bringing forth of what, please remember only out of ignorance, we call "That Which is Within the Caliph's Walls", springs similarly from *his* beliefs about the nature of change in the world, rather than from any specific knowledge. Also, of course, while the Commander of the Faithful does presumably know what it is that rests in his inner sanctuary, *his* will is guided by his perception of his own absolute power, or what, I should say, he regards as his absolute power. I have the profoundest respect (you must understand) for both these positions, even though I am aware that both worthy personages would fiercely deny that they are "positions" at all.

'However, in amending the Proposal to allow for limited access on a regular basis to That Which is Within, I hoped to suggest a solution (perhaps of an interim nature) which would produce satisfaction in all. Now, I am perfectly sensible that it has produced satisfaction in absolutely none. But I wish to persist (perhaps even to the point of 'immoderation', if I may say so) and recommend it to you once more, and to the Caliph, and to Zardin al-Adigrab, because (as I have said) I believe it is the best solution possible. This in fact, is my advice. (And I have explained my reasoning.) I cannot safely predict what Fate will unfold for you once I am hung, so I believe this is everything I have to say on the matter.'

There was now renewed rumbling among the populace, and a voice saying, 'Your reasoning is not reasoning at all! It is just *habit*, O hypocrite!' Then the Moderate Man began to speak again in a different vein.

'It is traditional now,' said he, 'for the man in my position to make a few remarks of a more personal kind. This is no doubt a fairly good tradition, though not, of course, necessarily to be followed *too* slavishly. However, as most of the essential elements of my life are so well perceived by all,' and here he smiled towards the populace, 'and since I have a request to tell a story about a certain golden smoking-pipe, I think I will neglect most of my confessional duties today.' At this there was a round of applause.

'Instead, since the story I am going to tell involves me personally, I will let it speak for itself – except on one particular. This is a matter of a certain charge frequently laid upon me these many years, and against which I wish to make a final defence. It has been said always, that I am *indecisive*, and that this is the true meaning of my moderation. It has been said, similarly, that I am merely *afraid*. Now, I can see that there is probably some truth in these criticisms. But let me please say in explanation that I have always hesitated to make decisions and judgements on matters about which I lacked sufficient information and understanding. *But*, that I have always felt at some point in my life (perhaps, even, the ultimate moment of my life), all the conflicting evidences *would* resolve themselves, and I *would* be able firmly to decide on every important question. You see, it was not that I was merely *indecisive*, it was that I was *waiting*, for illumination, and that, since one did not *yet* know all, moderation was the safest and most reasonable course to follow in the meanwhile.'

'The meanwhile is over, Salim bin Haubut!' shouted harsh voices.

'Indeed,' cried out one, 'now *hang moderately* if you can, Salim bin Haubut!'

'Well, this much said, I shall tell the story of the pipe, if you would like to hear it,' offered the Moderate Man. The populace indicated generally that it would.

The Tale of the Magical Golden Pipe

There once was a *fig merchant* in *Bagdad* who had two children, a son named *Salim* and a daughter named *Shelnar*. These two children, being twins, were inseparably joined by bonds of affection and familiarity so strong that no adult could ever imagine them. All day long they played about the chambers and garden of their father's modest house, and it seemed there was not a single possible delight they could desire more from existence, so contented were they with their situation, and with each other.

One day this *fig merchant* acquired at an unusually good rate a large number of fig bundles from the *al-Kharkh* market-place. His warehouse being nearly full already, and no caravan available that week to carry them where they might be handsomely sold, the *merchant* found it necessary to store one batch of figs in the back of his own garden. So he ordered his slaves to carry some of the fig bundles there, and those they chanced to pick up were some which had recently arrived by ship from remote islands in the eastern sea.

At first, little *Salim* and *Shelnar* were not much concerned with the figs in the garden as they went peacefully about their habitual amusements. However, when they came to play a game in which they were merchants of jewels, freely trading vast fortunes with the greatest civility and generosity, *Salim* wished aloud that they had some objects that might stand as tokens for the precious stones they could only imagine. 'Brother!' cried out *Shelnar* then. 'Stay here and I shall get some of those figs we saw in the garden, and these will serve our need very perfectly!' And she waited no other word but jumped up immediately and ran out the door of the chamber.

Left alone in the room, *Salim* began, as he often did, to reflect upon his feelings. 'How very happy I am today!' said he. 'How perfectly pleasant it is to be here playing with *Shelnar* in the cool house! How perfect she is too, and how lovely a place the world is to live in!' And he smiled, and laughed aloud, and sat in the room for a long while thinking these thoughts to himself.

Then, in the midst of this revery, he remembered that his sister had only gone out for a moment to get figs, and yet had still not returned. In sudden uncertainty he jumped up and went out to look for her. When he came into the garden he saw her straight away, lying still and dead on the grass near where the bundles were stacked up. There had been a spider – in reality a *jinni* in disguise – hidden in the figs, and his strong resentment at being transported unawares so far from his native island had provoked him to sting the first person he came upon. He lurked yet in a nearby tree, his appetite for revenge not entirely satisfied, and watched *Salim* approach the body of his sister.

'O *Shelnar*!' cried he. 'Do not be *dead*!' He then immediately plunged into an intense fit of grief, whose passion no adult could ever feel. Multitudes of tears rushed from his eyes and he sat down suddenly on the grass and wailed in an anguished voice, 'O *Shelnar*! O my happiness! Where are you gone!' His soul was seared with hot pains, and, perhaps worst of all, he simply could not comprehend what had happened, nor imagine how it could ever change.

'I was but a moment ago perfectly happy, and it was going to last forever! Now I am perfectly desolate with no happiness at all, and now *this* will last forever!'

So utterly mournful was he, and so reduced by grief, that even the cold foreign heart of the *jinni* was touched by pangs of pity and remorse. He began very slightly to regret slaying *Shelnar*, and to contemplate sparing the life of her *brother*. He resolved at any rate to discover more about the people of this country before he decided. Changing into the shape of a man he descended from the tree and presented himself to *Salim*, ordering him sternly to cease his lamentations. *Salim* looked up in surprise at the rich and brilliant figure which had appeared from nowhere, and spoken to him in such imposing tones of command. But while any grown adult would have been terrified into silence by so strange and elegant a perso- nage, all dressed in golden silks and jewels, with rings in his ears and nose, the little boy was not in the least affected but quickly began to weep again, even as he stared at the *jinni*.

'Be quiet while I speak!' cried the *jinni*, more loudly, but *Salim* wept on, caring nothing because of the depth of his sorrow. The *jinni* was entirely unaccustomed to being disobeyed, and he stamped his foot in exasperation, that was also a mixture of renewed animosity towards *Salim*, and feelings of guilty remorse for having caused such extravagant pain. 'Stop this noise!' cried he once more, but again without effect, and he considered angrily to himself how dreadfully unfair it was to have been first of all kidnapped from his homeland while sleeping, and then provoked so terribly in a strange country when he merely took his rightful revenge.

'Why are you crying!' he demanded, searching about in

his thoughts for a different method of approaching the *boy*. 'What is there to cry about?'

'I am crying,' said *Salim*, without ceasing to do so, 'because there is nothing but unhappiness in the world, and no more happiness in it anywhere!'

'Well, that's ridiculous, and quite untrue,' said the *jinni* bluntly; but it achieved nothing, as *Salim* continued to weep. This aggravated the *jinni* further, so that he wished to blast the boy from existence, especially as he found that he could not, in good conscience, quite do so. 'Tell me the one thing in the world you wish,' he cried out in desperation, 'and I shall grant it you, if only you stop this noise.'

'I wish for *Shelnar* to rise up and continue the game we were playing,' sobbed *Salim*, which did little to modify the rage of the *jinni*. Like all such spirits and personages, he was able to take away life, but as unable as you or me to create it.

'Well this must be stopped, by any possible method!' hissed he to himself, and drew from his robes a small golden pipe. 'Take this, and put it between your lips!' he commanded, but *Salim* did nothing but weep, so the *jinni* was forced to bend down and thrust it into the boy's mouth himself.

At the very touch of the pipe on the little *child*'s lips a remarkable transformation overcame him! He felt a coolness close upon his heart, and the tears that were obscuring the garden magically melted from his view. At once, the very *world* looked different; peace descended upon him, and he was filled with a new understanding. He stopped crying immediately, and he said, 'Well, if there is much that is bad in life, then there is also much that is good. I must only be patient, I suppose, and each will replace the other in turn.'

'Very good then,' said the *jinni*, and took the pipe from him, though the vision did not fade. 'Are you happier now?' he asked, somewhat impatiently.

'Well, yes, *happier*,' said *Salim*, 'if not exactly *happy*, if you see what I mean. I am not unhappy, or happy.'

'This is exceeding wisdom in one so young,' said the *jinni*. 'You ought to thank me.'

'Yes,' said *Salim*, 'I do thank you for this, although I do not thank you for being the cause of my *sister*'s death, as I imagine you are. But even out of evil comes some good, it seems.'

'Allah be praised,' marvelled the *jinni* in a sarcastic manner, 'but the pipe creates some wondrous philosophy in the people of this country!'

'Now, however, I can face the death of my *sister* with resignation,' went on the *boy*, 'and consider that, having been done, it can hardly be undone. And do I not have myself, and my revered *father* left? I shall retain my present frame of mind, and go forth into life and try to influence affairs what slight distance I can for the better.'

'Very commendable,' commented the *jinni*. 'However, it will be somewhat more difficult than you may imagine, because the effects of this pipe you have tasted last but a single hour, and then fade as if they never were.'

At these words little *Salim* did something which amazed the *jinni* very much, and this was suddenly to throw himself to the ground and fervently kiss his feet, crying out in beseeching tones: 'O great *master*, then you must please *please* give me that pipe of yours, that I may taste it again in an hour!' 'What is this?' thought the *jinni* to himself, 'How can it be? The pipe has ever before dispelled even the fear of its own absence. Yet this creature can feel it, even through the golden veils! What strange hearts have these talkative people out here!'

'O do not deny me this, do not, do not!' begged *Salim* most desperately and humbly, so that tears started up in his eyes once more.

'Not this!' groaned the *jinni* aloud. 'Desist, I say! The pipe is not mine to give! What is more, it can be touched only once in every day, or it loses all its powers! It cannot protect you from all things!'

But *Salim* would not give over his entreaties, and the *jinni*, surprised at the sudden reversal, grew even more exasperated than before. 'If I give it to you,' he cried, 'how shall I preserve my *own* peace of mind, in moments of need?'

'O you are very wise, great *master*!' responded *Salim*, 'and such a thing would never be hard for you!' and he fell to kissing the *jinni*'s feet all the more earnestly. Then suddenly an evil coldness came over the *jinni*, and he yearned strongly to kill the *boy*, yet once more he hesitated. Then a better idea came to him, and he thought, 'I shall give him another pipe, which will only increase his torment!' But just at that moment his eye fell upon the body of *Shelnar*, and he hesitated yet again in his design.

'O but the complications of this country are such to drive a spirit to madness!' he cried in a fury. 'Is *nothing* simple and direct!' Then he rose up suddenly in the air, and hovered, still uncertain in his mind whether or not to kill *Salim*. But finally, in a passion, he flung down the pipe on to the grass beside the wailing *boy*, and called out, 'Here then! *Here*! Perhaps there is no worse I can do you anyway, in this worthless, tiresome, unclear place!' And on the instant he disappeared in a jet of purple smoke.

Salim seized the pipe and, catching it up close to his person, directly became calm and resigned once again. When his *father* and the servants came out into the garden a while later and discovered *Shelnar* dead, *Salim* told them only the story of the *spider*, as he judged it would do no good to tell any more, at which they might demand the pipe of him. Through eyes streaming with tears for his dead *daughter*, *Salim*'s *father* saw the *boy*'s mild attitude with much surprise, and said to him, 'You are very moderate, O my son, at the death of your dear *sister*.'

'Yes, my *father*', said *Salim*, 'for I see that it must have been as Allah wishes, and its meaning is probably beyond our understanding.' And even in the midst of his dreadful grief, the *fig merchant* could not help wondering greatly at this response.

At the end of an hour, *Salim* discreetly excused himself from his *father* and the whole party of wailing *servants* and *neighbourfolk*, saying that he wished to mourn and pray in solitude. Then he went straight to a secret place he knew in the house, where he was struck instantly with pangs of terrible grief that caused him to weep and cry aloud, just as the rest did. But presently he discovered that one characteristic the *jinni* attributed to the pipe did not hold entirely true, at least for him: the effects of its comfort *did* linger, for though the grief returned, it did not return with quite the same inconsolable fury it had an hour before. Somehow the most desperate moment seemed past, and with weeping he was able gradually to ease the bitterness of his heart. Nothing else could have prevented him from hazarding another touch of the pipe, whatever the *jinni* had said about the effects this would have produced.

Each morning for a year after, the *boy* touched the magical pipe once to his lips, and thus was able to begin his day with calmness, and so endure his loss. Then at the end of this period, when his *father* and the rest of the household put aside the tokens of mourning, *Salim* hid away his pipe, and went out into the world with a clear countenance.

As he grew older, the boy's *father* gave much thought as to what career his *son* should undertake. The marketing of figs, while prosperous enough, did not seem to him a sufficiently worthy activity for someone of such solid common sense and modest perseverance as *Salim*. One day at business in *al-Kharkh*, however, he chanced to buy a goodly number of fresh oranges at a bargain price. As his *son* had just then reached the age proper to independence, he made a present of them, saying: 'Here is your entrance into the life of trade and business. Take these oranges and go to *Basrah*, and see whether you may not make a good account of them, for I have heard they are mightily short of this fruit now in that city.'

Salim set about this task immediately, and with the greatest of eagerness, hiring a ship and setting out for *Basrah* the very same day. As soon as he arrived there, he discovered that oranges were indeed in very short supply, and a quick survey assured him that he could command a magnificent price for his shipment. His mind filled up with impetuous visions of the profit that could be made, and the joy and pride his *father* would feel at his success, and he hurried back to where he had moored his vessel, calling as he went for porters to bear the oranges.

Before he arrived there, however, he was accosted suddenly on the street by a voice he had never before heard. Looking up, he found his path blocked by a tall and imperious *personage*, whose gesture for his attention the young man could by no means ignore. He was dressed in the finest and most exotic of silks, and his hands sparkled with diamonds and sapphires, while all around him stood a party of the tallest, richest clad and most elegant *slaves* the *fig merchant*'s *son* had ever seen. 'Are you the vendor of *oranges* lately arrived from *Bagdad*?' he demanded in a loud voice.

'Yes,' replied *Salim*, 'I am he that has brought oranges.'

'Know then,' said the *personage*, 'that great good fortune has befallen you, and that wealth, position, and a bliss as near to absolute as the world may offer are available for your enjoyment if you will but stretch out your hand to take them!' *Salim* was greatly amazed by these words, and hastened to inquire what their speaker had meant by them, and how they could relate to one as humble as himself.

'Your confusion is not to be wondered at,' came the reply, 'but you may soon know all, if there is somewhere we might comfortably convene to speak of our business.'

Being full of a natural curiosity, the *young man* did not hesitate to lead the *stranger* to his ship, which was docked nearby, to seat him as well as he could in his own cabin, and bring forth a collation of coffee and sweetmeats and oranges.

'You doubtless crave to understand how I am able to offer you immense riches and fame and other benefits,' began the *man*, when he had eaten. 'But I assure you I *can*, as you shall hear:

'I am an emissary from the most potent and magnificent monarch of the world, the *Emperor of China*, and I bring from that earth-striding *Power* a demand of the greatest possible urgency. The realm of *China*, due to the workings of a malevolent *spirit*, has been deprived this year of its customary orange crops, and the *king*'s entire household, including his famous retinue of the one hundred most beauteous *slaves* in the world, have fallen deathly ill for lack of this fruit, which in better seasons used to constitute their entire diet. To any man who can soon enough arrive with sufficient oranges to save them (especially the *slaves*) the *king* has unconditionally offered one tenth of his inconceivable riches, and the hand of his second or third *daughter* in marriage, maidens, you may be assured, who have neither of them equals in the universe for beauty and pleasantness (unless it be his first *daughter*, who is *not* offered). Many lands have I scoured for oranges, but the *spirit*'s curse (spread by an evil variety of moth) has stretched far and wide, even to this port of *Basrah*, where, as you know, an orange shortage is acute. However, now that I have found you, all you need do is set sail immediately with me in this ship, and with God's aid we shall reach the shores of *China* and claim the reward!'

At this discourse, the mind of *Salim* filled up with shining visions of possible felicity, and accounts of the fabulous wealth of the famous sea merchant *Sinbad* echoed in his ears, so that he was almost overcome and could not speak. The *emissary* smiled and said: 'I can see that a choice of this superb nature cannot be made instantly. I shall withdraw some minutes to allow you to contemplate your good fortune, and what you stand to gain. When you are decided call me – but do not delay, for tide and wind are right, and we must hurry if we are to save the suffering in *China*.' Then he went up on the deck to confer with his *minions*, leaving *Salim* alone in his cabin.

'O this is a strange and wonderful opportunity indeed!' cried he to himself. 'First, it is an unparalleled chance to achieve immense wealth and happiness and the good regard of my father! But then, secondly, might it not also be an invitation to great dangers and peril? How may I trust this *emissary*? Suppose he were a *pirate*, desiring only to lure me out into the open ocean where he could

attack me and seize my ship and my oranges and cast me
into the water with an anchor tied round my body? Or
suppose, even if he were sincere, that we were ship-
wrecked, perhaps by some great storm raised by that vile
spirit who poisoned the oranges in the first place? It seems
possible either to gain all, or lose all utterly! What kind of
terrible choice is this!'

As he paced about his cabin in a manner near distracted
with the difficulty of his decision, *Salim*'s eye fell inadvertently on the golden pipe the *jinni* had given him, where it
lay among his possessions. Hardly thinking what he did,
with a small movement he took it up and put it to his
mouth and began to suck on it as he walked to and fro.

'Well,' he said then, 'there is certainly no end of unexpected and perhaps unimaginable things that *could*
happen to one on as long and difficult a voyage as this,
though none of them necessarily *will* happen. On the
other hand, it is clear that if I remain here in *Basrah*, I *will*
sell my oranges to good advantage, I *will* make a handsome profit and an admirable start in the business of being
a merchant, and my *father will* be quite pleased with me.
If I go to *China*, any number of things might not be as
they now appear. It might be too late, and all the *king*'s
slaves may be discovered dead already. Or they might
have already been succoured by someone else who arrived
first with oranges, which would greatly decrease the profit
I might gain from mine. Or, even, however fair the *king*'s
second and third *daughters* were, I might accidently fall
in love with his *first daughter* and bring down the full
force of his vast displeasure upon me!'

Gradually, as the pipe worked its magical effect upon
Salim, he grew more and more peaceful at heart, and
settled down upon a pillow with a sigh, saying: 'Well,
now, no man shall deny that this offer of the *Emperor of
China* is exceedingly generous and attractive. And I have
no doubt that in his age the weatherbeaten *Sinbad* did
richly enjoy his hard-gotten wealth. But am *I* the man for
such things as these? Am *I* the man to marry the *daughter*
of one of the two greatest monarchs of the world? No, no,

Salim bin Haubut, this is something we are quite unable to imagine!'

And so eventually he called the *emissary*, and told him he would not go, and the *emissary*, greatly surprised and disappointed, left him immediately and found another, more venturesome *sea captain* who accepted his offer. *Salim* took care then to sell all his cargo to this *man* at the greatest possible profit, and shortly returned to his *father* who expressed great pride and pleasure at his success, and showed him how best to spend his windfall in establishing himself as a merchant. Not a word did *Salim* ever say to him concerning the elegant *stranger* he had met from *China*.

Some years after this remarkable event in the life of *Salim bin Haubut*, the youngest of the *slaves* of a certain rich *cloth merchant* in *Bagdad* gave birth to an unexpected *daughter*. The merchant, whose name was *Firuz Hamaden*, was greatly incensed with this occurrence, because he could not remember having had congress with the *slave* in the year past. As soon as he heard that she had been taken to bed he rushed in upon her, even as she was surrounded by her attendant ladies, and began to accuse her of vile practices, and of lying with his house-servants.

'O my master,' cried out the *slave*, whose name was *Nassileh Moon-Hair*, 'do not so upbraid me! You yourself lay with me when you were much with wine, these nine months past!'

But the *merchant* cursed her as a harlot and swore it was not so, and demanded her to remind him of the circumstances if it were.

'O my master,' said *Nassileh*, weeping, 'do you not remember calling all your *slaves* together, and boasting that you could satisfy every one of us in a single night? Before you fell asleep you took indiscriminately several, and I was one of these.'

Firuz was enraged to hear of such folly, nor could he remember the slightest detail of it, so he grew more and more convinced of the *concubine*'s crime, and he screamed at her so that flecks of white foam fell upon his beard. 'Who was it?' cried he. 'Who was it, that I may revenge myself of this dishonour! Was it one of my idling porters, then?'

'O my master,' wept *Nassileh* once more, 'it was none but you yourself!' And then just at that moment the newborn babe began to cry in the arms of one of the women. Taken in a fit of ungovernable rage, the merchant *Firuz* seized the child and rushed with it out into his garden and drowned it in a fountain. Then he ran from room to room of his house calling to his *secretary* to bring him a scimitar.

The members of his household were very familiar with these furies of their master *Firuz*, and knew they could do nothing to calm him until the humour vanished of its own accord. But *Nassileh* was a favourite among them because of her sweet and placid nature (and because, not being much loved by the *master*, she was resented by no one), so they wished to protect her from his vengeance if they could, knowing that soon enough he would become just and reasonable once more. While the *secretary* risked a terrible beating by trying to delay him with remonstrances, the other *slaves* wrapped up the weeping *girl*, though she could hardly yet walk, and hurried her out of a back gateway and down the street.

It was only barely done when *Firuz* knocked his *secretary* senseless with a great blow of his hand and took up a weapon. When he could not find *Nassileh* he slew one of his *porters* in the yard instead, and commanded that she be searched for everywhere, promising instant death to any who were discovered to have helped her. Then he went into the room where she slept and cut apart all her clothes and her couch and smeared the tapestries and curtains with the *porter*'s blood from his sword and smashed her brushes and combs and whatever else he could find that was hers, weeping with wrath as he did. Then finally he threw down the scimitar and fell asleep on her couch, even where it was all chopped and ragged from his anger, and slept there without rising for three days.

Meanwhile, when the two *slaves* had hurried *Nassileh* to the next street, they were forced to stop and consider the peril of their situation. 'O sister,' said one to the other, 'our *master*'s retribution will be terrible indeed if he discovers we are gone. We must return quickly!' 'But what is *Nassileh Moon-Hair* to do?' cried the other. 'For how can we help her now?' 'She must look somewhere for refuge,' said the first, 'for she will never be safe in our home, and if we go further ourselves, our death will be the only reward.'

Nassileh, all this while, said nothing to their distressed words, but only wept in great confusion.

'You must go somewhere for help, or you will die,' said the *first slave* in agitation. 'But you must not tell them who you are or cause them any great trouble or the truth will surely come to our master and it will go badly for all of us.' 'Yes, yes,' cried the other, 'go somewhere and be a maid or a servant, but take care that you do not make a nuisance of yourself. Make yourself small and insignificant and all may be well.' 'We must run back now,' cried the first. 'We are sorry *Nassileh Moon-Hair*, but we must, or we will die. Go out and look for help.' 'Come sister!' cried the other, and hastily kissing *Nassileh*, they ran back down the street.

After standing motionless for several minutes, *Nassileh* turned and went slowly forward and walked through the streets of *Bagdad*, turning here and there, regardless of direction, but knocking upon no door. The people of the city looked at her with surprise, for she was unveiled and her clothes were bloody, but she did not speak to them, but only wept and wailed quietly to herself.

Finally, after she had gone about for many hours, some children who were playing in a lane took her by the hems of her garment and led her to the *Cady* of their neighbourhood. The venerable *Cady* knew not what to think of her, and asked her many questions to which she made no answer, but only looked at him with wide weeping eyes like a madwoman, which is what he took her to be. But she could not be left to the mercy of the street, and he called to mind that the *servants* of a certain household nearby were of a particularly kind-hearted and passionate disposition, and that their *master* was a prosperous and generous man, and so decided to convey her there and see if they would not shelter her.

This was the house of *Salim bin Haubut* and when his *porter* answered he greeted them with all the politeness and compassion the *Cady* could have hoped for. As they stood conversing, the last of *Nassileh*'s strength finally left her and she fell down. Many hands quickly lifted her up and carried her in and laid her upon a sofa, while some of the *servants* who clamoured about them in excitement ran to inform the *merchant* himself.

The *young man* was at this period rising rapidly in the world of *al-Kharkh* commerce, so that it was his good fortune to enjoy the society of many worthy and respected men. Some of these he had this day with him, sitting together and drinking wine and savouring a treat of rare and exotic fruits that one of *Salim*'s ships had recently brought him from the east. The conversation among them was light and pleasant and witty, and two of his companions were just teasing their *host* upon having attained all the attributes of a man of substance except the possession of a wife, when several servants burst in to inform him of the arrival of a strange *girl* at his door. 'Oh, *bin Haubut*!' cried his friends then. 'Here she has come now, at the very mention of the subject! Clever God has brought you your partner without delay – on our advice, of course!' *Salim* laughed with them at this jest, and rose excusing himself, going immediately to see what it was all about.

After the *Cady* had explained to him everything he knew, his *servants* conducted him to the sofa where *Nassileh* lay and the *young man* gazed upon his unlooked-for *visitor*. He was utterly stupified by what he saw. The *girl* lay still, breathing uneasily, her sickly pallor terrible to see and her strange silver-veined black hair strewen in disorder all around her. But in her face there shone a delicacy which was infinitely touching to him, and fire kindled suddenly in his heart. All of her form and pitiable condition moved him as no other lady ever had, and, in short, upon the instant he fell deeply in love with her.

When he could collect himself and speak, he turned to his *servants* and said: 'What do you think is the trouble with her?' 'O master, master!' cried several of his *women* at once. 'It is clear to us that, unaccountable though it may seem, the *lady* has only this very day given birth to a child!' 'A child!' cried *Salim* in surprise, and also somewhat in dismay. 'How can this be? Where is the child, and can it be that she is some other man's, then?' 'O master!' cried back the *servants* all at once. 'We fear it must be so, but that she must someways have been terribly spurned, and no doubt most unjustly! Let us keep and protect her, for the goodness of Allah! O master, let us do this!'

'Well, we shall,' responded *Salim*, his eager eyes returning again to the *girl*, 'at least until we discover from her the nature of her trouble. Carry her into an inner chamber, and tend her with the utmost care. Report to me immediately of any rising or falling of her condition.' With glad cries everyone assured him that they would and set about the task with fervour, while *Salim*, leaving with much difficulty, made his way back to his guests, his heart full of love's tumult.

When he re-entered the room where the other *merchants* were set they all turned to look at him and, before he could begin a short speech of apology for the interruption, all burst suddenly into a loud clamouring: '*Oh Oh! Oh! Bin Haubut!*' they cried, with vast amusement and delight. 'Worthy gentlemen—' began *Salim*, but he was allowed to go no further, as all his friends had risen with alacrity from the table and were patting him on the shoulders and laughing and shouting, '*Oh-Oh, Oh! Oh Bin Haubut!*' Then, without further ceremony they began to take their leave of him, letting him speak or explain nothing, but only responding, '*Oh! Oh!*' repeatedly, and laughing and kissing him affectionately. At length he could do nothing but submit and, when all had gone, return again to the chamber where *Nassileh* lay.

For two days she remained unaware of all things, and her life was very near to extinct, so that *Salim* and his *servants* were in anguish for fear that she might die and never speak to them. Then finally she began to improve, and a natural blush to come very slowly back to her face, so that presently she even awoke and opened her eyes and saw those who were crowded around her.

'Sweet surprising *Lady*,' said *Salim* then, in the kindest, most comforting voice, 'we little expected your arrival at this house, but we are very happy to have you, and we shall keep you safe and tend to all of your needs as long as you may desire.'

At these words the eyes of *Nassileh* turned to *Salim*, but she said nothing. The *orange merchant* quickly had his people bring food and drink for the *lady*, which she was much in need of. He watched in satisfaction as she ate and drank some little bit, and waited until she was well finished before speaking again.

'This food, dear *lady*, will slowly restore you to full health, with Allah's help. Now that you are finished, may I inquire of you only some few details of your situation, your name, and your sad plight, in order that we may help you further?' But, to *Salim*'s astonishment, the *girl* replied nothing, though she met his eyes unflinchingly, and tiny droplets appeared on her face from some hidden emotion which he could not guess.

'Dear *sister*,' attempted then one of the *serving women*, 'you may trust us, be sure of that. We can see you were but recently delivered of a child, but we know not from whence you came, nor where that child may be.' At these words *Nassileh* turned to fix her gaze upon the *woman*, and her eyes filled instantly with tears that did not flood over but only lay like small pools, and she made no sound.

All the *servants* then began to make a great uproar of pity and wonder, but their *master* quickly quietened them and said, 'Well, we shall no more press upon matters which are very grievous to you at this moment. It would be far better for you now to rest and tomorrow we shall converse again.'

But the morrow was no different, nor was the next day, and though the *merchant* ever attempted to inspire her confidence and demonstrate with a thousand small smiles and gestures gentle and polite that his regard and sincerity outstripped even that of a *host*, still long weeks went by and the *girl*'s lips were not unsealed. Again and again *Salim* pondered her shy and enigmatic demeanour, and courteously greeted her and received in return the seeming acknowledgement of her eyes, and an intense and unspeaking gaze that made him speculate a thousand unsettling yet delicious things. But she said nothing. When her strength returned, she arose wordlessly and began to work with the others as a maid.

So it continued for months, and the love he held for the *lady* grew and grew within him, so that he hardly knew what to do, and began to neglect his business and his household, both of which were fortunately well taken care of by his very capable *steward* and his zealous and irrepressible *servants*.

In the household of the *cloth merchant*, meanwhile, matters had taken a different turn. When *Firuz Hamaden* arose from his long sleep, all traces of his fury had disappeared, and he looked around at the ruination of his *slave*'s chamber with great confusion. 'What is this that I have done?' he cried forlornly to his *secretary*, who stood near, awaiting his commands. 'O master, a general rage was upon you,' he replied, and then explained, in as discreet a way as was possible, what had occurred.

'O this is very foul and terrible in me, to do such things!' wailed *Firuz*, when he had heard all. 'O great sorrow it is, that I cannot ever control myself, and am ever causing myself and others such pain! O poor *Nassileh Moon-Hair*, what has become of you!'

'This we do not know, O master, for it seems she has quite fled,' replied the *secretary*.

'I must make amends to her, that is certain!' exclaimed the *merchant*. 'I must heap wealth and affection on her, I must redeem my terrible hastiness at once, *at once*, for I cannot by any means endure this anguish I am presently feeling!'

'O master,' replied his *servant*, 'we know not even if she lives or has died.'

'Find her out!' cried *Firuz*, 'or it shall be your woe! Spare no effort, but bring her to me! I shall marry her, certainly, to cleanse myself of this thing!'

And so immediately, the *secretary* sent for all the household, but was delayed by his *master*. 'Only note this,' added he. 'Let no one describe the circumstances, but merely inquire for her by name. It may be that my infamy has not been noised abroad, and perhaps the sweet *Nassileh* will even now have refrained from sullying the good repute of her *master*.' And with this further command, the *secretary* dispatched the *servants* to look for her. But for many days they came back empty-handed.

After *Nassileh Moon-Hair* had lived in the house of *Salim bin Haubut* for one half of a year, the young *orange merchant* decided he could abide no longer the feelings teeming in his heart. One day, as he sat with her at a meal, he summoned all possible courage and spoke as follows:

'O most strange and wonderful *Lady*, I can conceal the truth no more. I know that I am most likely not at all worthy of you, and that I do not even know your name, and I fear that what I am going to say will cause you the greatest imaginable offence, but say it I must. Since you have not, or can not speak to dissuade me from my course, I confess I have fallen deeply in love with you, and I now wish to marry you. This is what I have pondered thoroughly and feel must be so. All is prepared for the ceremony to occur tomorrow, and I wait only for you to indicate the strongest possible unwillingness for it to happen, for this is all that may prevent it.' But even at these passionate words *Nassileh* still said nothing, but only met *Salim*'s eyes with her usual intense stare that was dark with unfathomable feelings. 'Well, then it shall be so,' said *Salim* presently, and rose and left her.

The next day everyone in the household rose early, and the *women* greeted *Nassileh* with joy and bathed her and worked industriously to prepare her long silver-streaked black hair. *Salim* bathed as well, and, giving orders for the best of foods and wine to be bought, and invitations to be sent out to all of his acquaintance, dressed himself in his richest clothes. Soon guests began to arrive, and many presents were given and received, and *Salim* was congratulated on the joy of his heart, while musicians began to play and his *servants* rushed here and there in delight. All day the festival went on and the food and wine was consumed. In the evening *Nassileh* was brought to *Salim* where he sat, dressed in a robe of saffron, with pearls around her neck and jasmine in her hair, and he sat her beside him with the utmost pride and pleasure. And she seemed to acknowledge the greetings of the *guests* with solemn modesty, even though she still spoke not.

Finally, after singing and dancing and eating of the finest sort, all the *guests* rose and saluted the *couple* and left in a happy company. *Salim* took his *bride* by the hand and went into the chamber prepared for them, accompanied by the *household* who chattered and argued loudly as they lit the lamps and warmed the bed and helped undress *Nassileh*. When at last they could be encouraged to leave however, and the *bride* was in her bed, *Salim* found a deep uneasiness come over him.

'*My fairest mistress*.' he said, 'I fervently hope that everything today has been to your satisfaction. Now that I am your *husband*, I am at liberty, of course, to command you in all things, but please realise that as I am also your *lover* there is nothing you may not ask of me and be sure to receive.' To this, though she regarded him steadily, she said nothing.

'I have proceeded on this business entirely upon my own will,' said he, then, 'which I feel I was certainly right to do. But I cannot help but be sensible how little I know what your true inclinations are. Did you wish this to happen? Are you glad to be my wife?' Still, *Nassileh* said no word.

'I almost fear that your silence rebukes me,' said *Salim*. 'It is like the silence of the earth that will not give out a clue to its truth. I have heard it before. I wonder, is it that I am unworthy to know? Or is it simply that there is no truth until it comes directly before men's eyes? Is it that you care not about this marriage today, that you simply have no inclination one way or another?' But she answered not, and a long silence fell upon them, during which the listening *servants*, assuming the best, gradually became bored and retired.

Then at length, *Salim* said, 'You cannot, I imagine, fail to recognise that to be married to me is of the greatest possible material advantage to you. You, before, had nothing, and were unable to speak for what was rightfully yours. You had no status from which to derive respect. All these things I now freely and gratefully give you, because it happens that I am able to do so, and they matter little to me.' She did not blink or look away at all as he said these words, but only regarded him with earnestness.

'As for the love that is normal and desired between *husbands* and *wives*,' he went on, 'you can see, I hope, that I hold it for you, but you must realise that I shall never command it *from* you in return. I have had my will in marrying you, but for the conjugal delights we might enjoy together, I have decided to wait upon some sign from you, some indication that they are desired by you. Otherwise I will assume that they are only obnoxious or offensive, or that you cannot partake in them for some reason that you are unable to tell me. It is not necessary for you to speak articulately, but only give me some manner of sign.' Then he turned and looked to her and she returned his look from where she lay in bed and their eyes were locked for many long minutes. But he could not fathom her, and so he rose and blew out the lamps and retired quietly to his own bed.

The next night he went to her once again, and asked the same question, and once again she seemed to give no answer. As before, after some minutes, he returned to his own bed without having touched her.

On the third night he came again and asked his question, and the result was the same. But *Salim* was most agitated in spirit, and as he extinguished the lamps and prepared to leave, he felt as though all the heaviness of passion in his heart had drained into his limbs and was forcibly preventing him from moving. For many long minutes he stood frozen in the darkness, and she lay absolutely still in her bed, the silver shining in her hair the only thing he could see.

Finally, his will deserted him utterly and he turned and went back and entered the bed with her and embraced her with the greatest imaginable eagerness. Throughout the night he enjoyed her, and thought of nothing else. When the sun rose and the *servants* bustled in to open the window gratings, he found himself lying with his arms around her and their faces close together on the pillows. He could smell her. The warmth of her body beat upon his body, and the faintly bitter taste of her mouth, like a faint taste of lemons, was in his own mouth. She smiled a very small smile at him and her eyes looked modestly away. He rose full of joy and went about his daily business.

For many days *Salim* came thus at night to his *wife*'s chamber and enjoyed her in his passion, until one night as they lay together half-asleep he was utterly amazed and stupefied to hear her suddenly speak in his ear in a low whisper.

'O my master *Salim*,' she said, 'I am with child by thee.'

'O my beloved!' cried out he. 'You speak! O tell me my *joy*, my *wife*, tell me thy name!'

'I am *Nassileh Moon-Hair*,' whispered she.

Salim bounded in joy from the bed and rushed out shouting, 'O my *household*! O my *servants*! My *wife* speaks! and her name is *Nassileh Moon-Hair*! and she is with child by me!' And when everyone shouting and clamouring and weeping with happiness had gathered in the bedroom, she responded shyly to their entreaties and in a very low voice told them briefly all her history, except to whom she had belonged.

Then she whispered, 'I have my baby back within me,' and all were moved to tears and joy and there were loud cries for food and wine and celebrations, which were immediately produced and which the happy *household* enjoyed right there in the bedchamber, even at that very late hour.

However, the next day the truth of her identity

inevitably escaped into the market-place and was heard by the *servants* of *Firuz Hamaden* who rushed back at once to tell his *secretary* the news. The *secretary*, who knew of *Salim bin Haubut* and knew him to be a lesser merchant than his own *master*, immediately dressed himself in the finest silks he could find, and put jewelled accoutrements around himself, and gathering together a retinue of servants, set out for the *orange merchant*'s house.

Salim bin Haubut could not help but be impressed by the dignity and elegance of the unexpected and jewel-laden visitor who was ushered into his foyer. 'Respected sir,' said he, 'you may be sure that anything I can do to be of service I gladly will.'

The *secretary* acknowledged this deference with only the slightest bow of his head, and then replied in a cool and official manner: 'Worthy *orange merchant*,' said he, 'I am surprised that you do not know me, or that you do not know my errand. But since you ask how you may oblige me, I will tell you directly: I am come to claim for my *master*, one of the greatest men in all our city, indeed in all the realms of our all-powerful *Caliph*, a certain *article* of his property which I have reason to believe is presently within this house.'

Salim, much surprised at this speech, asked immediately, 'What article might this be, since I am sure I do not know of its existence?'

'It is a *slave*', replied the *secretary*, coolly. 'One *Nassileh Moon-Hair*, property of the great *Firuz Hamaden*, who escaped some months past, and who must now be returned without delay.'

Salim was all aghast when he heard these awful words and for many moments his mind was in utter turmoil, especially because he was very aware of the power and magnificence of the great *Firuz Hamaden*. Then finally he spoke, saying, 'I hardly know how this can be, but I must assure you that the *lady* in question shall never be relinquished by me. You must take me straight away to your *master*, and we shall talk the matter out.'

So the *secretary* carried *Salim* back to the house of his

master, and after first advising *Firuz* of the *orange merchant*'s condition, brought him into the *great man*'s presence.

'I hear,' commenced *Firuz*, ignoring the greeting proferred him by *Salim*, 'that you have a *slave-girl* of mine, that I want back.'

'Nay, honoured sir,' responded *Salim*, 'the *lady* you speak of is my beloved and treasured *wife*.'

'She can hardly be my *slave* and your *wife* at the same moment,' said *Firuz*. 'She could only be your *wife* if I had given her or sold her to you, which I have not done and will not do, because I have done the poor creature a grievous injury, and I cannot rest until I have compensated her and married her myself.'

'I am sure that all the world admires such generous sentiments,' replied *Salim* respectfully, 'but you can hardly marry her unless I divorce her first, which I certainly will not do, because she is very dear to me, and is also bearing my child.'

'No *divorce* is necessary,' responded *Firuz*, in growing anger, 'because she is in no way *married*. Only a slave's *master* can marry a slave. You have stolen her from me, and you must return her to me!'

'I am sure my *master* is sensible of the trouble you have gone to,' broke in the *secretary*, 'in the keeping of this *slave*, and of feeding her and clothing her. He will, I have no doubt, be quite willing to recompense you very richly for this service, indeed, much more richly than a man like yourself could ever look to expect, especially from such a negligible affair.'

'No amount of money,' replied *Salim* steadfastly, 'could recompense me for this *woman*, so it need not be offered.

'I on the other hand, since I seem inadvertently to have married another man's *property*, would be very willing to recompense *him* for the loss, to the best of my ability.'

'This is in no ways acceptable to my *master*,' replied the *secretary*, 'for he is set upon having her back, and nothing else will answer.'

'How can this be!' cried out *Salim* suddenly to *Firuz*.

'You would have killed her when you had her last, and even when she was yours, she was not at all your favourite or much looked on by you!'

'I am a man of deep feelings!' responded *Firuz* in outrage. 'And my feelings often carry me to great heights of passion which ordinary men do not know! Such a passion led me once to threaten her life, but now another and opposite passion has filled me with remorse, and I will not rest until she is returned to me, so that I may do my duty towards her. I am overcome with pity now for her, and I must have her back, so that I may wrap her in forgiving tenderness. Until I do I shall be the most miserable of men, which I will by no means abide!'

'This may be and be and be!' replied *Salim* wildly. 'And you may be great and passionate and you may be all that you are, but I say still that you shall not have her!'

'It seems this is a matter we cannot here decide,' said the *secretary* then. 'So let us call in one of the *Caliph*'s own ministers of justice, and let him give us a ruling on the problem.' This was agreed to by both *merchants*, for *Salim* felt certain of the rightness of his case, as did *Firuz*, who also was confident in the power of his name, and neither was willing to concede to the other.

Accordingly, an urgent message was sent to the court of the *Caliph*, and it was promptly answered by the appearance of the *Second Grand Under-Vizier* himself, who called first of all for *Nassileh Moon-Hair* to be produced, who was the object of the quarrel, and this was done. Then he listened with the greatest possible care and deliberation to both sides of the argument. When both were finished, he stood silently in contemplation for many minutes, then finally he spoke as follows:

'This is a matter which is not at all easily decided, and one of a sort I have never seen before. As a matter of law, it is a question of whether *ownership* shall take precedence over *marriage*. To whom does a *woman* truly belong? Does not *Firuz* lose his title to her, by attempting her death and driving her from his home? Does not *Salim*'s marriage to her remain void, because he has not recompensed the original owner and because she was never properly his to marry? Surely she belongs to neither! As to the matter of *feelings*, which the *Caliph* bids all of his *servants* never to forget, esecially when the law is unclear, there seems to me no answer supplied by them either. Both of these men are overcome by *passions*, and who is to say which is more true? Do they not both partake of guilt and falsehood to some certain degree? And how should a man judge the passions: by their strength? by their purity? by the actions they inspire? or by their rectitude in the eyes of God? I shall not pretend to have the eyes of God.

'For this reason I have chosen a third way of resolving this question, which it seems you have been unable to resort to on your own judgement. And that is to ask *Nassileh Moon-Hair* herself, and allow *her* to decide completely to which of these *merchants*, if either, she will go.'

At once all eyes turned to *Nassileh*, who had been listening to all the proceedings and arguments with the greatest possible anguish and distress, weeping all the while, and whispering that she was of no consequence and did not want all the trouble that was being created about her. At the words of the *Under-Vizier* she stopped weeping and stood stock-still, gazing at those around her with horror-filled eyes.

Then suddenly *Firuz* fell down upon his knees before her and began loudly to implore her to choose him, and promised her great comforts and honours and benefits and assured her of the prosperity of her *child*. *Salim*, who expected to be chosen immediately, was made wild by this action of his *rival*, and he cried out to *Nassileh* and tried to meet her eyes. But he saw only the same strange mute stare with which she had responded to his questions before her pregnancy! Terrified, he too fell upon his knees before her and began shouting to her of his love and respect and all that he could provide, attempting to drown out the *other*.

But *Nassileh* only covered her mouth with her hands and wept, looking wildly from one to the next, as the din was increased by the shouting of both *Firuz*'s and *Salim*'s servants and the voice of the *Under-Vizier* calling at them all to desist. Finally she ran madly from the room into the back of *Firuz*'s house, and when she was followed she was found to have returned to her old chamber, which her first *master* had fully repaired and hung with rich curtains and laid with gorgeous carpets. This the *Under-Vizier* took as a sign that she had chosen *Firuz* and he awarded her to him, and ordered *Salim* to return forthwith to his own house.

Salim could not think to do other than as he was told, being in a state of unspeakable dismay and shock. As soon as he arrived once again in his own surroundings he burst into anguished tears and sobs and began to beat his breast and cry out, 'What! What! Have I been dreaming! Can this possibly have happened!' All of his *household* were no less distraught than their *master* and they quickly added their cries and lamentations to his own. Presently, however, they began to wax fierce and defiant and called upon *Salim* to lead them back to *Firuz*'s house that they might try to rescue *Nassileh* by force. Some of the *women* advised *Salim* to try to enter the house in disguise, so that he could talk his *wife* out of her folly. Still others urged that they rush to the *Caliph* himself and beg on their knees for his wise intervention.

But *Salim* for the present was so torn with grief and confusion that he knew not which of these plans to pursue. His *servants* rushed everywhere tearing their hair and arguing amongst themselves and sharpening weapons, until he bid them carry him to the sofa in his own chamber (for he found he could not walk) where he would rest and try to think upon the situation.

When they had done this and *Salim* was alone the true import of what *Nassileh* had done struck even more deeply at his heart, and he began to grieve immeasurably. But straight away this very grief reminded him of other, earlier trials, and at once the memory of the peace that had entered his soul at those moments came to his mind. He did not hesitate, but reached instantly for the golden pipe where it lay long disused among his things.

'O power of this pipe,' he whispered, 'whatever is thy

source, let thy might be equal to the keenest anguish ever suffered by any mortal man!' And he put the pipe between his lips, where it shortly began to take effect. The tears retreated back into the depths of his eyes, and his wild moans subsided gradually into sighs, and presently *Salim* began to reason this way to himself:

'All these plans suggested by my good-hearted *slaves* are but vain, and bound to fail, that much is clear. Would the *Caliph* contradict his own *Vizier*? Could our little force prevail against the savage power of the great *Firuz Hamaden* and his extensive household? I should think certainly not.

'As for talking to *Nassileh Moon-Hair*, where is the sense in that? Is that not the whole problem, after all, that she has not chosen me? There is no point in pursuing a woman who has not chosen to be with you, for what is the value of *love* which does not choose to bestow itself, but is only forced to comply, or argued into existence against the *beloved*'s will? One may resist anything and everything in nature, except this: when a woman makes her choice. This one must accept, or what is the value of what may be gained?

'I see that I have made a very immense error in this whole matter, and this is probably the source of all my grief and loss! *I have not waited for a sign.* I have gone forward out of pride or will or desire, and inevitably crushed the very thing I wished most to have. If I have lost *Nassileh Moon-Hair* it is because I did not wait, but went ahead and took my desire. All else followed from that, and has not Allah paid me back precisely in kind for my fault?'

So *Salim* made no further effort to recover his *wife*, but did his best to calm his household and turn their minds back to the ordinary businesses of life. The next day he sent formal notification to *Firuz Hamaden* that he divorced her, and plunged himself once more into the buying and selling of oranges. On many occasions he was stricken with remorse and doubt, so that he had need to resort to the golden pipe every evening for ten years. But gradually he was able to put her from his mind, and he married a handsome and well-to-do *lady* who was of a cheerful and self-possessed disposition and who (he made certain) took him quite as freely as he did her. By her he had two fine *children* who gave him the greatest possible pleasure, and his *friends* and *neighbours* congratulated him (again) upon his wise choices and his prudent marriage. He was open and friendly with every man in *Bagdad* except *Firuz Hamaden*, who eventually died a violent death at the hands of one of his own *slaves*. It was only then that it was learned that he had murdered *Nassileh Moon-Hair* and her *child* many years before in a fit of rage brought on by some mention of her first *husband*.

As his life progressed *Salim bin Haubut* found he had less and less use for his pipe, for the effects of moderation and philosophy had ingrained in him deep habits of restraint which needed no magical assistance. Indeed, today, the pipe has touched no man's lips for fully seven years.

There was a surprised silence as the story came to this slightly abrupt end, and then the courtyard filled with a deep roar of applause. The Purple Man stepped to the edge of the platform and held out the pipe for all to see, as the applause continued. Then gradually it all died down, and the Purple Man cleared his throat.

'I am sure, O Bagdad,' he cried, 'that you are all as entranced as I am to learn the true source of the Moderate Man's moderation! Our thanks to him!' This too was greeted with a loud noise of appreciation.

'Now, however,' went on the Purple Man, 'he must hang. But I feel certain that none would object if we offered the Moderate Man a taste of his own pipe in order to settle his mind for this somewhat trying event.'

'This is a very generous offer,' replied Salim bin Haubut, 'and you must not doubt my appreciation of your kindness. However (as I have said), I little need the pipe's effects at this period of my life, and what is more, I intended it as a gift for the Caliph himself. I would hate very much to disappoint our honoured Commander of the Faithful should he want to taste of it this very hour, for you recall that the pipe cannot be used above once a day, or its power is lost.'

'O Moderate Man!' exclaimed the Purple Man, stepping back. 'This is magnificence itself! Do we understand then, that you are prepared to hang?'

'Well, if the –' began Salim bin Haubut, but the next sound that came from his lips was inarticulate because the Purple Man had triggered a lever that caused the entire front half of the platform to collapse, tumbling a number of attendants head first into the crowd and leaving the Moderate Man hanging in mid-air by the neck. 'O!' cried the populace at once. Then a great sigh of pleasure shuddered through them.

Then there was no sound at all for several long minutes as thousands of eyes watched the feeble strugglings Salim bin Haubut made as he swung slowly from side to side in the sunny air.

Then a shrill wailing flute began to play, and was quickly joined by the shivering metallic note of a zither. Tablas began to pummel softly, and here and there, from different sides of the courtyard, all the musical instruments started to give voice, producing a peculiar, but subtly harmonious and touching din.

The Purple Man presently commenced to speak over it, saying to the people, 'Well, well, O Bagdad, this has been an interesting and significant affair today, that no man can deny. Can anyone say they ever dreamed that the Moderate Man concealed a secret source for his amazing moderation? Or did any man predict that this superb moderation should extend to the very end, or,' and here he gestured with a sad smile to where Salim bin Haubut was suspended, '*almost* to the very end?' A ripple of amusement passed over the people.

Then the Purple Man held up the golden pipe again and examined it, as the band continued, softly, to play, saying: 'Is it really to be imagined? Such unnatural power, from such a modest object! Now here is a question I must put before you all. Do you really suppose that the *Caliph*, being the impetuous monarch he is, would have much use for a gift such as dear Salim has left him? For what need has *he*, who is absolute, and has everything, and need be disappointed in nothing? For you see,' he said, winking to his audience, 'I am of a mind to try the pipe *myself*!' There was another rumble of excitement and laughter from the assembly, and several voices cried out, 'Do! Do! O Purple Man!'

'Well, now,' said the Purple Man, 'I certainly have need of it, to console myself for the loss of such a fine character as our dear Salim.' There was more laughter. 'What is more,' he went on, 'I do believe that true moderation is perhaps the *only* sensation I have yet to experience!' This was greeted with a great roar of laughter and appreciation, and while voices urged him on, the Purple Man smilingly lifted the pipe to his lips.

On the instant he gave a terrible cry, dropped the pipe, and to the intense amazement of all, fell choking to the platform, where, within the space of a few seconds, his face turned quite black and he died in horrible convulsions.

Another great roar of sound rose from the people, drowning the music, as everyone commented excitedly on this unlooked-for event. 'Well,' cried many, each to each, *'Moderate Men are not what they once were!'*

And in general the people disapproved of the trick Salim bin Haubut had played.

A party of the Purple Man's retainers went to the house of Salim bin Haubut with a cage containing a brilliant green singing bird. They knocked long and hard on the door but received no answer. (For the faithful eunuch of Salim's children, upon receiving the message his master had sent him, knew it to be a sign long before agreed on between them, and took the children and household safely away. Neither they nor any of their descendants were ever seen or heard of again in Bagdad.) Growing impatient, the visitors broke down the door, and finding no one there, departed in anger. The last man took the singing bird from the cage and threw it on to the roof of the house, where it burst violently into flames, starting a fire that burned the house to the ground.

The gradually descending sun approached the domes and roof-tops of Bagdad. The small shadow cast by the hanging body of the Moderate Man crept slowly eastward on the marble floor of the deserted courtyard. From the great city beyond the silent walls a woman's voice rose in solitary wailing.

'O Salim bin Haubut do not die! You are all that saves us, all that stands between the terrible opposites that paw the weary earth! O Moderate Man do not hang! Do not leave us!'

But it was impossible to know if the intent of this was ironical or not.

3   They Are Not Pleased

Through the secret, woman-scented corridors of the Inner Palace hurried the Grand Vizier, muttering aloud to himself.

Stars expanded upon stars in geometric rhythms on shadowy walls and marbled floors. A dull, beating sound came steadily from somewhere nearby. With it, the sound of the Vizier's footsteps syncopated strangely. With it, the echoes of his aged voice competed fruitlessly.

'*Something* has happened,' he was saying. 'Something *has* happened. Something has *happened*!'

He brushed through an embroidered leather doorway, and turned a corner into a new area of the Palace.

'But how will it affect the Empress? Events are not to her liking. They offend the Immutables. They bring down the wrath of her Relatives, the supposed *Inhabitants of the Stars*. She does not *like* events, unless they are *her* events. But why do I care? And *why* do I call her "Empress"?'

He strode on in the murky air, passing through long corridors hung with elaborate tapestries on celestial themes.

'She is not an Empress at all,' he told himself. 'She is only one of the Caliph's old, used-up concubines. What happens to old, used-up concubines? Some die. Some sit in corners and smoke hashish. Some retire to the country and plant azaleas. Others take over the government.'

The old man sighed heavily.

'Now popular theory believes that the *Grand Vizier* rules all with a heavy hand. The Grand Vizier admires this idea, but has other impressions! One day he finds himself Grand Vizier, with various responsibilities and honours. Next day he happens to look out of a window and notices the Purple Man hanging all his Under-Viziers. Why might this be? It very much tends to undermine trust and co-operation among Council members when one catches another hanging all his assistants. Why did no one mention it to him? What good is a Grand Vizier without Under-Viziers? Then there is today's event. Has someone made a decision? Whom you think has made a decision locates you in the toils of Bagdad accountability. Of course, there will be those who feel the Vizier has really done it, but the Vizier himself is not of that opinion. He has only just found out, having been told by a kitchen maid.'

Passing through several floating wisps of silk, the official now entered a dim antechamber. This was occupied only by a muscular black man, squat and scantily clothed, who held a naked scimitar and sat, with eyes closed, on a pillow beside a small flickering lamp. Beyond him was a further doorway, and darkness.

'Ibn, hail!' said the Vizier.

A smile very slowly grew on the sitting man's features.

'I see you, old one,' he said presently.

'Matters of great urgency for your mistress and her Council!'

Ibn slowly opened his eyes and examined the Vizier. Then his smile grew even wider.

'I see that you still fear death, old one,' he said.

The Grand Vizier sighed and clicked his false teeth.

'What should happen if some day I came to this door, and this was no longer so? You might needs trust my loyalty then.'

'Loyalty, without fear?' Ibn shrugged. 'Probably I would just kill you, to be sure of you.'

'Well,' said the Vizier, 'at least I would not care.'

'The Empress rules over all those who desire Life,' said Ibn, and he smiled even more and beckoned with his scimitar. 'Enter, by all means.'

The Vizier could hear the shouting well before he reached the Council Chamber, which was also the Empress's bedroom. A half dozen senior civil servants were accusing each other of having hung the Moderate Man. The deep, unpleasant voice of the Empress herself was thundering over all, calling them a catalogue of foul names.

Coming to the open door, the Vizier's eye caught the eye at once of the only unfamiliar figure in the room, a handsome young woman who lay naked on the bed beside the vast and sweated Empress and gazed back at him with a frank, bright curiosity.

'The Empress,' he said presently, clearing his throat, 'lies with a splendid new woman.'

The Empress stopped shouting, while the others went on unabated, and swivelled her massive head towards him.

'It is called *Amina*,' she said, with heavy, possessive pleasure.

'She is indeed fulgent,' he murmured, 'possessed of a form whose full charms can but narrowly be surpassed. Supple, lithe and lissom – another certain disquietener of poets. With such thick black hair, and visage exotic and sharp-boned, like a figure slashed from subterranean rock by the scimitar of some pre-Adamite sultan of the lower earth.'

'Yes,' agreed the Empress, and she sighed. 'And she does not talk too much, although she is clever. And she cries out in an agreeable manner, and has a great many pleasing wiles.'

Now, however, one of the other council members had noticed his arrival and was waving a sharp finger at him and shrilly accusing him of ordering Salim bin Haubut's hanging.

'If I had the power to hang anyone,' earnestly replied the Grand Vizier, 'I would not have hung the Moderate Man, I would have hung *you*.'

Someone else shouted out that perhaps the late Purple Man had gone mad and thought of it himself.

'He had not the imagination to go mad,' pronounced the Vizier.

'*This is not the point!*' ponderously roared the Empress. '*The point is: the People in the Stars are not pleased! They are not pleased with the shattering of the tranquillity which has occurred!*'

A discouraged silence descended.

'And what do your celestial relatives now recommend?' asked one of them warily.

'Do not imagine, however, that I was not warned!' The Empress continued to shout, as though above other voices, although the other voices had ceased. 'Last night a cousin of mine from the Glittering Plain came to me and warned me of the impending danger! He *warned* me of the death of a moderate man! He warned me of a certain ragged band of vagrants who would seek to steal away my son, the Prince of Stars, the Caliph's only child and heir, and hide him in a dark cavern from which he never would escape!'

'Truly, your Grace,' remarked the Vizier, 'fears that the Prince might grow up have ever and again proven groundless.'

The Empress, though, went loudly on, so that the Council members all winced.

'*Immediately*, of course, I perceived that he could only mean this unruly crew now infesting us, who are spoken of as the fruit party!'

'The Ripe Fruit Party, I am sure Your Majesty means.'

'I do not study their pretensions! But my cousin believes we have tolerated them far longer than we should, due only to our exaggerated mercy and compassion!'

'They feel just so regarding *us*.'

'The words of my cousins are not meant to be taken lightly, thou feeble factotum!' bellowed the Empress. 'We have hardly been living up to our supernal models so well that we can now afford to ignore their advice! *They* are reality! *They* only! Anything else is *unreal*! And it is not the *unreal* we should heed, but the *real*!'

'You may be certain, O Magnificence, that all your subjects are throughly attentive to that,' murmured the Vizier.

'They *should* be!'

'They are carefully supervised, be assured.'

'*Tomorrow*,' the menace of the word was deafening. '*Tomorrow* ripe fruit shall hang from new trees! *Where* are they hiding, the notorious Zardin al-Adigrab and those young ox-droppings that have risen up to follow him? *Where*?'

'It is said only that they hold court on the other side of the river,' said the Vizier vaguely, 'somewhere in Rusafah district.'

'Then, at first light, let Rusafah be burned down to the earth, street by street, until they are found! Ripe fruit is ripe to rot! Without the Moderate Man to cover them in confusion and doubt, the populace will easily be persuaded that it can be no other way!'

'It is the day!' a Kazi roused himself to say.

'It is the hour!' shouted the rest of the Council.

The Empress finally breathed in with satisfaction.

'The populace,' said the Vizier, 'may easily be persuaded of any number of things. (Except, perhaps, the inhabitants of Rusafah district, who might be temporarily overcome by selfish subjectivity.) But what, this very night, of the immediate intentions of the Ripe Fruit Party?'

'I care not for their "intentions", should they have any. No more do I care for the intentions of a fig, or of an orange. Bagdad will sleep once more in her disease, before feeling the lancet of the healing surgeon. It is not the way of the Commander of the Faithful's bright sun to shine in the natural darkness. We will begin at first light. By tomorrow's dusk the Caliph will have cast his doom *publicly* on them, and their rank breath will have been stopped in the courtyard of the people, before the eyes of the city!'

'Will the Commander of the Faithful agree, do you think?' suddenly asked Amina, the young woman on the bed.

'These are his very designs!' shouted the Empress angrily, before an embarrassed pause could begin. 'This is his utmost desire!'

'It is the day, the hour!' quickly agreed Amina. 'The situation is desperate!'

'*All* situations are desperate,' said the Vizier, 'simply by being situations. Only when we are able to banish situations completely, will we be free of desperation.'

'This is not the moment for your tiresome remarks, Vizier!' exclaimed the Empress. 'Perhaps you are unable to see it, but a great purifying change *is* under way! Tomorrow all these disorders of ours will begin to end, and the peace of a single understanding shall descend upon us. *All* our questions shall find their answers! By our own hand shall these things be done! We shall draw aside the curtain – the shadows will vanish!'

'When two tygers are thrown each other for food,' sighed the Vizier, 'order will soon enough be restored.'

'Go to the Captain of the Guard,' commanded the Empress, ignoring this, 'tell him to look to the doors! Tell him to look to the beasts and the traps and all the defences! Then go to my son, the Prince of Stars, and – you know where he is?'

'Indeed,' was the Vizier's unenthusiastic reply, 'I have kept track of that most precious jewel of your soul, our semi-divine inheritor of the virtue of the stars. He is where he *always* is.'

'Where is that?' asked the Empress coldly.

'In the *games* room,' said the Vizier. 'At the very centre of the Palace. Far from every eye.'

'Go to him, and awaken his spirit to the vastness of the day, the hugeness of the hour! Urge him to emerge awhile from the imperial tranquillity of his mind, to come and stand boldly by the side of his towering father!'

'I will try to get him to quit playing chrochinole,' said the Vizier, not hopefully.

'Go!' the Empress commanded the whole group. 'And defend always the *true* reality!'

The Vizier and the other Council members filed morosely out past the immobile Ibn, leaving only the Empress and Amina, and presently the last of their footsteps died away into the clammy marble passages.

Ibn smiled, opened his eyes, quietly set down his weapon and crept back to the doorway to listen.

In the white bedchamber beyond a majestic silence also gradually descended. A silence like that in the furthest deeps of the sky. Long moments lengthened and coalesced and drifted in a directionless manner, like eddies in an immaterial river slowly going nowhere. So empty, so smooth, unfeatured it was, that presently the little antechamber, the Palace itself, perhaps the entire universe, appeared almost to begin turning, to *move*, to rotate, with the vast and magnificent feeling that *nothing whatsoever* was happening.

There was a heavy rustling sound.

A voice cried out. Suddenly yet softly, startled but expectant, full of arch overtones of submission.

Ibn's smile grew even wider and he padded back to the

centre of his room, picking up his weighty scimitar and making a few noiseless practise passes in the air, so that the great silver blade flickered with the fearsome speed of a tongue darting from a serpent.

4 Something *Is* Happening

The Grand Vizier broke in on the Captain of the Guard just as he and his two wives were finishing their evening meal.

'Glad tidings for soldiers!' he shouted, causing them to drop their implements and scramble to their feet.

'*Enemies*!' the Captain cried. 'O Majid Shair-al-Walahan, do you bring me genuine enemies? There is no true battle without enemies! No true struggle that will purify the soul. Without enemies, there is nothing but surrender!'

'Nothing but *wives*!' cried Su'ad, his taller and handsomer and elder wife. 'Nothing but wives and dinner parties!'

'And tales!' added Hind, his smaller and prettier and younger wife. 'Nothing but wives and tales and dinner parties and idle conversation!'

'I bring you Zardin al-Adigrab,' said the Vizier grimly and turned to leave again.

The Captain's harsh features brightened perceptibly.

'You think he will fight?' he asked.

'He is war itself,' said the Vizier. 'He dwells in it as others dwell in houses and tents.'

'Life *has* been so dull!' shrilled Su'ad.

'Nothing has *happened* in such a while!' agreed Hind.

'They mock,' growled the Captain, 'but I discern in you, O venerable friend, a great new seriousness!'

'In these few hours past, you will know, was destroyed not simply a Moderate Man,' replied the Vizier, turning again, 'but also an *Amendment*. It *is* an event of the greatest seriousness. The Amendment itself would have been no final answer, of course, no complete solution. But it softened the harsh edges of the Absolutes. It delayed, it modified. It held people back from knifing each other in the street. It appeased people.'

'It kept enemies apart,' said the Captain.

'Yes, but now Zardin al-Adigrab –'

'*Zardin al-Adigrab!*' cried the two wives in delight, clasping their hands, as though the name of a new arrival at a party had been announced.

'Now Zardin al-Adigrab is left face to face with the Empress,' went on the Vizier. 'He will most certainly regard 'himself as provoked. He will suspect she is intending new deaths. Indeed, he will have reason to. In short, each faction will no longer tolerate the other's existence. The balancer topples. Destruction and dissolution loom.'

The two wives smiled brightly at the Vizier, and the Vizier smiled back mirthlessly at the wives. A maid-servant shuffled into the comfortable dining-chamber and began gathering up their plates from the low table.

The brawny Captain fairly rippled with eagerness as he took a pace to one side and back again, his hands grappling fiercely.

'What do we *do*, then?' he demanded.

'The Life-loving Empress, most characteristically, feels that we should hang Zardin, his followers, whoever else is convenient, and burn down large parts of the capital. You may be gratified to note she is remaining admirably calm, considering the crisis.'

'It is all the Commander of the Faithful's will, of course,' muttered the soldier intensely. 'It is all as he must intend it. But we, who can see so much less, cannot but fear, and think he must beware where he sets his teeth among these tainted fruits!'

Majid Shair-al-Walahan leaned back against the doorpost, and with an exhalation regarded his friend. 'It is a wondrous loyalty,' he said, 'by which all confusions are rendered as order, all darknesses as light. However, informed opinion might tell you that the Caliph has not really set his teeth at all. They might hint that all his teeth have fallen out. Matters unfold. Fruits fall. Men hang. People make speeches, take actions. My own suspicion is – let me tell you, purely in an unofficial capacity, of course – my own suspicion is that *either* these things all *must* happen, *or* that there is no point or need in them happening, but that they merely *do*.'

'Yes, but what is the Caliph's mind in all this?' came back the Captain impatiently, as his wives made a show of suddenly sighing and sitting down again at the table. 'Why did he not just send horsemen and crush Zardin and his followers at once? Has he not told you his intentions concerning this hanging today? Things do not happen *entirely* without causes or intentions! Does he court disaster then, in his age?'

'Why, how old is he?' asked the Vizier, with a start.

'Well, older than he once was, at any hazard.'

'I will tell you,' then said Majid, 'that the Caliph is as a moonless night to me, as to all men. I know him not. One hour he is one man. Another hour he is another. It is as the clouds and winds that change expression across the broad face of the earth. He who is *absolute*,' he added with some bitterness. 'He is as changeable as Zardin is, as every man is now in this city. He is no thing, no truth, but *himself*. And *himself*, it is never still. It is his pride to be thus, you comprehend it.'

'No, I do not,' said the Captain, and they both fell into a muse.

The wives seized the opportunity to interrupt, calling from below.

'Speak you of *Zardin al-Adigrab*, prince of the rebel fruits!' cried Hind.

'Mean you that same famous *Zardin al-Adigrab* who so boldly proposes to bring forth the whatever-it-is from within?' demanded Su'ad.

'Of course,' replied their husband glumly.

'Then there is much *we* can tell you!' cried Hind in glee.

'Have you information?' asked the Vizier, despite himself.

'Oh well,' said Su'ad, 'listen then to –'

The True Origin and Ancestry of *Zardin al-Adigrab*, Leader of the Ripe Fruit Party

There once was an honest but humble *riverboatman* who had a beautiful wife. She too tried to be honest but humble, but did not always succeed, largely because Fate and her undeniable beauty were against her. Thus it was that one day, while her *husband* was out ferrying goods up and down the river Euphrates, the *lady* was surprised in her bath by a perfectly monstrous *Ifrit* who steamed with desire for her. 'What means this!' cried she, but it little availed because the *Ifrit* at once seized her in his muscular arms and flew away with her to a beautiful island that lay green and placid in the sparkling eastern sea. The air here was soft and delicious and the grass was very like the richest and deepest carpets in the *Caliphal* apartments. But the *lady* roundly cursed the *Ifrit* and told him that what he had done was outrageous, although this unfortunately only caused him to laugh and lust for her all the more. She, of course, fell to weeping and wailing and tearing her hair but this was useless too.

The *Ifrit* produced a sumptuous repast for them and proceeded to talk to the *wife* in the most cunning manner imaginable, until finally she decided that necessity being what it was she might try to make the best of a dreadful situation, in the following ways: First, she promised to yield to the *Ifrit* if he would in turn agree to return her to her proper home before the arrival of her *husband*, and that he would leave no mark upon her to allow the *husband* to guess she had been another's. To this the *Ifrit* agreed, because, despite his present desires, he was a mature sort of *Ifrit* and well guessed that after having once or twice availed himself of the *wife*'s person he might no longer have much craving for her and would not much mind returning her. Besides, if she turned out to be so extremely enjoyable that he wished to keep her nothing would prevent him from breaking his promise, being an *Ifrit*. Second, she resolved that the only means she had at her disposal of protecting her *husband*'s honour (seeing no practical way of killing herself without the *Ifrit* noticing and stopping her) was to enjoy the ravishments of her abductor as little as she possibly could. Being so determined she bravely submitted to him and suffered him to carry her beneath a shady tree and achieve his desires. Now the *Ifrit* had great powers and the *wife*'s struggles to resist the fawning unworthiness of her own person were very terrible, but she was just beginning to hope that her humble *husband* would not be *too* badly dishonoured when, suddenly – lo! – a *fruit* – I know not what variety! – fell from the tree and hit the *Ifrit* on his bare back, causing him to jump with surprise! This in turn set into action a fatal motion within the *wife* which all in a rush began to deprive her *husband* of the last few tatters of his self-respect. 'O! O!' cried out she in her chagrin. 'The *fruit*! The *fruit* is ripe! O! O! Ripe Fruit!' When all was done, the *Ifrit* (perhaps finding this rather silly) cared not to keep her and dutifully returned her to her house in *Bagdad*, where she contrived to lie with her husband that same night, rightly fearing that she had conceived with the *Ifrit*. The child, of course, was none other than Zardin al-Adigrab, Son of an *Ifrit* and a *woman*, patron of ripe fruit!

The wives were now up again and cavorting about the table, giggling and singing. The Captain and the Grand Vizier had both sat down on the carpet and were picking listlessly at the dessert plate.

'I dreamt we were all saluting a *new* Caliph,' said the Vizier vaguely. 'We were down on our knees. We were trembling with fervent fear and love. His beard was black, his manner stern, his eye was full of power. *The Caliph Haroon al-Raschid!* we cried, *The Caliph Haroon al-Raschid!*'

'I have never heard of him,' said the Captain sourly. 'He is not among the chronology of Caliphs in the histories. We *have* a Caliph. It is disloyal to speak of any man – past, future or present – as the Caliph, if he is not.'

'Well,' said the Vizier, 'perhaps it is not disloyal to dream it. I shall tell you something else we said. You will like it even less. We said, *Truly, we declare that there is but one word, and the word is* God!'

'I've never heard of *him* either,' said the Captain.

'Well, I heard our own voices say it,' sighed the Vizier.

He clambered to his feet and the Captain followed. In the entrance way to the Captain's Chambers they turned face to face.

'Urgency is everywhere!' announced the older man, attempting to summon his lost animation. 'I must to the Prince and you to your soldiers! Not a moment is to be lost!'

'Yes, yes, you men of State must produce some martial business now!' sang the voice of Su'ad from behind them. 'It is the day, it is the hour! The tales have all been told – too often – and the songs sung – too loud – and the wives just get sillier and sillier! And all the while, poor strong soldiers go soft in their houses, with their red blood wasting in their skins like old wine trapped in wine bags!'

The laughter of the younger Hind drifted after, but with uncertainty.

'In the morning there shall be new orders,' said the Vizier, as they parted at the end of the hallway. 'But for this evening be especially alert: it is an uncertain period. The palace is a lamp left unwisely alight. The night is dense with events, winged and inchoate, blundering towards it through the darkness.'

'My scimitar is bright, and so are those of my men!' cried the Captain. '*We shall resist anything and everything*!'

The old man made his way inward through the palace. Presently he came to a small circular courtyard, where in daylight those who sought audience with the Caliph would gather and wait. Now it was deserted, and he stopped by the dried-up fountain and looked contemplatively around him, clicking his teeth and sniffing the air. The sun was gone below the level of the walls, and shadows filled the arcades above him.

He sighed and raised his foot to rest on the cracked basin. Then he threw back his head, and half closed his eyes, as if attempting to recollect.

'Evening...' he said, after a moment, and paused. '*Evening*...' he then repeated.

'O *Evening*,' he began again, in a voice which attempted to be fervent, 'O lovely evening like *a young girl's breasts* ... like birds in flight ... or the *still bosom* of the *sea* off *Basrah* ... *Evening's spell*, much like the *memory* of the *earth* rising, with closed eyes and parted lips ... And the *jasmine scent* mixed with that of *various other flowers*, the distant yet near *sounds*, the *sweetness* and *sadness* ... the presence of the word *God* ... the strange *air* of Evening, and its *coolness* upon the soul, purifying, frightening, saddening ... filling one with *hope* ... and yet ... with *none*.'

Then he stopped, and another sigh escaped him. Then he smacked his lips and drew in his breath and sighed once more. Then he fell silent and looked in several directions around himself.

'Indeed,' he said in a low voice, 'It *would* appear that it's evening.' Then he fell silent again. Then he brought his foot down and walked a few steps from the fountain. 'Life is long,' he said bitterly, 'art short.' And proceeded quickly on his way.

Soon he was descending a curving set of stairs and passing through a series of unguarded portals along a lower hall. Everything here was bare and grey and dusty, the chambers entirely without ornament, deserted and perfectly silent. Even the air seemed stale and lifeless.

Behind him he left a single trail of footprints across the unswept stones.

'And this the *navel of the universe*,' he muttered.

He came then unannounced into a cool, circular room, the terminus of four similarly empty corridors. At the centre, beneath a dim, guttering lamp hanging from a brass chain, stood a low hexagonal pedestal, the top of which was a marble chrochinole board. Over it bent a thin young man of slightly below average height, dressed in a faded blue garment, and across from him a dwarf eunuch wearing a stained pink turband. Off to one side, on the raised stone dais that ran all around the walls, sitting on cushions about a small coffee-pot, were three figures: two middle-aged eunuchs and a boy.

'This is called the *Changing World Club*,' the Vizier reminded himself, '(formerly the *Eunuch's Club*), and is devoted entirely to conversation about current topics.'

The eunuchs on the pillows had noticed him and were anxiously beckoning him away from the figures in the centre of the room.

'Venerable authority!' cried out one. 'What pleasure! Such an absence! But come and have coffee with us, and do not yet disturb him!'

'Wait at least until his game is complete,' urged the other. 'He will be unpleasant and unsociable, but perhaps less so!'

The boy said nothing but smiled cheerfully.

Glancing first at the chrochinole players, the Grand Vizier reluctantly accepted the invitation, pulling himself up on to the dais and reaching for a threadbare pillow.

'Coffee then, to fortify myself against the soul-destroying arguments of our admired young monarch,' he agreed.

'Immediately! Immediately, O excellent man!' cried the first eunuch, looking about for a cup. 'There *was* another,' said the second eunuch, 'I saw it. It was under Gharib's pillow.' The boy jumped up and looked under his seat, and then cried out, 'No, truly! You slander me once more, Gondrat!'

'Perhaps it is among the slippers,' said the first eunuch.

'It is more likely *lost*, now,' said Gondrat gloomily, feeling among the slippers. 'Didn't the Prince take it?' asked the boy. 'No, of *course* the Prince didn't take it!' exclaimed the first eunuch. 'The Prince *never* takes it, foolish boy! Because the Prince says coffee drinking causes his finger to shake and his aim to decay.' 'He only says *that*,' said Gondrat, 'when he is in an optimistic frame of mind, and does not see the whole process of the universe in it.' 'In the name of the Mother of Compassion!' cried out the first eunuch, 'look under the Vizier's pillow there!' 'It is she who has hidden it,' muttered the other. 'The Mother of Compassion hides things and the Father of Demands makes us make mistakes,' explained Gharib to the Vizier. 'It's not true!' cried out the first eunuch, 'She also causes them to be found as well, and He allows the Prince now and again to win games if he does not try too hard.' 'It's not there,' said Gondrat, withdrawing his hand from under the Vizier.

'I am experiencing,' said the Vizier, 'a marked lessening of my desire for coffee. I must speak to the Prince.'

'No! No! But you must have some!' cried all three members of the club, and redoubled their efforts.

'Truly Fhumdullah!' exclaimed Gondrat testily to the first eunuch as they scrambled about various sides of the Vizier on their hands and knees, 'you are full of words on every matter, but you cannot even keep the coffee gear in order! Surely coffee for a guest is more important than an *Alladin's Warehouse* full of your opinions!' 'But who is Alladin, and what is this about his warehouse?' said the boy immediately, sitting back on his heels and tilting his head at the eunuch. '*Alladin*,' pronounced Fhumdullah from behind him, 'is an excellent example of how fortunate a man can be if Father, Mother and Fates all smile upon him.' 'Well, it is a short tale, and easily told,' said Gondrat, also sitting back.

'Would they be impressed if I were to mention that I was about an errand of great urgency?' the Vizier asked himself aloud. 'Would it concern them if I were to assert, in a general way, that every moment was precious, every passing instant an irrecoverable treasure?'

'Soon! Soon!' cried Fhumdullah, looking wildly about.

'Well,' said Gondrat again, 'it is most simply called – '

The Story of Alladin and the Magic Warehouse

Alladin was a singularly tiresome youth who showed very little sign of promise. His *mother* even despaired of him, which shows how truly unremarkable he was, because mothers are notoriously incapable of perceiving reality. Then one day a *man* approached him in the street where he was playing idly with a piece of broken brick. 'Come with me,' said the *man*. 'There waits a *spirit* a short way from the city who wishes to bestow great wealth upon you.' 'Why should he want to do that?' said *Alladin*. 'This only he himself and God know,' said the *man*. 'But come along.' So *Alladin* went with him and presently came to a very *old man* (or *spirit* – *Alladin* never discovered which) sitting on a rock with his hands on his chin. 'Is your name *Alladin*?' asked the *old man*. 'Yes,' said *Alladin*. 'Well,' said he, after a moment's looking at him, 'you will suffice.' 'Suffice for what?' asked *Alladin*. 'Know this:' said the *old man*, 'I have been on the earth for twenty-seven hundred years and yet feel the experience has been quite worthless. I have more power than any other living being in or above the world, but nothing pleases or displeases me sufficiently to want to exercise it. I am probably in despair, except despair is probably not a powerful enough word for one such as myself. Besides which, it implies an intensity of feeling which is decidedly absent from my heart. I purpose shortly to throw myself into an erupting volcano, which is in all likelihood the only natural hardship sufficiently cruel to put an end to me. Before I do this, however, I do desire to make a small gesture.

'In considering my long life, I have concluded that through the great majority of it I have – whatever I may have thought at the moment – been treated with immense indifference by all humankind. The amount of active *good*, or even active *evil* shown towards me, has only been enough to amount to generally good or bad fortune in the lives of two ordinary men. This offends me deeply. I have decided, therefore, to do but one solitary man a good deed, and but one solitary man a bad deed, before I depart existence.' 'Which am I?' asked *Alladin*. 'You are he who shall receive good from me,' said the *old man*. 'I was at some difficulty as to how to make this choice. The more I thought about it, the more I felt there were indeed no ways to distinguish the deserts of most men. In the end I ordered my *helper* to prepare a list of all imaginable names. This was jumbled into a leather bowl from which I happened to draw out the name *Alladin*. I ordered him to procure me an *Alladin*, which he has done.' 'Am I permitted a choice of what my favour shall be?' inquired *Alladin*. 'No,' said the *old man*, 'because it is quite probable that you would then choose to your own ultimate detriment. This would not satisfy my design. I have contemplated you, seen through your nature entirely, and have decided to give you a *warehouse*.'

'A *warehouse*?' said *Alladin*. 'I had indeed begun to hope for *beautiful women*.' 'A *warehouse* is better, in my opinion,' said the *old man*, 'but you may pursue beautiful

women just as you please. You may even obtain a few
because this warehouse will probably make you wealthy
despite yourself. This is because, squander it as you may
it is a self-replenishing *warehouse*, and will always be ful
of cheap, low-quality, basic goods for you to sell. (I do no
fill it with riches, so as to protect you from *thieves* and
officials.) Here is the key, with the address written on it.
And he handed *Alladin* a key. As *Alladin* was preparing to
go, however, he thought to ask what the *old man* was going
to do to the other individual, and who this unfortunate
victim was to be.

'These are not things I am prepared to tell you,' said the
old man. 'If you are at all curious to know, look about you
at your neighbours. Of them all, know that only *one* wil
truly not deserve the harm that befalls him, just as you
have by no means deserved what you will have. Perhaps i
will entertain you to try to guess which man that is.' With
these words the *old man* and his *helper* faded away and
Alladin returned to the city and found the *warehouse*. I
did just what the *stranger* said it would, so that *Alladir*
became quite wealthy. He was able to obtain a certair
number of fairly *beautiful women*, but they had littl
affection for him because he remained just as tiresome a:
he had been. His *mother*, however, was delighted witl
him, and indiscriminately thanked the heavens for giving
her a son who eventually made good.

'Why do you always tell moral tales and never ones witl
fighting and jinns and exquisite ladies!' complained Gharib
'I told the tale' said Gondrat, 'only to demonstrate for you th
meaning of my metaphor, and to show how good a metapho
it was.' 'Unfortunately,' said Fhumdullah from the floo
below, where he was still searching, 'fine as your metapho
may be, you have not found our guest a coffee cup.' 'Indeed
I *have*!' said Gondrat suddenly, reaching across and snatch
ing up Fhumdullah's cup, which caused Gharib to giggle and
cover his mouth. Tossing away the contents and cleaning i
out with a pillow-tassel, he handed it to the other eunuch
who was just clambering back to his seat. 'You see! You see!

exulted Fhumdullah. 'In equal portions deal out the Parents of us all! This was finely done, Gondrat!' 'Well, it was,' agreed Gondrat, watching him pour out the cup from the silver coffee pot.

Taking the proffered drink, the Vizier turned impatiently towards the centre of the room, where the steady clicking of the game-pieces continued.

'*Not yet!*' whispered both eunuchs noisily.

With a sigh he turned back to them. 'So,' he asked, 'what matter has the club had under consideration today? What new alteration should our city heed now?'

'Well,' said Fhumdullah, 'we have been discussing *Love*, and how it is not as it once was but has changed and now is quite different.'

'Remarkable,' said the Vizier. 'Changed do you mean since last we spoke?'

'Changed,' said Fhumdullah, 'from what it has always been before.' The club, all nodding, settled themselves more comfortably on their pillows.

'Indeed,' added Gondrat, 'and no one seems to realise this is so.'

'Do I gather the club to have had recent dealings with the populace,' murmured the Vizier, 'thus to sound their ignorance?' 'I well know what you are suggesting!' retorted Fhumdullah. 'And it is not just and it is not fair!' 'So do I also!' added Gondrat. 'Nor is it!' 'What do they mean?' asked the boy. 'He implies, as do all men, that we can know nothing of these things, being *eunuchs*, and you being a *boy*,' said Fhumdullah. 'But we think it is very indiscreet and inelegant of him even to mention it!' 'Our condition affords us an objectivity that well allows us to make judgements on the general state of things, and measure the drift of our city, which we could not do if it were otherwise!' asserted Gondrat.

'Well,' said the Vizier calmly, 'if it is only a matter of this, I can assure you that all men tend finally to be eunuchs.'

'Well, I have claimed, and I continue to claim – and it is true – that the populace shows little sign of being aware of the great change which has occurred to *Love*,' said Gondrat. 'It is not as it once was. It is quite different.'

'Yes, for example,' said Fhumdullah, 'it was once the case that men would perish utterly if they failed to achieve a specific lady. Well, that's now considered to be quite ridiculous, and is no longer done. Have you, in fact, heard of any recent instances? Lovers used to believe that death would result from their emotions, but they are discovering, day by day, that this may no longer be so.'

'Yes, and they used to fall in love in quite different ways,' said Gondrat. 'It was once possible for a man and a woman to fall in love at the slightest thing – and was frequently done, also. But a man is now no longer willing to become irrevocably enamoured at the mere glimpse of a lady unveiled. A lady will not fall in love with a man simply because she hears a few good things about him. That is no longer possible. Love is no longer like that, and people have realised it.'

'Take, for example, this matter of weeping tears for love,' said Fhumdullah. 'This is much less likely to happen.'

'Or poor people marrying the daughters or sons of kings or Sultans,' added Gondrat. 'This is being recognised in most cases to be an illusory possibility, or a mere fantasy. People no longer look for these sorts of occurrence to happen, and do not expect a great host of other strange events to come about either.'

'Such as being seduced by beautiful princesses in the wilderness, or that sort of event,' agreed Fhumdullah.

'Not *all* women have damask cheeks, ruby lips, gleaming teeth and beautiful and comely shapes any more, either,' said Gondrat.

'Perhaps that is why love is no longer the same,' remarked the Vizier.

'In general,' said Fhumdullah, 'chance plays a much smaller part in it all, and people are not nearly as silly and ridiculous as they once were.'

'Well,' said the Vizier, 'this is very heartening progress we make.'

'Not necessarily!' cried Gondrat.

'That is true,' agreed Fhumdullah.

'People do not feel the ecstasies they once did either. A smaller number of wives have children than was once the case, and in general, a smaller proportion of love affairs turn out happily.'

'Lovers are not so clever,' added Fhumdullah, 'and do not write such nice poetry as they did in the silly old days, even though the poetry, fine as it may be, is not sufficient reason to return to how we once were – so it is generally felt.'

'A certain kind of music and delicacy has vanished with the great reduction in dishonesty.'

'On the whole, however, this is felt to be worth the price.'

'Well, this is excellent information,' said the Vizier, 'and fills me with amazement.'

'Very little escapes us,' admitted Fhumdullah, somewhat proudly.

All three members of the club then released a sigh and sipped their coffee, except Fhumdullah, who reached for his but couldn't find it.

'It makes you wonder what will happen next,' offered Gharib, tentatively.

'So have I ever said,' agreed Gondrat.

'Perhaps *nothing* will happen next,' said the Vizier briefly. 'Now, tell me, what has been the condition and state of mind of the *Prince* thy master these last weeks?'

'O, it has been very much as it ever was,' replied Gondrat, looking vaguely across at the Prince of Stars.

'He plays chrochinole a lot,' volunteered Gharib. 'Mainly he plays with Menshalla, but on occasion Menshalla gets tired, and so he plays with us. We play very poorly, and he accuses us of deliberately losing games, in order to give him pleasure. It is not true, of course, because we are not sure whether losing or winning pleases him. Mainly neither do. But he is the best chrochinole player in the world. We have seen him score one hundred and three consecutive shots into the centre-hole! That was when he was practising and he thought no one could see him. On occasion he wins games, but more frequently he makes mistakes near the end and loses. He has never ever won two games in a row. If he wins one game he gets very dreadful and makes a great number of mistakes in the next game, which he always makes someone play immediately.'

'Does he ever ask you about doings in the world outside this room?'

All three members sighed again heavily, and Fhumdullah gave up looking for his cup.

'No, not ever,' said Gondrat, sadly.

'He shows not the slightest interest in what we have to say,' said Fhumdullah. 'He commands us to silence when he sits with us to eat (which he only rarely does, and very little) and he utterly forbids us to interrupt him at his game.'

'Well,' said the Vizier, rising uncomfortably from his pillow. 'Now there are things he must hear, forbid them or not as he may.'

'This is not wise, in truth!' anxiously exclaimed the two eunuchs.

'You may set him to losing,' said Gharib. 'This can be most awful for him. He once began losing somehow and lost seven hundred and ninety-two games in a row!'

'What put an end to it?' inquired the Vizier thoughtfully.

'Absent-mindedness,' said Fhumdullah.

'And some most excellent shots by Menshalla,' added Gharib, 'that cleared away his own players while seeming to attempt to clear away the Prince's in a very lifelike manner.'

'Nonetheless,' said the Vizier, turning from them, 'he *is* the Prince of Stars, paragon of great Bagdad's very mind, heart and soul, and must be persuaded of the fact before these are all extinguished.' And he crossed the floor.

The two players were standing motionless on either side of the pedestal. The thin young man was staring fixedly at the patterned board, across which were scattered a number of small black and green marble disks. So intense was his inner involvement with the arrangement of these markers that the reality and colour of his person seemed almost to be shrinking slowly back from his peripheries, leaving his skin pale and lustreless, his outlines uncertain in the weak light. Only his eyes appeared to have being, and they were dark and brilliant.

'He is twenty-five years of age,' announced the Vizier, stopping within a pace and considering him. 'At once the oldest and subtlest of sophistical sages, and the unripest

half-grown child. Like either, he is extremely argumenta-
tive, but *his* sole desire is ever to be defeated. He is passionate
also, like a lover, like the woman the lover loved, like her
furious prohibitive father, like his squirming aching rival,
like the scandalous populace in the market-place at their
report, like the cool poet watching their agonies, who
marvels at the unconscious artifice of their suffering. Like
Alladin with his warehouses – he is a very tiresome young
man. He is *all* the people, born and unborn and never to be
born, all their hopes and defeats combined. Mainly,
however, he is a young man of whom many things are
expected, and from whom nothing but the meaningless
shooting of inconsequential chrochinole pieces at an abstract
target is ever received.'

'Prove to me that it is not here as it is everywhere,'
murmured the young man, without looking up from the
game.

'In the great world beyond these walls,' said the Vizier,
'not all men are blessed with chrochinole boards, or players.
They must strive, even now, with their hearts, their bodies,
their souls, their scimitars, their wits, their money, their
courage.'

'It is all one,' said the Prince, as he reached slowly for a
piece. 'It is all striving. But observe here: this next shot of
mine is the last of the game, and decides the outcome. All I
need do is propel this marker in such a way as to eliminate *one*
of those of my opponent, and leave my own piece on the
board. It is a rudimentary shot. I have made such a shot on a
hundred thousand occasions – quite literally. Is there any
reason why I should not be able to make it now?'

'The Prince of Stars is pleased to be hopeful, I'm sure.'

'It must be confessed,' pursued the Prince, turning his
eyes intently on the old man, 'there *is* no reason. It works as it
might should a man, any man, myself even, see dates upon a
platter, and think: "I will have myself a date, then," and, so
deciding, reach out his hand. How should it be that he
should not have the date in his mouth, as he has willed?'

'Perhaps,' suggest the Vizier, 'errant birds will suddenly
have carried them off, or snakes or jinns. Or perhaps, as

apparently occurs now and again, the dates will have on the instant been transformed into maidens.'

'No, but these are ridiculous things and do not happen,' said the Prince seriously. 'Indeed, there *is* no *real* cause that he should not have the dates.'

'Well, and if it happens,' remarked the other, 'then it will necessarily have been for a cause that is *unreal*.'

'You may say that,' said the Prince grimly, and bent once more to the playing-board. 'And you may say numberless other sayings. But you cannot deny that what I have asserted is true: that there is no reason.'

'Hearkening and obedience, O valiant Prince,' murmured Majid Shair-al-Walahan.

An emptiness descended upon the entire room, as Menshalla, who had been rocking slowly from foot to foot, became still, and the low voices of the Changing World Club by the wall fell away. For a long moment there was perfect silence, and an absolute absence of motion. Then the Prince fired his marker. It glanced off one of Menshalla's and then careered from the board, while that which it struck bounded to one side striking two more of the Prince's colour, causing them also to slide smoothly off into the gutters, as their antagonist, after a short roll, remained in place.

'I win,' said Menshalla, after a pause.

'*Of course you do*,' said the Prince, deeply bitter.

'That was an exceedingly poor shot, your gracious highness,' said the Vizier. 'It was a pimp to aged eunuchs as a true man might be a good shot.'

'There *was no reason* why I should not have done with that shot what I willed!' exclaimed the Prince passionately. 'There *was no reason* – except that there *was* a reason to do it! Do you see how I fail!! Do you see how it is!! I fail *only because* there is some slight importance to the shot! One game won or lost, when life for me is an endless stream of games won and lost, and none more consequential than the last, except perhaps that some tiny desire in me *wished* to win it. You see, were *no* shot ever to have that curse upon it – Significance, Importance – I should never miss! But even the warmth of a desire as cold as mine burns to ashes that which it desires, destroys it utterly, no matter how trivial, and I squirm with self-hatred and remorse, as all things are denied me! For if I cannot do *this* simple thing, how can I do *any* thing?'

'Well, Menshalla,' said the Vizier, 'how do *you* feel after this, your latest remarkable victory?'

'Indeed,' said the dwarf modestly, 'I did not win this contest upon the pure merit of my shooting. My opponent was in a position to triumph, were it not for this last unfortunate attempt of his. But, though he is most certainly blessed with greater gifts and abilities for this sport, as in all things (as befits one of royal blood), it is still true that nothing is ever certain. A mistake may intervene at any moment, likely or unlikely. It is thus with me, just as it is with him.'

'Perhaps it was this coffee you have been drinking,' said the Vizier to the Prince, noticing a cup sitting among his spare markers. 'Perhaps it decayed your aim with nervous vibration.'

'No,' said the Prince, shaking his head. 'That cannot be, because I have made such a shot as this should have been on a thousand days and more when I have also drunk coffee. There is *no reason* for me to have done as I have done.'

'Did you know,' said the Vizier in a conversational manner, looking about himself, 'that men have called this room the very *Navel of the Universe*?'

This rather different remark occasioned a longish pause.

'No,' said the Prince, then, with evident disinterest.

'Well, their reasoning for it is peculiar, but it is so. For, though we, so blessed by *Caliphal Intimacy*, are ever looking *outward*, you should know that the great commonality of men – even now! – gaze *inward*, upon us. Remarkable! Marvellous! It is almost as if they wanted something! But you must understand how they conceive of the matter.' He settled in to explain, leaning his hand against the board and crossing his legs.

'Well, they say to themselves, here we are upon the *earth*. (How curious. How droll.) Is there any better earth than this earth? A pointless question, entirely. But, then, are there better or worse places *upon* the *earth*? Much less pointless!

'Well, they persist, one to another, who is the ruler, properly speaking, of the *earth*? The *Caliph*, needless to say. Now, one half of the *earth* heeds the rod and rule of the *Commander of the Faithful*, and one half does not, so surely this first half is the better! Certainly, so is this first half, this grand *Caliphate*, this widely spreading realm, the first in importance. May I describe it to you?'

The Prince made no answer, but began silently clearing up the pieces from the board.

'So far and glimmering, from west to east, ring the names!' exclaimed the Vizier. '*Andalusia* in the north, with horses racing across plains, *Magrhib*, tranquil by the great glittering western sea, *Libya*'s deserts and groves, and wondrous *Egypt*'s speechless stones; the ancient noble realms of *Arabia*: *Hejaz* and *Yemen*, the *Hadramaut* and *Oman*, *Mahra*, *Hezer* and *Bahrain*; and in the mountainous north *Armenia*, and *Persian Khorosan*, with lightning dogs and fierce-eyed hawks; and the wild eastern lands, *Kerman* and *Mekran*, and all the varied countries even out to strange and exotic *India*. They stretch like a vast jewelled garment, tawny and green and glinting with silver rivers embroidered, rumpled with mountains and valleys, sewn with shining cities.

'In the bosom of these lands, protected and served in north and south and east and west by their strong fresh limbs, lie the sweet lands of *Syria* and *Mesopotamia*, and towards these rich domains the eyes of all men are ever turned. They are not turned to *China*, where men are barbaric and eat meats warmed under their saddles. They are not turned to the godless north beyond the mountains, where there is only gloom and snow and neither warmth nor wine nor light. They are not turned to fabled *Abyssinia*, which probably does not exist at all. They are turned to the true glory that they can *see*, and *know* to be real. And what lies in the true geographical heart of that Glory?

'Well, they say, none other than the queen of the world, the Abode of Peace, the treasure of the universe, the preserve of civilisation itself: the great metropolis *Bagdad*. *Bagdad*, with its myriad mosques and domes and minarets catching the gentle morning light – *Bagdad* with its teeming markets and canals choked with commerce, and its thousands of wealthy palaces. But, then, there are even degrees of magnificence within *Bagdad* itself! For what sits in the midst of this grandest of all places?

'Well, they say, of course, this every man knows. It is the ancient *round city* of *al-Mansur*, whose perfect symmetry and ageless beauty are the marvels of the universe. Whose twelve rings of wall are impregnable, whose white features are even and unbroken and unblemished. But does not something occur at the centre of the *round city* also? So they ask.

'Indeed, they say, does not the great *Palace* of the *Caliph* stand there? Well, it does! Then, truly, they cry, herein must lie the *navel of the universe* itself! And they gaze upon it with the utmost satisfaction, determining its various parts. For it is like the honied bee-comb, complex and connected, dripping everywhere with sweet gold, they say. Here on one side is the *Courtyard of the People*, here opposite are the famed *Women-Gardens*, here again the *Preserves of the Empress*, and here above the *Hall of the Caliph* himself! But what is it that lies in the centre of the centre of the heart? What room is it we see, isolated, but connected to all, which is at the very core, the hub of the irresistibly outward-spreading pattern?

'Ah, they say, it is the *Chamber of the Prince of Stars*, wherein abides our *future hope*.'

The Vizier stopped speaking, and fixed upon the young man a regard which had been growing increasingly grave.

'O *Prince*,' said he at length, 'my mouth is full of a dreadful bitterness. In my inner mind, a foul Ifrit whispers: "*Would they were here*, the men of the world, to *see* this marrow, this core, this hub. To know the emptiness that it is."

'Today was mysteriously hung one *Salim bin Haubut*, the famous Moderate Man. It is a development of the greatest imaginable peril, for he was a true retainer, a binding for the frail sheaf of the city's passions. What will come of it cannot be said, but you must prepare yourself to go to your people, and play properly the role God has chosen for you.'

'Are they *my* people?' asked the Prince of Stars in a very

low voice. 'The Empress my mother feels they are *hers*.
Likewise the Caliph my father calls *himself* their owner. This
man Zardin al-Adigrab, says they are *his*. Or *no one*'s.'

'I believe your grace knows in what relation he actually
stands to the people,' replied the Vizier. 'They do not look to
you, because they do not believe in you. You are forgotten by
them. But the moment of succession, of decision, may
nonetheless soon be upon them. Their world is filling up like
a deep pool with death. Only *you* are their life.'

'Life,' said the Prince vaguely.

'You must *be* what you are!' cried out the Vizier.

'Be,' said the Prince, and looked down at the board, now
cleared of all its players. He took a single disk and put it in
shooting position. 'Well,' he said, 'if you see that this room is
at the centre of things, do you see that this board is at the
centre of this room, and that yon hole is at the centre of this
board, and...' He paused, bent down, and after a long
moment's concentration, snapped the piece with his finger.
It slid forward and stopped just short of the hole. '... and
you see?'

At this moment all six people in the room became aware of a
very unwonted sound. Someone, in fact, a number of
people, were approaching rapidly down all four long-disused
corridors. They were accompanied by a growing commotion
of shouting and excitement, and of a sudden a large crowd of
eunuchs and slaves with torches burst excitedly from every
side into the chamber, all crying and exclaiming together in a
great clamour: '*Something very dreadful indeed is happening! Something very dreadful indeed is happening!*'

5 Bagdad by Night

The first evening stars glimmered beyond the curving dome of the mosque. Nighthawks and swallows were chirruping in the cool air. Gajaba, the lamp-maker's wife, sat ruminating with her three sleeping children by the trunk of the banyon tree, and the brown canal water at the foot of the deserted laundry yard glinted velvet purple in her eyes. 'It all becomes so clear,' said she.

'Was I dreaming these many years, to feel, and yet not to see the truth about the life I live? Now the myriad cruel and unperceiving acts of my husband march through my memory like numberless ranks in the Caliph's army, every one of them tormenting me with their grossness and disrespect. But it need not have been thus! I was not born to be a vulgar man's thrall! Had I been who I *truly* was I would have been one of the palace slaves instead, and a great court lady, like the Empress herself. Who am I that *this* should be my life, that my beauty should ever and again be squandered *here*, in this squalor, on a man who is not as me, nor by any means worthy of me? O, could I but call back the day when this ill-matching life was made!'

Then Zardin al-Adigrab slipped noiselessly by in his boat, whetting a glinting scimitar.

Mustaffah al-Raman crouched in the darkened house-barge doorway behind his brother, who was sitting on the steering block and whittling a wooden bird. Mustaffah al-Raman listened to the little scraping sound the blade made against the wood in the quiet evening, and stared at his brother's back, and thought: 'He is but one year older than I, and look, I am even a little taller and a little stronger than him. And I am certainly quicker, and wiser, and more fearless in every way. But who *am* I, and what hope have I of joy and happiness, who am but my father's *second* son? Were I to push him suddenly, he might fall upon his knife and die. Or I might knock him down into the canal and he might drown to death in the water. O, that would be better, than to crawl once more into the narrow bed we share, and pull the single blanket over us, and spend once more the long darkness intimate with each other's smell and breathing. How Allah must despise me, that I was not born first!'

Then past his brother's bent head he saw Zardin al-Adigrab poled swiftly by.

Sadim bin Tialimat settled himself by the water on stiff knees like knobbed reeds, and prepared to make evening prayers of adoration. Little curls of mist drifted on the dark still surface, and the cool of oncoming evening made the elderly man shiver, while the cries of the Muezzins hung reverberating in the air. 'O true God,' said he, before even beginning his prayer, 'I am one considered pious and happy. But I know that in my body's core I am not as I seem – nor am I contented. There *is* but one God, yet false gods spring up in all my desires. The smile of a man, not in reverence for my good habits, but because I too am simply a man – that is a god. The children that have never sprung from my loins – the children I shall never have – are small dark-headed gods, haunting me with running and laughter. A tall horse, a swift tasselled camel, that might speed me across the land with the wind in my beard – these are truer gods to me, who shuffles so slowly in the endless courtyards before the veritable God. Who am I, so impure, so compromised with unbridled thought, to be bending my head again at dusk, with an unhappy heart and a mind still hungering for the god that hand might touch and eye might see?'

Then ripples lapped at the paving by his feet, and he looked up to see Zardin al-Adigrab glide by, his eyes on fire, and his gaze fixed before him.

Shahnez Lakhani came down the steps to the water's edge with stones concealed in her robe. Behind her from the lighted doorway drifted wailing music and the laughter of drunkenness.

'So, and though they all say to me: *it shall be* – it shall *not* be, no, not ever,' whispered she. 'And though my father brings me his young man, and though my mother says it is ever thus, and though my sisters all of them have done it –

indeed, and say they are happy – and though my brothers laugh and say I should be beaten. And though the Imam himself is kind and says, that they gain the gifts of God who resign their will to him, and though whatever and all else – *it shall not be*!' The lights of the wealthy palaces around her glimmered on the still surface of the canal, and beyond, over the dusky white walls of al-Mansur, the round city, the shape of the Palace rose dark and silent.

'Yes,' said she, 'and my father says it is because I dote upon some other that I will not marry his choice. Once in the square I did see a cameleer's son, who was clean and happy, and smiled kindly at me. I think if there were one as he was, I might so choose and be content. But who am I to marry one as good as he? It is a sad thing that I should have seen him at all, for such hopes are only bitterness and cruelty to me now! It is certain that I shall marry no one, but the water shall have me first. I am not the shining Princess Badroulboudur, nor am I the beautiful Naomi, nor soft Marina of Tyre. There may be such happy conclusions as theirs, and there may always be, but yet I shall be dead, or I shall be defiled, and that will not change, no, whatever else may go well for an eternity of heroines, rising in lovely triumphs . . .'

At that moment the boat bearing Zardin al-Adigrab arose suddenly out of the dusk, swerved to avoid her, and passed quickly on, disappearing once more into obscurity. Lingering only a space to watch him go, the young girl presently plucked up her weighted draperies and stepped delicately down into the water, wading forward until she was immersed up to her waist. Then she spread her arms and pushed off gently towards the centre of the canal, where she was pulled slowly down into the black water and began helplessly to drown.

Zardin al-Adigrab had signalled for his boat to stop at a corner where the canal washed against the very walls of al-Mansur.

'This place only I know,' he whispered, 'and it shall lead me inwards, if I have the courage.'

'O Zardin al-Adigrab,' whispered back his boatmen, 'do

you?' And Zardin al-Adigrab laughed a low laugh, quickly stripping off his shirt and baring himself to a loincloth. Then he took his scimitar in his hand.

'When shall we see you again?' asked his followers.

'At sunrise,' said he.

'O Zardin al-Adigrab.'

Zardin al-Adigrab had pulled a short length of cord from the bottom of the boat and tied it through the grip of the weapon so that it formed a loop. This he passed over his head and arm, letting the scimitar lie along his back. Then with a sudden agile movement he slipped over the gunwhale and was gone down into the water.

The boatmen waited wordlessly for long moments. Then one to the other whispered: 'We may say we saw him at the last.'

But Zardin al-Adigrab was diving downwards with fast, hard strokes, feeling the cold surface with his hands. Soon he reached a square iron grate set in the wall, and between it and the stones on one side there was a narrow gap, through which he struggled like a squirming eel, coming with difficulty into a long submarine passage. Along this passage he darted with desperate undulations. Long and long he went, going faster and faster, till finally, when no man could live an instant longer without breath, he emerged in a small dark chamber, gasping terribly. Said he, after a moment, 'That is one breath.'

Then he swelled his chest and dived again and swam for an even longer distance through the underwater conduit till he emerged once more into a tiny lightless air-pocket. 'I have breathed the second breath,' he whispered, when he was able. 'And it remains to be done but once more.'

So he drew in the damp, stale air to his fullest capacity and, descending again into the well-channel, swam forward with great strength. On and on he passed with fierce strokes and kicks of his legs but the dark passage continued ever before him. Soon the blood began to protest sharply in Zardin al-Adigrab's head, and his eyes bulged and went dim and his lungs seemed to fold up within him, but he only persisted in swimming forth. Then presently, as he swam ever and ever, the desire for air and breath lessened in him and there came before his eyes a bright virgin in the water, saying, 'All is well, Zardin al-Adigrab, for you have nigh achieved what you desire.'

'Nonetheless,' said Zardin al-Adigrab with his mind, 'it is important that I breathe.'

'Well, truly,' said the fairy, 'for that all you need do is open your mouth, and the cool water will refresh you just as air would have.'

'That it would not,' said Zardin al-Adigrab with his mind. 'And, indeed, thou knowest it.'

'In the end, in the end,' chanted the virgin, who had unexpectedly become two virgins, 'water is but air, and earth is but fire. Trapped, trapped, that is all!'

'In truth,' replied Zardin al-Adigrab, 'I am surely entered into a glittering palace of false deceptions!'

'But otherwise you will die, certainly,' said the virgins, with a concerned air.

'Water is water. Earth is earth. That is their virtue,' said Zardin firmly in his mind.

'Death is death, Zardin al-Adigrab, after all,' replied the fairies.

'This is not dying,' said he with his mind. 'What they do elsewhere is dying. But I shall not myself die, because I am not one of them, of the dying sort.'

'O poor Zardin al-Adigrab,' said a great number of virgins, 'deception, *deception*! It is *you* who art by your very self deceived! Little point there is in our warning you, or telling you the true nature of things, since *now* indeed you *must* die!'

At this very word, however, Zardin al-Adigrab felt stones come up under his feet and in another instant his head broke forth into air.

At first he could but suck helplessly, rocking with desperate heaving gasps, as if his convulsing body would turn itself quite inside out in its agony for breath. For many long moments he endured a sharp suffering worse than the worst moments of his swimming, while his throat and rounded mouth let forth a pathetic whistling, piping sound, like that of a duck. But gradually, with larger, deeper, more gratifying breaths, he began to be slaked and sight returned to his darkened eyes, and he said, at length, 'Now may I perform with purity that which I am born to perform!'

Then he began to look around himself and see that he was in a large underground apartment, where a single torch burned and many pots and jars and barrels were stacked against rough-hewn stone walls. 'Certainly I have dreamed aright,' he said to himself, 'for I am in the very well-room of the Caliph's palace, where the water is drawn.' And indeed, he was standing, still half-submerged, in a low circular basin which was the well itself. Then he heard people approaching, so he clambered out and hid himself behind some jars.

Soon there entered from a dark hallway a line of young women, poorly dressed, evidently slaves, who cast a forest of shadows about the room. They sang softly in unison as they dipped their jugs in the well and went about the work of cleansing the Caliph's golden meal dishes. The dishes flashed and glinted, and rattled as the slaves stacked them, and their motions while they sang and toiled were slow and lethargic, like those of dreamers, or those entranced by drugs:

> O pretty falcon scything in the sky,
> You have a wondrous lustrous coat,
> You have a brilliant angry eye;
> Your mistress awaits you soon
> Where the cliff-tops burn with moon.
>
> O lovely fish glitt'ring in the stream,
> Your scales are as silver as a spoon,
> You move like sunlight in a dream;
> Your lovers want you by them
> In the cool of a sparkling fountain.
>
> O delicate fly drifting by the grass,
> Your wings are blue as the sapphire gem,
> Your eyes are glinting balls of glass;
> Your unknown lovers call you from the field
> Your million lovers call you from the field.

Zardin al-Adigrab was much affected to hear their haunting voices, and found it necessary to wipe a tear from his eye.

But the slaves remained oblivious of him, and went steadily about their tasks. Presently, the leader of the Ripe Fruit
Party noticed that as they finished their washing and slop-
ping many of them retired to a corner of the chamber and,
raising their garments, calmly squatted to relieve themselves, as it appeared this was another function of the place.
Zardin observed them with reverence and interest. For it was
a sight not he nor any other man ever before had viewed.

'This too, can I find beautiful!' he at length cried out in a
low voice.

Soon all the washing was done, and each woman placed a
filled jug on her head and knelt to gather up the dishes. Then
one by one they filed out through the narrow hallway and up
the set of curving stone-cut stairs it led to. On quick
noiseless feet he followed them, even all dripping with water
as he was, taking care to stay a few steps back and conceal his
presence.

Upwards for several minutes they passed, turning in a
slow spiral, the women soon falling silent but for the soft
padding of their bare feet on the stairs. Then at last the
column stopped, and voices could be heard ahead, male,
then female, speaking in short phrases, repeating something
over and over. Now the line moved forward slowly, in halts
and starts, and Zardin, peering cautiously forward, could see
the outlines of a massive marbled doorway over their heads.
Closer and closer they drew until finally, edging forward, the
Ripe Fruit man was able to see what was transpiring, a sight
which filled him with amazement and outrage.

Before a tall, tomb-like entrance way there stood a eunuch,
thin, sallow faced, with an expression of extraordinary
cruelty and contempt upon his features. His garments were
all of red, and a gleaming yellow stone shone from the centre
of his turband. Before him stopped each of the kitchen
slaves, and setting down her burden, raised her garment over
her head and displayed herself to him in full nakedness. In
this posture each paused until he was satisfied, and pronounced these words:

'Well, it is you, and only you!'

To which they replied:

'Yes, O Alcash of the blue-eyed ones, it is I, only I.'

Then the eunuch would say:

'Go forward, for the good of the Caliph!'

And the next slave stepped forth.

'He has not the lover's right!' muttered Zardin al-Adigrab. 'Such is ever the vile practice of this place, from top to bottom. But it shall not endure!'

Even as he spoke he reached behind himself and drew his long scimitar over his head, rapidly undoing its rope and winding it tightly around his wrist. Then, clenching the weapon in a firm and loving grasp, he stepped forward behind the last of the maidens. Just as the eunuch began to swing closed a great iron door, he cried out:

'You cannot close this door without *me*, O leering one! Take your steel in hand, for I shall not be denied!'

'Who art *thou*!' cried the eunuch, leaving hold of the door and backing up in his surprise.

'It is I and only I!' jeered Zardin al-Adigrab, advancing to the threshold.

'For some that is enough, for others it is not!' said the eunuch.

'I whom you wish to forget! I whom you wish to debase! But I whom debasement has made pure! *I* who am more of you than you are yourselves!' cried Zardin. '*I* who shall *not* be denied!'

'You cannot enter here!' was the only answer he received. 'Already you have come so far that death can be your only expectation!'

'And yet I expect *life*! Draw forth your weapon and continue to resist me if you wish!' exclaimed Zardin al-Adigrab, making ready to rush upon the eunuch. But this Alcash called out suddenly and surprisingly in a loud voice:

'*O blue-eyed ones*! *O blue-eyed ones come forth*!' At his words arose a great clattering in the darkness beyond, and before Zardin could well prepare himself there came from the shadows a rushing band of blue-eyed *apes* screaming and chattering and all holding bludgeons and knifes in their crude hands!

'Destroy this treason!' cruelly commanded the eunuch, and pointed to Zardin al-Adigrab.

In an instant they were upon him, battering him with blows and slashing at his skin with knives, so that Zardin al-Adigrab was hard pressed to save himself and fled in terror back down the steps. But this gave him no respite because the apes came clamouring after him in ungainly bounds, screaming and hissing and clashing their teeth.

When he arrived back at the well-room he turned to face them with his scimitar in hand and at once the battle grew savage and deadly. Many did Zardin slay with his cruel cuts, lashed out here and there in desperation, so that their blood ran into the cracks in the stone floor, but he could not resist their numbers. And the more he fought the wilder the blue-eyed apes became, foaming at the mouth and screaming in such a fashion that Zardin's flesh involuntarily shivered.

At last he leapt to the top of a large barrel, with the apes bounding all around him, and cried:

'O apes! Do you not know whom you slay!'

But the apes heeded him not, but instead began to rip up stones and tiles from the floor and hurl them at him.

'O apes!' cried Zardin, trying to shield himself and reason with them. 'Are we truly enemies?'

But once again the apes did not respond, and one of their number pulled himself up by his hands and bit Zardin al-Adigrab savagely on the foot. Flinching with pain, Zardin al-Adigrab struck him down, uttering as he did a wild cry, a cry which, once begun, grew long and tormented, becoming at first a snarl and then rising to a mad, unbearable scream, such as seemed to burst from his very soul.

Even the apes were taken aback by the power of this grim and awesome sound, and they hesitated, then shrank back in confusion, eyeing him uneasily. Zardin could see that he had their attention, and drew in his breath. '*No more, O apes!*' he thundered, and the apes all gibbered nervously. '*No more!*' he roared again with furious authority. The apes began to drop their weapons with a clatter to the stone floor. Gradually a kind of peace settled on the well-room.

Zardin bent down and transfixed the assembly of crouching apes with a terrible stare, peering slowly from one to the next. 'O apes,' he whispered, 'do you not know why I am here?' The apes looked about vaguely. Some played uncomfortably with their toes.

'I am here to bring forth That Which is Within!' he cried. 'That Which is Within – do you not know what it is? Does it not beckon to you also, from behind the dark doors of its seclusion?'

The apes replied not, but bared their teeth.

'O apes,' whispered Zardin al-Adigrab again, 'O blue-eyed ones, it is yours as much as it is mine! It is what is within you, as much as within me! It is what is *truly* within you. And is it truly within you to kill *me*, who am here to deliver it forth?

'O *apes*!' he shouted suddenly. 'Have you never wondered who you *are*!'

The apes rolled their eyes and babbled.

'Have you never wanted to *know*?' went on Zardin, rising to his full height. 'Have you never wished to look into your own veritable hearts? Have you never been allowed into the secret chambers of your own souls, to see for yourselves! What *is* it that destroys your curiosity, that lies smothering you, making you mere bestial apes? What prevents you from rising?'

At these exhortations the apes began covering their eyes with their hands and whimpering. The voice of Alcash the eunuch called down faintly, 'Obey, apes, obey!' But Zardin did not relent.

'O what would you *do*, what would you *be*, if only you *could*!' he challenged them in ringing tones. 'Imagine, apes. Imagine!'

There was silence now among the motionless apes.

'*Imagine*!' cried out Zardin again.

The apes were shuddering.

'*Imagine*!'

Trembling.

'*Imagine*!'

The hands began falling from the apes' faces. But every eye that was revealed was the eye of insanity! Suddenly they released such an uproar of screeching and babbling that even Zardin was staggered and amazed. Capering wildly, they snatched up their weapons and rushed in a rout from the room, swarming back up the stairs, gibbering as they went in a fashion so horrible, so deranged, that only a nightmare could convey its uncontrolled and murderous frenzy.

Zardin, as he sank down from the barrel, sweating and quivering, whispered hoarsely after them:

'I am here to bring forth That Which is Within!'

Soon all sound ceased, and he rose and walked unsteadily to the well-basin and refreshed himself with its water. Then, limping because of the bite on his foot, he slowly ascended the curving staircase once more.

'O mercy!' cried the small voice of the eunuch from above.

'That cannot be,' said Zardin al-Adigrab gravely, continuing to toil upwards.

Shortly he could hear other sounds, unearthly shrieks and thumps and clashings of weapons. He hurried onwards, painfully, as best he could. Approaching the top, the leader of the Ripe Fruit Party heard all the noise above slowly die away.

Emerging, he was confronted with a most unpleasant and strange spectacle. The hideous remains of the eunuch Alcash, all battered, serrated and dismembered lay here and there in testimony of the inverted fury of his former minions. But the pathologic wrath of the blue-eyed ones had no end at his destruction, and had evidently expressed itself further in fratricidal and even suicidal butchery. Some of the apes lay as if gone quietly asleep, but many were dead of horrible wounds, some clearly self-inflicted. Certain it was, however, as Zardin shortly discovered, not a single one of them continued to breathe!

'These,' said Zardin al-Adigrab, surveying them, 'were no ordinary, natural apes.'

Looking about, the leader found himself to be in a large,

dark storeroom. Bales of cloth, and jars of wine and olives lined every wall. There were several doors, and he was in great confusion as to which to take.

'My purpose is clear,' said he, 'but how may I find my direction?'

Then a faint glistening on the marble floor caught his eye, and he saw that the kitchen slaves' feet had left a small moist trail through one of the openings.

'I am the vengeance!' cried Zardin al-Adigrab with suddenly renewed energy and optimism. 'All shall be revealed!'

Then he set out to follow the trail, which led him down long corridors and through storeroom after storeroom filled with goods and foods and heaps of weapons and fineries of every sort. After some walking he became aware of voices and the clattering of implements ahead of him.

Approaching stealthily he soon came to a brightly lit doorway, through which he peered with caution. Within was a large bustle of people and activity, and the air was filled with laughter and singing and the shouting of instructions and questions. Great iron stoves lined the walls and from them issued many mingled aromas, while every different sort of food was heaped up on long rows of wooden benches.

'These are likely to be the Caliphal kitchens themselves,' said Zardin al-Adigrab. 'Perhaps my purpose may be achieved by a simple poison! But there is no sure and certain method, truly.'

It was evident that a meal was very near completion. Some of the slave-girls were piling brightly coloured fruits on to golden platters, and trays of lovely sweets were being taken from ovens. Stewards were ladling out dishes of sauce and vegetable ragoos, and jugs of wine were being decanted from large jars by the walls. It was obviously to be a meal of such magnificence, subtlety and variety, that it could be intended for none other than the Caliph.

Still, though all else was present, Zardin al-Adigrab could not discern what the main course of meat was to be.

Then an elderly male slave, who had been judging and ordering all, clapped his wrinkled hands and called out: 'Bring forth the three fishes!' To the secret watcher's great enchantment there were then produced from a hamper near the door three beautiful pink and green striped fish, of a variety he had never before seen.

'Bring me the pan!' now cried the old slave, and when this was produced all the other slaves and servants crowded about him. With great care, he began to fry the fish.

'Retire and prepare to take up your appointed burdens!' commanded the old cook, as he turned each fish once. 'Hearing and obedience!' cried they, and immediately hurried back to form a Procession of Food, each with their own platter or bowl or sweating wine jug. At the end of the Procession were placed three beautiful young boys, dressed alike in azure and silver garments, and carrying three covered dishes of bronze. As the cook finished each of the fishes he was cooking, he placed it reverently in one of the bronze receptacles and the boy lowered the cover over it. When the three were done, a quietness came over the whole party, their smiles being quickly replaced by a uniformly stiff and ceremonious expression, and they all fell to making small last moment preparations. With great dignity, the old man set down his pan and fork, and crossed the kitchen to a large bare area of wall directly opposite the watching Zardin al-Adigrab. Here there dangled a long, golden-fibred cord.

'Is all in Absolute Readiness?' he demanded.

'Yes, O Master-cook,' responded the line as one, 'all is ready.'

Then the old slave pulled twice slowly on the cord, and with a great roaring and grinding sound, the wall swung majestically open to reveal a long, candle-lit gallery of stairs leading upwards. The candle-flames all flickered momentarily with the gust of air from the doors, then became still, serenely beautiful once more.

'Praise be to Appetites!' quietly exclaimed Zardin al-Adigrab. 'Harbingers of freedom! Betrayers of tyranny! I shall find my access through the lusting of the evil one's own stomach!'

The Procession began at once to ascend, and in a short while had left only the Master-cook in the kitchen, watching them go. As the last of them, the three fish-bearing boys, passed through, the great doors rumbled together again and Zardin al-Adigrab leapt forward from his hiding place.

'Now, old master!' cried he. '*Does* that food go to the Caliph himself?'

The slave turned to Zardin al-Adigrab in amazement, but he replied: 'At this late hour the Caliph will be asleep. This food is only the food that must sit at his chamber door, in case he should awake in the night and be hungry.'

'Does it often happen thus?' inquired Zardin in great eagerness. 'Does the Caliph awaken each night and call for food?'

The cook looked wonderingly at Zardin al-Adigrab, obviously marvelling at him and his fierceness and his beauty. When he answered, it was slowly, as one entranced. 'It has *never* happened,' he said. 'But, you see, we must prepare in case some night it should. These pink and green fishes I have cooked because they are renowned for their ability to stay warm. All these other foods are imbued with great power to induce gentle and restful sleep.'

Zardin al-Adigrab at once bounded to the hamper by the door and drew forth another fish.

'This is good, good!' cried he. 'Fry this fish for me without delay, and give me also somewhat to wear, that I may join the Procession.'

'O, but this cannot be!' replied the old slave quickly. 'There can be but three fishes, and that is all it is my liberty to cook.'

'Well, and I urge you to fry another fish, and so thou shalt do it!' Zardin turned a furious eye on the old man. 'I am not to be resisted and denied, simply because you take it into your head that you "must" cook but three fishes!' And so speaking he seized the pan and thrust it into the other's hand, throwing the fish down in it, so that it began to sizzle with the heat remaining in the metal.

The Master-cook looked at the fish with an air of enormous sadness.

'It is for me to cook but three fishes every night. That is all that I do, and you must not ask me to do more.'

'Come come,' said Zardin al-Adigrab, as he began searching about for garments. 'And suppose the Caliph *should* awake, and suppose he should be *terribly* hungry and wanted a fourth fish? Might he not praise you for anticipating his needs, and fill your mouth with gold and give you a lovely houri? Begin, begin, for I can have no delay!'

And so the cook set the pan down on the stove and began, slowly and vaguely, to fry the fish, saying:

'It is for me to cook three fishes, and only three. I do not go to the ocean to see the fishes caught. I do not go above the stairs to see the fishes being eaten. You must not imagine that I have any choice about these fishes.' And presently, as he cooked the fish, large tears began to run down his aged cheeks.

Having found a discarded set of garments, Zardin returned and stared at the old slave with incredulity. 'Have you never wondered to know *why* it is but three fishes thy tyrant master wishes?' he asked. 'Might it not be that there *is* no reason? Verily, when That Which is Within comes forth, a man shall cook two fishes or four fishes, just as it suits him!'

'That is unthinkable,' said the cook in great despondency. 'What is more, it suits me to cook three.'

'Yet it shall be thought! And much else besides,' calmly announced Zardin al-Adigrab. 'For I tell you that this cooking of three fishes is but death disguised, and tyranny, and you shall do it no more. For death, will be substituted life!'

'Who are you in any case?' demanded the cook, as he watched Zardin don the clothes, which were yellow and green, and quite unlike those of the other fish-bearers. 'And why do you come thus at night with perilous cruel orders and commands about the cooking of extra fishes?'

'I am the vengeance,' replied Zardin al-Adigrab. 'What is more, I may tell you that I am not unknown to you, though you may have forgotten me and denied me.'

'Well, you have done me a great harm about this fish,' said the cook, with the tears now fully pouring from his eyes in renewed sorrow, 'for I did not wish to cook it.'

'Come, come,' said Zardin al-Adigrab again, taking the fish from him and slapping it rudely on a silver chalice he had found. 'A man may cook another fish or so and still be a man.'

But the old cook replied not a word but only made a small, pathetic coughing sound, and sat down on the floor and leaned his head against a bench.

'Now, you must open the door for me, and rapidly,' said Zardin al-Adigrab when all was arranged. But the Master-cook did not move, and when Zardin approached him he found to his surprise that he was quite dead.

'This is odd,' said he, 'and also to some degree pitiable. For here, for the very fear of it, is one who shall not see the great dawn. But this is no doubt as it must be, and I too must continue upon my task.'

Going to the bare section of wall, he pulled twice on the golden cord, just as he had seen the cook do. Once again the wall parted with a large noise and the long gallery of stairs was revealed.

Up these sped Zardin al-Adigrab with all possible stealth (his foot now, in his eagerness, seemingly all forgotten), bearing his fish in its silver warmer. His hastiness was rewarded shortly, when he reached the top and discovered the last of the Food Procession just then filing through a large ornate doorway. These he joined, and in such a deft manner that none noticed his arrival.

On the other side of the doorway was a large, brightly lit chamber, full of milling officials and armed guardsmen, and the newly arrived kitchen slaves, whose orderly line disappeared as soon as they passed through the door, and now walked about here and there, still holding their food. Against one wall of the elegantly furnished room, beneath a magnificent crimson canopy, sat a Chief of Kazis on a throne, surrounded by sumptuous maidens. Laughter and conversation filled the air, as everyone, soldiers, slaves and all, mingled on terms of greatest familiarity.

'All that which is destined for the lips of our Noble and Auspicious Monarch – whom God eternally ratify! – must first pass the testing of his lesser subjects!' announced the Chief of the Kazis over the noise. 'What is more, the honourable Empress has urged me to especial care this evening. Who knows but what poison may lurk in these meats, who knows what evil is intended by these vegetables! Therefore, since the hazardous task has been granted to only *me*, bring forth the first dish!'

This speech was greeted with words of agreement and encouragement, and the first carrier, a comely lass of some fifteen years, came forward in a sprightly manner, and presented him with a platter on which stood a single pear. The Chief of the Kazis tasted it with some ceremony.

'It savours clearly of sweetness and innocence,' remarked he after a pause. 'But let further trials be conducted on it, for one man's judgement can never be relied on in isolation, when the life of the first Ruler of the world hangs in the balance. Pray, young maiden, let its juices be sampled by some of my inferiors here.' And so the slave merrily took the half-eaten pear to a soldier she favoured and together they consumed it. In a similar manner was all the rest of the food treated, dish by dish, and jug by jug, while one of the kitchen girls began to play indolently on an oud, and others joined in impromptu songs. Nor was the wine spared either, so that soon none were hesitant or shy, but all were happy and talkative. Finally it came the moment for Zardin al-Adigrab to present his fish to the Kazi, who had by this point eaten much and drunk more, and was passing the dishes by with the most superficial of sniffs.

'Come forth, young man,' he cried gaily, 'and let us inspect your pretty little dish.'

Zardin al-Adigrab advanced with a bowed head, and obsequiously presented the Chief of the Kazis with his burden. The Chief of the Kazis lifted the cover with a sigh.

'He who has created this fish has indeed succeeded admirably,' he said, 'and deserves our regards and praises for his efforts.'

But then a confusion seemed to come into his mind, and he stopped, and said:

'But is this a *fish* I am shown?'

'Indeed, O Chief of the Kazis, it is a fish,' replied Zardin al-Adigrab in a low, humble voice.

'But have I not been shown three fish already?' asked he. 'It cannot be a fish!'

'O inspector,' said Zardin al-Adigrab, politely taking the cover from his hand and replacing it, 'it is a fourth fish.'

At this moment a great silence fell upon the room, and all turned to gaze upon Zardin al-Adigrab.

'A fourth fish!' cried the Chief of the Kazis. 'And what are these improper garments you are wearing! Who art thou, and what is this you are saying: a fourth fish!'

'A fourth fish! A fourth fish!' cried all the soldiers and officials and kitchen slaves.

In a fury Zardin al-Adigrab threw down the fish so that it made a great clattering on the floor.

'Is it as if I were to say the Sun rose in the west, or the stars fell down, or the mountains blew away with the wind?' he cried. 'What signifies it if there be one more fish!'

All the soldiers and slaves let out a great sigh at this boldness, but the deeply agitated Kazi leapt up and cried:

'Who art thou, I say again, who art thou!'

'I am the vengeance,' said Zardin al-Adigrab.

'And why have you come thus concealed and deviously into our midst, and how have you done it!' cried the Kazi. 'Do not admit to me that it is treason! Do not reveal to me that it is an impure design!'

'For the pure all things are pure!' returned Zardin al-Adigrab in defiance. 'I have come to bring forth That Which is Within! I have come to end the realm of evil, to open the eyes of blind tyranny!'

At these forthright and chilling words the Chief of the Kazis grew horribly pale, started to choke, and then abruptly fell down dead, scattering dishes and cups and half-eaten food as he went.

Zardin al-Adigrab threw off his garment and drew out his scimitar, as did all the soldiers in the room. The gasping slaves and officials withdrew hurriedly to the corners.

'*Who are you!*' demanded the soldiers.

'You know who I am,' replied he.

They stepped towards him, and he made a few light passes of his glittering weapon in the air.

'That will not do,' said they, and approached another pace. 'Explain yourself!'

'I weary of explaining,' said Zardin al-Adigrab. 'I am the vengeance.'

'For what?' demanded the soldiers, coming still closer.

Zardin al-Adigrab made a gesture of impatience. 'For all these unanswered questions! I am their answer!'

The soldiers shook their heads and glanced grimly at each other.

'Lock the doors!' ordered one, and people hurried to lock and bar the doors on several sides.

A tall, heavily bearded man confronted Zardin al-Adigrab, blade in hand.

'It is my duty to kill you,' this man told the advocate of ripe fruit and vengeance. 'Those are the orders of my commander, Hamid bin Talal.'

'Do your *duty*, then,' mocked Zardin al-Adigrab.

The man growled fiercely and rushed at him. But Zardin ducked easily under his scimitar and cut him down dead with a backhand stroke.

'But perhaps when you *truly* know why you act you will have some chance of succeeding!'

Another man leapt out, furious at the sight, brandishing a spear.

'You are not *allowed*, evil man! It is not *right*!' he cried as he lunged forward, attempting to impale Zardin al-Adigrab. But Zardin al-Adigrab jumped backwards on to the chair where the Kazi sat, causing the attacker to stumble. As he tried to rise Zardin lit upon him and quickly sliced off both his hands, which made him fall into a swoon and shortly die.

'Obviously, there are deeper moralities,' commented Zardin al-Adigrab.

Angry soldiers were now jostling forward in their eagerness to kill him.

'For the love of the Caliph, our true and rightful monarch!' shouted one, advancing on him with flailing passionate strokes. But he could not overcome the speed and agility of his opponent, and within moments a deft blow by Zardin blinded him so that he dropped his sword. In another instant his heart was punctured by a scimitar tip and he collapsed heavily.

'Might there not be greater things to love?' Zardin al-Adigrab rhetorically wondered.

A fourth soldier leapt forward, spittle bubbling furiously on his lips.

'But nothing worse than you to *hate*!' he fairly screamed. '*Revenge*!' And he also wildly engaged Zardin al-Adigrab, who writhed and wriggled to avoid his maddened blows. For a long minute they danced across the marble floor slashing and faking, until finally Zardin al-Adigrab executed an uncannily swift feint which caused the soldier to misjudge his stroke and trip over a discarded food dish. As he tried to struggle to his feet Zardin snuffed him out.

'Not until hate is *also* love, passion also indifference!' he told the watching crowd. 'Not until That Which is Within has come fully forth!'

When they saw that no single champion seemed able to destroy the mysterious interloper, the rest of the soldiers resolved to attack him together.

'We are soldiers,' they cried, 'and we are men! Unless we are *all* to die, we must put an end to this dangerous person!' So they rushed eagerly forward, their hands full of thirsty steel.

Then was the fighting of Zardin al-Adigrab truly wonderful. Amid a thousand strokes he danced a weird and skilful dance of evasion, as if every step had been planned before. Back and forth and up and down he whirled and leapt gracefully among the flickering edges, as the soldiers struggled in mobs to bring him down. Yet they could not, for they were all but entranced with him and with his motion, so that they continually staggered and stumbled at his dodges and quick turns and spins. So spellbound also were the kitchen party, who watched as the fighters swirled about the chamber like a strange festival, that the girl holding the oud all without thinking began once more to play and vaguely sing, with the clanging of the scimitars weaving rhythmically into her composition.

Longer and longer the struggle continued, but it seemed

Zardin al-Adigrab would never tire but only danced on and on in his marvellous dance. And even as he avoided his enemies' attack he dealt out dire stroke after stroke of his own, so that a great number of them were killed or hurt.

After much bloodshed, however, the soldiers did manage for a moment to drive the leader of the Ripe Fruit Party into a corner of the hall, where they strove in a desperate fury of desire to destroy him. Now even Zardin al-Adigrab seemed endangered, and as he battled them back he called out in a cunning voice to the kitchen slaves and officials across the room. 'O my comrades!' cried he. 'I am you and you are me! Come, step forth, and free yourselves, for you see your freedom here fiercely pressed! Come, you have known me before, and all our partnership was long ago arranged, arranged in our very blood, in our birth, in the beating of our hearts – come, in order that the inevitable may occur!'

The slaves and officials were thrown into great confusion at these words, but the maddened and frustrated soldiers had little doubt of their import. 'Traitors!' cried they. 'Traitors and betrayers all! Indeed, *this* is how he came here!' In a strange access of ferocity many of them turned and fell upon the others, killing their former friends indiscriminately amid a rising tumult. Thus distracted, the remainder were not prepared as Zardin al-Adigrab made a great slashing bound and whirled free with liberated death foaming and glittering along the edge of his pitiless scimitar. Terrible now was the disorder as the fighting raged redoubled amid the cushions and wine-jars and remains of the meal, and man fell wildly upon man all unknowing who his enemy was. Until suddenly, before one could well comprehend it, a last scimitar fell shivering to the floor, and everyone but Zardin al-Adigrab was slaughtered – men, women, officials and all – and the room descended into a morbid, dripping silence.

'Well,' panted Zardin al-Adigrab in a moved voice, looking about himself. 'What do all these noble motivations have at bottom but mistrust and fear and wilful blindness?'

As there came no answer to this question, he slowly doffed the rest of his borrowed clothes, and wiping his scimitar briefly on the robe of a fallen woman, addressed himself again to his mission. Somewhere nearby the Caliph himself must be hidden!

Looking around the room, he quickly discovered a narrow entrance way concealed behind the folds of crimson canopy which hung about the Kazi's throne. Through this, at the end of a short, dark corridor, as yet another set of stairs leading upward into obscurity. By the light of a single candle burning motionless in a silver bracket at the foot, Zardin could see that its walls were made of the finest grey marble, ornamented with elegant designs of jade and sapphire, and that the staircase was draped in glittering materials, laced with precious thread, and exuded a faint, dry odour of old perfume. But somehow also an atmosphere of fear and inexpressible terror pervaded the dim shaft, and a strong wave of reluctance to go further came over even the stout champion of Ripe Fruit.

'Indeed, it *is* a nightmare,' he whispered, 'vivid and horrible! Evil petrified will has formed the stone, and the scent of unhealthy decay is in the shrouds! Yet to overcome even the worst of dreams all we need ever do is *press on*, neither quail nor wake, but sleeping still approach the hidden and terrible thing itself: the beast in the cave, the dark and strangely smiling mother, the father with his rod in the upstairs room. Approach, but approach and see! But touch, and *be* touched. Eat, be eaten, possess, be possessed, slay, *be* slain! Then should we slumber in peace forever, smiling like the little dreaming child, rapt in unqualified joy! Between such a blissful dream, and drugged and drowsy waking, there lies only the barrier of ourselves, and our fear! But courage and holy murder shall carry me past it, even as I am!'

So Zardin al-Adigrab began with great caution to ascend on bare and silent feet, his scimitar poised ready in his hand. He had not gone far when he discovered that the pathway he followed was a tall spiral, and that as soon as he had turned one full turn the air was tinged with a soft blue radiance. A few turns more and there arose in view a set of glittering silver characters, which burned like stars high up in the wall over the head of the stairs. Climbing, Zardin al-Adigrab found them to read as follows:

Obedience so Utter that to Hear is Already to have
    Obeyed
To Know is to be as the Pot in the Potter's Hand
To Think is to have Abandoned all Thought
To Be is to Believe
To Live is to be Ready to Die.

'Modest demands for poor mankind!' said Zardin al-Adigrab bitterly. 'O mad old perversity, when will we be free of thee?'

Then he took a firmer grip on his weapon and answered his own question. '*Now!*' he cried, and leapt forward through the doorway.

He found himself in a narrow, carpeted chamber, with unadorned walls. At the far end was a huge ebony door, beside which sat a tall, unbearded Chamberlain, fast asleep, his head nodding forward on his breast. Over the portal were engraven more letters, which read:

The Unwavering, the Omniscient, the Indomitable, the Auspicious, the Terrible, the Majestic – Nothing Escapeth Us!

'Indeed,' breathed Zardin al-Adigrab, stropping his scimitar on the tail of his loincloth. Then he boldly approached the Chamberlain, and, taking his chin firmly in the fingers of his left hand, sharply raised up his head and drew the blade across his throat. 'Awake!' he cried. The Chamberlain opened his eyes and contemplated Zardin al-Adigrab with a sleepy expression, but said nothing, until presently his eyes closed once more, and Zardin lowered his head upon his chest, so that the outflooding of life could not be seen, and one could hardly distinguish death from a deepening sleep.

'What use is vigilance,' asked he softly, 'when the enemy is one's own hidden self?' Abruptly the Chamberlain gave a loud gurgle and fell over on his side, whistling pathetically.

'No protestations avail us,' remarked Zardin al-Adigrab, as he once more cleaned his busy scimitar. 'It is now the hour of upsurging Revelation. No eyes of will can see the danger.

No ears of concentration can hear its approach.' The Chamberlain lapsed into silence.

Stepping lightly over the body, he pushed open the great, silent door with the tip of his blade and advanced cautiously into the room beyond.

Even the fierce spirit of the leader of the Ripe Fruit Party, however, was not entirely prepared for the splendour that greeted him. His eyes were immediately filled with a soft, silver light from a dozen unflickering lanthorns, and his heart was nearly subdued by an overwhelming opulence of brocade and drapery and precious cushions. The walls were hung with tapestries of glinting silk that were like curtains of wavering light itself, or like the great cold waterfalls of colour that rustle in frigid northern skies. The room was ornamented everywhere with coral and cornelian, with porphyry and ebony, with marble and lapis lazuli blue as the veins on the breasts of heavenly houris. The floor was covered in a thick carpet of jet-black hue.

In the four corners stood exquisitely wrought censers burning aloe-wood and ambergris and subtle foreign musks, so that an aroma of amazing complexity and sweetness drifted insidiously into Zardin al-Adigrab's nose. Glinting here and there in the profusion, as if scattered by some careless child, were emeralds and sapphires and brilliant diamonds of truly staggering dimensions.

But the strangest feature of all in this strange chamber was a deep pool sunk centrally in the floor, and edged with tiles of jade and green crystal. Instead of being filled with water, the pool was brimming with shining quicksilver, that undulated and pulsed in a slow but ceaseless motion, like a bared heart, reflecting on its rounded and changing facets every glinting and glowing wonder of the room. Standing over it, Zardin stared at a queasy elongated image, an image that swelled and burst, narrowed and swam, a dark, ghastly vision of a soul drowning in the heavy flood, emitting silent screams of horror and groaning with nauseous despair – the reflected image of his own face peering upwards from the gleaming murk!

Zardin al-Adigrab, though, only smiled grimly and turned his eyes away.

'What scene of putrid and imaginary slakings do I view here?' he asked aloud. 'Do you dream that *you* can possess the power of the Senses? Do you think them mere treasures, that *you* alone can *have* and *own*?'

No answer being heard, he went on slowly through the chamber, the carpet veritably burning with softness under his sensitive feet. Everything around him was laid out as if it were a bedchamber, except that there was no bed, and no sleeper either, so that he was filled with puzzlement, and also consternation.

'Where are you hiding, O vile old father?' whispered he. 'Why do you conceal yourself from me? Is it that you fear to sleep, knowing I shall come there? It is night, O frozen one, my hour, and deeper slumbers shall soon overcome the tyranny of your waking!'

Then Zardin al-Adigrab perceived an aperture beneath a cloud of white silk, leading once more into darkness. Advancing, he brushed aside the soft stuff, which floated like cobwebs in a faint draught emanating from beyond, and quickly found himself in a dim clothes cupboard hung with many rich and jewelled garments. All of them were familiar to his eye, for he had ever seen them adorn the distant person of the Caliph when he appeared before his Diwan. Here was the scarlet suit of Anger, and here the white and blue dress of Peace, while beside them hung the golden clothes of Forgiveness, the black of Death, the green of Festivity and Happiness, the purple of Law-Giving, and white of Sobriety, and many others beside. Pushing these aside as well, he passed on into a tiny inner foyer, lit by a single, motionless, blue-flamed lamp. Here, each at the top of a dozen small steps, there were three ebony doors.

Zardin al-Adigrab looked from one door to the next, and saw without difficulty that they were all perfectly similar, and could not be told apart.

'Thy life is a game without meaning or cause, evil one,' said he aloud. 'But you may be sure that I have both the patience and the inclination to try all your doors, for though you attempt to hide from my eyes and ears, yet I sense you nonetheless, I sense the emptiness where something *should* be – so, I know it is you – I know you are here.'

Gripping his weapon resolutely in his hand, he stepped up to the door on the right and pushed it with his foot. It swung open soundlessly on a tiny room. In it, on a narrow couch, lay a man sleeping in magnificent robes, with a shining crown on the pillow beside his head that lit up the enclosure with a soft, white radiance. On a finger of the hand that lay curled by his cheek was the great Sapphire Signet of the Realm.

'Caliph!' whispered Zardin al-Adigrab. 'Thy domination is at an end!'

The man instantly awoke, and stared up at him. 'O now, young man,' he said after a moment, 'do not be so hasty that you make an error!'

'I am the vengeance,' said Zardin al-Adigrab, 'I make no errors.'

'Well,' said the Caliph, 'in that case it may surprise you to learn that in actual fact you have been misled. I am not, as it happens, the Caliph. Indeed, I am but a double, a mere chimera for the eyes of the unwary. Many, like you, might *call* me Caliph, but truly, it is not so.'

'Surely you do not imagine that I may be put off!' cried Zardin al-Adigrab. 'Thus have you ever underestimated me, vile one! And shall I swim here through rivers of blood, burn in ordeals of fiery hatred, freeze in frozen heartless wastelands, and be told that there is a *mistake*, that this is not the palace of the Caliph, that this is not a scimitar in my hand, and that you are not the Caliph?'

'Well, in pure truth,' answered the Caliph, 'you must concede that your having swum in rivers of blood and the rest does not make it necessary that *I* be the Caliph. And indeed, were I you, having gone through so much, I should want to be most particular that I assassinate the correct man. And I once again most passionately assure you, I am *not* he!'

'Come, come,' said Zardin al-Adigrab now with a smile, and folding his arms, 'what are these rich robes you are wearing? What is this crown on your pillow? What is this ring on your finger?'

'Ah assassin, assassin,' urged the Caliph, as if very concerned over Zardin's welfare, 'do not enter the confusion so common to your kind, and mistake the trappings for the *essence*! Many a crown has there been with no royalty beneath it, many a mosque has been built with no God inside it, many a word has been spoken with no signifying about it!'

'A word spoken is a word spoken,' said Zardin al-Adigrab bluntly, 'and may cause offence. A crown on a head is a crown *worn*. Let me hear no more of your malingering "essences"!'

'Ah,' said the Caliph brightly, 'but you see I am not wearing it, the crown that is.'

'Come, come,' said Zardin al-Adigrab again. 'Do you persist in this folly so unconnected to that which very clearly is the truth? Do you sit here, upon the Caliph's couch, in the Caliphal palace, with the crown of the Caliphate beside you, and persist in saying to me you are not the Caliph?'

'Indeed I do!' said the Caliph. 'But you may better believe it if you hear how it is I come to be in this situation.'

'You must put aside your words and stories!' shouted Zardin suddenly. 'You must put aside your evasions and excuses and talk of "essences" and "appearances"! You must admit to nothing but the simple *truth*! I am about a great mission, and I have suffered, and will suffer, no interruption of its inevitable progress! That Which is Within shall come forth! Therefore, tell me whether you are Caliph or not, and die at least with the truth upon your tongue!'

'I am not! I am *not*!' shrieked the Caliph, as Zardin raised his arms. 'As to That Which is Within, you may do with it as you wish! Bring it forth! Do! I will help you!'

'Die then denying thy way and thyself!' cried Zardin al-Adigrab grimly. 'For Truth is come and Falsehood banished!' With these words, and both hands on the grip, Zardin al-Adigrab brought his scimitar down furiously on the man on the bed. The blow cut his head off, and those that followed hacked to pieces the rest of his person, even as it lay all unresisting. Nor did he stop then, and so profuse and savage were his continuing strokes, that presently he cut through the very foundations of the bed and it gradually collapsed with its burden into a bloody and disordered pile of wood and cloth and flesh.

When at last he had done and came out of the little room, wiping the sweat from his glistening brow, Zardin al-Adigrab noticed the other two doors still unopened, and said: 'It may be that there is more to be done here, for I cannot deny that I sense him still.'

So he mounted the stairs to the middle door and kicked it open. Here he found a second man lying on a couch, who was identical in every respect to the first. Beside him on the pillow was a second crown, equal in lustre, and upon his finger was another and similarly brilliant signet ring.

'Caliph!' cried Zardin al-Adigrab hoarsely. 'Thy domination is at an end!'

The Caliph woke, and pulled his beard, and said, 'I am no Caliph. I am no *true* Caliph.'

'To *be* Caliph *is* to be false!' cried out Zardin. 'Never has it been so clear to my eyes! To *be* is but to pretend to be! O appalling!'

'By no means do I even pretend to be Caliph,' interjected this Caliph. 'I do not claim it, though you and others before you have tried to press it upon me. But I turn my back upon this power, this prestige and wealth. And why, you most certainly may ask? Because I cannot in truth say that it *is* me, for I *am not* he, and conscience and the respect for Allah with which I am filled prevents me from claiming it. I *am not* Caliph, nor was ever meant to be!'

'*Meant* to be!' cried Zardin al-Adigrab. 'Was one ever *meant* to be this odious thing! No, but men *have* been, just as you, O deceiver, most assuredly *are*!'

'By heaven and earth, *I* assure you it is not so!' answered back the Caliph. 'Indeed, I am one of *you*, O liberator, and you should know that I have long awaited this gratifying moment! For truly, I desire nothing so much as to be able to follow you down to the beloved sea and soil!'

'Come, come,' said Zardin. 'Do you suppose me susceptible to vanity? What is this nonsensical talk you raise between us like a veil? Thus have you ever underestimated me, and spat upon the purity of my mission! Yet the *fact* that confronts you now is that I am *here*, and your reign can endure no longer!'

'O but *I* reign over nothing!' cried the Caliph. 'It is all fraud and imposture! I assure you by all the verities of what is natural, that I, in truth, *am* no Caliph!'

'Well,' said Zardin al-Adigrab, raising his scimitar, 'you may assure me, and I may assure myself.'

'*O the irony of it!*' cried out the Caliph, almost angrily, but Zardin upon the instant brought down his weapon, and after a few minutes' furious exertion had reduced him to exactly the condition of the first.

When he finished he returned to the foyer, where he saw the third door still closed. 'It cannot be but that I must open this door also,' he said.

And so he went up the steps and pushed open the door, finding once more a man identical to the others, dressed in rich robes, with a crown by his side and a ring upon his finger. He, however, was awake, and spoke at once, saying: 'I imagine that they have told you I am the Caliph.'

'Do you deny it?' inquired Zardin al-Adigrab.

'Most emphatically I do!' cried the third Caliph. 'It is indeed the very worst of slanders! I, the Caliph! Most absolutely and relatively and universally *not*!'

'If none of you is the Caliph, where is he?' asked Zardin al-Adigrab.

'As for that, I am not informed,' replied the Caliph, 'and it seems there is some confusion in the minds and hearts of men upon the matter, for I have on many occasions been wrongly mistaken for him. However, I imagine that it is one (or perhaps even both) of my two neighbours that is, or was, he whom you seek.'

'I cannot doubt that there are excellent reasons why you lie here, not the Caliph, but in the Caliph's bed, with the Caliph's crown, wearing the Caliph's ring, in the Caliphal Palace,' remarked Zardin al-Adigrab.

'These are only circumstances,' replied the Caliph, 'and they have no force in the question of who I truly and veritably am.'

'Then who are you, truly and veritably?' asked Zardin

al-Adigrab, leaning back against the chamber wall and pretending to inspect the blade of his scimitar for nicks.

'Indeed, I am most delighted that you have asked this,' replied the Caliph, 'for it gives me an opportunity to tell you a strange fact which will amaze you and fill you with interest. Although I appear to every outside eye to fill the place of the Caliph, in fact this is but my purpose, and leads me towards my actual intent. For it must be explained, I am in actuality a double in every physical trait to the real Caliph, and I have been placed here so that I might, given the right circumstances, verily assassinate him and take his place!'

'Perhaps that is what you have already done,' said Zardin al-Adigrab. 'Perhaps you are now the true and only Caliph!'

'O most certainly not!' responded the Caliph. 'For you must understand, the wonderful development in the matter is that I have, in fact, *changed my mind*! I do not *wish* to be Caliph! It no longer holds the slightest attraction for me!'

'Come, come!' cried Zardin al-Adigrab, losing patience. 'You *are* Caliph, and your domination is at an end!'

'Absolutely not!' cried back the Caliph with equal force. 'That has been vilely and falsely imputed to me!'

'You *are* the Commander of the Faithful!' shouted Zardin al-Adigrab angrily. 'You rule all the known world in name and in tyranny! This very day you were so utterly presumptuous as to order the hanging of the Moderate Man, because of his Amendment, and because you are madly determined to keep That Which is Within from ever coming out!'

'Nonsense! Nonsense!' cried back the Caliph in a passion. 'There *are* no Faithful! There *is* no known world! There *are* no Moderate Men! There can *be* no Amendment! *And there is nothing ... nothing ... NOTHING within!*' There were flecks of foam upon his beard.

'Evidently,' said Zardin al-Adigrab, stepping back, 'you are suffering from a great and final derangement. So long and so bitterly have you denied your own being, the soil you stand on, the blood in your veins, and the force that drives it forward – that now even your mad domination means nothing to you! What have you left *me* to destroy? Your evil has consumed you – nothing remains but an evasion of an evasion! O Caliph, it is but a small favour I do you, then, to darken this sputtering fuel-less lamp of thought, that flickers so frantically and pointlessly here in the empty skull of your once glittering palace!'

'I am not the *Caliph*!' screamed the Caliph in a terrible voice, leaping up and rushing at Zardin al-Adigrab with his bared hands.

'Indeed, you *must* be!' sternly replied Zardin al-Adigrab, and struck him down with a savage blow.

When he had cut this third Caliph into pieces, a task which, grunting with effort, he performed with even more passionate energy than before, the leader of the Ripe Fruit Party descended slowly to the foyer and made his way back through the clothes closet. Here, to his dull amazement, he found that every trace and vestige of the rich garments had vanished! Going on into the marbled chamber, he saw it also altered, the fabulous furnishings gone, the lights extinguished, the quicksilver pool empty, and the room standing strange and bare to its cold stone. And now, in its centre, sat an ancient and bony woman wrapped in mourning veils, who was wailing steadily in a cracked voice, and singing this lamentation:

> O that they would what they were,
> Then would the one sun be one,
> Then would the one moon be many!
> O that they would what they were,
> O that they would, O that they were!

As Zardin al-Adigrab approached, the woman abruptly ceased her noise and adjusted her veils.

'O venerable mother,' said Zardin very politely, 'what signifies this strange song you sing? And who art thou, and why are you here? And who were these other men in the bedchamber of the Caliph?'

'I am not *thy* mother,' answered the old woman in a hostile manner. As the Ripe Fruit man stepped a step closer, his nostrils detected an intense, foul odour rising from her that disconcerted him and made him hesitate.

'May your head prosper, aged one,' replied he, 'but I did not speak thus literally.'

'Ask me nothing,' said the woman.

'I came here with a strong heart in order to slay the Caliph,' said Zardin al-Adigrab. 'But, instead of one man in this bedchamber, I have found three. Pray, *do* answer, *who* were these others?'

'Have you slain them all then?' asked the old woman in a low voice.

Before Zardin al-Adigrab could reply, however, there came like a living thing into the room a dark rivulet of blood, flowing quickly, almost purposefully along the marble floor from behind him. As the old woman drew in her breath and Zardin stared grimly, this horrid reminder passed between them and hurried on across the room, exiting at the stair-well, as if bound determinedly for the lower regions of the palace.

'As you see,' said he at length, 'it is their very souls departing.'

'Then you have, indeed, slain the Caliph,' said the woman slowly.

'Certainly then,' cried Zardin al-Adigrab seriously, '*Truth is come and Falsehood is vanished*!'

'This is not for you to say,' muttered the woman.

'May I not speak, in a triumphal hour!'

'You *may* do just what you *can*,' replied the woman bitterly.

Zardin al-Adigrab laughed, and put his scimitar down on the floor, settling himself beside it. 'So I have ever found,' he said, and laughed once more. 'But now you must tell me who these other men were, and how they came to be in this place. And, indeed, you must tell me who *you* are as well.'

'All this I *will* tell you,' presently replied she, 'on the condition that you perform for me one certain action when I am done.'

'Well, that I would gladly,' said he, 'but it only must conform to my nature and deep principles.'

'Do not fear,' said the woman. 'That which I will ask you is very much in your practice.'

'Then I agree, and you solve for me these mysterious matters.'

The old woman sighed deeply and bitterly, and rested silent and motionless a long moment.

'Know then that I am the natural mother of the Commander of the Faithful, he whom you have presently destroyed,' she said finally. 'But yet for all that I cannot tell you which of these that you have slain is truly my son. And the reason for this must be sought in –'

The Tale of the Three Caliphs

Once, as there should always have been, there was indeed a *Caliph* proud and fierce and just sitting in the jewelled chair before the great *Diwan*. Then, as always, was he absolute in his decree, and he needed but think a thing and lo! It was. Once, I say, there most certainly *was*, as now there never more shall be, a *Caliph* in majesty, and sun gleaming on the lands.

But then, upon a certain day, when all the *Kazis* and *Chamberlains* went in to wait upon the *Prince of True Believers*, he said, 'Describe to me this day just as it is.'

None knew how to answer him, until finally the Grand Vizier, *Majid Shair-al-Walahan*, a true Jewel of the Realm, took it upon himself to speak, saying:

'O Mighty Leader of all Civilised and Peaceable Peoples, it is a good day and fine of aspect, warm, with a fresh breeze out of the east, and no clouds in the firmament. The sun is lying like a golden ship upon the verge of the world, and the voice of the Muezzin has already called the believers to prayer.'

'Yes, and the sun shall rise no doubt,' replied the *Caliph* angrily, 'and set also no doubt, amid the prayers of the believers! But tell me how this day differs from any other day that has ever been!'

The *Kazis* and *Chamberlains* looked from one to the other in some perplexity and perturbation and were all lost for an answer to make to the *Commander of the Faithful*. Then another senior *Emir*, who was *Consul* of

Commerce and *Captain* of the Port, stepped forward to speak, saying:

'O Fount of Auspicious Majesty, this day is graced with many fair signs betokening prosperity for *Bagdad* and for thy realm. This morning at first light were berthed a convoy of six ships bearing fine *aloe-wood* from the far isles of the east. Also arrived is a large ship of *Tin* from the north, and another of *Ivory* and *Women* from the south. Expected today are ten more ships bearing *spices* from *India* and *Ceylon*, and other far places. With the opening of the gates this morn were ushered in several *caravans*, one of eighty camels loaded with *dried fruit* and *sugar*, hearkening from distant *Fez*, another of *corn* and *paper* and *diamonds* from *Cairo*. In addition to this God has willed that a very great one from *China* should arrive safely by the *Nishapur* route, having no less than two hundred and fifty camels loaded with the finest *silks*. Further to this, and God allow it so, we expect fully a dozen more such to enter the city before the gates are closed this evening, and trade promises to be proportionately active and profitable.'

But at this information the *Caliph* only raged, and cursed the *Emir*, and said, 'Is it not ever thus, and do not trade and ships and camels repeat themselves ever and ever? And have I not wished to know something about this day which is particular to it and has not happened before and shall not happen again?'

Once more his advisors were thrown into confusion, but promptly enough the *Caliph*'s personal *Chamberlain* stepped forth.

'O honoured Scion and Potent Soul of the Faith,' said he, 'it is today the such and such day of the such and such month of the such and such year since the Hejira, and your Eminence has attained the fortieth year of life. Thy son the *Prince of Stars* is this morning five years old, and is beginning even now to learn of the blessed *Alcoran*. Thy handmaid the *Empress* approaches the thirtieth year of her life, and you have at present three wives, of eighteen years, twenty-two years and forty-four years of age.'

'Cease these numbers!' cried out the *Caliph* in a passion. 'Is there not more to a day than *numbers*! Tell me no more of numbers! Has all been reduced down to numbers! Tell me of *Life*, just as it is upon *this* exact day!'

It happened that there was a wise and holy *Imam* among them, and he now undertook to placate the *Caliph*, saying:

'O Commander of the True Belief, how may one begin to speak of Life in your realms? Thy people spin and sweat and wish for that which they do not have. They laugh and drink forbidden wine and sing the poems that the poets have written, and they also weep, and fall down in grief and pain, and kneel before their God contrite, hypocritical, pious, and doubting. They fight, with their tongues and weapons, they murder with daggers and poison, they entertain each other hospitably and give one another gifts. They lie down together on couches and beds and straw-covered floors and enjoy one another, and give birth to one another, and bury one another, often at the behest of God, and just as often not. They are happy, sorrowful, prosperous, miserable, energetic, slovenly, worthy, unworthy, pure and impure. And if God is willing that it should be so, they shall be all these things tomorrow as they were yesterday and yet, O Prince of Believers, it is these things and these things only which are particular and distinctive of today.'

But the *Caliph* was in no way satisfied with this response, and cursed the *Imam* for a sentimentalist, and swore that his *advisers* merely sought to conceal from him that which he desired to know.

'Understand that my soul is not to be placated with a day which is no day at all!' he cried. 'For if thou and this day will not be more than this paltriness which you have laid before me, then shall I not be the glorious *Caliph* either, unless it please me! For why should I, who am absolute, partake of such a homely *ragoo* of relatives and comparisons and dull habits and mere numbers as this? Does one sun but willy-nilly replace another, and shall we therefore say it is ever the same sun? I shall have thee know that *I* too am a sun, but upon this day I shall *not* shine, for that is what pleaseth me!'

And so, to the amazement and concern of all, the *Caliph* retired to his own bedchamber and allowed none to approach him.

Then did we confer together in secrecy, the *Empress* and the *Chamberlain*, the *Purple Man* and the *Kazi* and I, that we might find some means of remedying the misfortune, before it was noised about and made to benefit the *Caliph*'s enemies, both near and abroad.

And the *Purple Man* advised us of a certain man in his prisons who awaited hanging. The man had been seized for but one reason – and this was that he bore a resemblance of the closest imaginable kind to our *Caliph*. 'And is it doomed and inevitable that he must die?' we demanded of him. 'It is doomed and inevitable that *a man* must hang,' replied the *Purple Man*, and so we contrived in the following manner. The *Purple Man* seized at once upon a man for whom he had a certain dislike and, covering his face and head with dark cloth, carried him before the people in the place of blood. 'Here is one who would imp the *Caliph*!' cried he. 'And indeed, so well has his birth suited him to this impious design, that his face must remain hidden from the common eye!' And then he was hung, and he who resembled the Commander of the Faithful was conveyed to us by stealth.

Quickly we arrayed him in the robes of Forgiveness, and, giving him careful instructions, carried him before the assembled *Diwan*, where he was accepted without question by all, due to his astonishing likeness.

'*Kazis* and *Courtiers*,' said he, 'I have chosen to forgive you your failings and petty treasons of this morning – provided that you strive to improve yourselves.' And the *Kazis* and *Chamberlains* kissed the earth, and blessed the magnanimity of the Commander of the Faithful. 'Indeed,' continued he, 'I am ever of a forgiving nature. Ye may fear my wrath, but ye may also know my love. However, let now the day's affairs begin.' So excellent was his imitation, and his quickness of wit, that the day proceeded without the smallest of hindrance, and what was more, we did not hesitate to make use of him on many other occasions when the true *Caliph* refused to be himself.

This serviceable expedient endured for some years, until it gradually came into the head of the second *Caliph* that he *was* indeed *Caliph*. This was made much worse when he once discovered us in the error of mistaking him for the first *Caliph* and the first *Caliph* for him. Then, when he felt himself the veritable Prince of Believers, he became (who could be surprised?) just as the original *Caliph* was, and soon began frequently to refuse to perform his official functions. At last, at a certain grand banquet he threw down a plate of oysters on the marbled floor and cried out:

'Take away these excessive meats and wines from my presence, for they weary me to an unspeakable degree and I will have no more of them!'

So the *Chamberlain* and the *Steward* approached him in a solicitous manner.

'O Prince of the Pious,' said they, 'perhaps there is something else which would delight and solace your majesty?'

'What have you?' replied he.

'Perhaps, O blessed one,' suggested the *Steward*, 'you would take pleasure in the graceful dancing and singing of your *artists*, performed to accompany the lute.'

'Did we not have them yesterday?' demanded the *Caliph*.

'Better still, O Auspicious Leader,' said the *Chamberlain*, 'might we not tour through the endless storerooms of the Caliphal Palace, to admire the illimitable wonders and beauties therein contained?'

'Did we not do that the day before?' returned the *Caliph*.

'In that case,' rejoined the *Steward*, 'may I suggest Your Majesty have recourse to the vastness of your *harim*, where there are not only delicious and eager concubines who have not felt your hand for over a year, but even in fact beautiful and delicate maidens both domestic and imported who are entirely clean and unsullied and untasted! Beside which, of course, should your inclination be towards the familiar and comforting, there are your three wives to consider.'

(Though, of course, even the *Steward* had not temerity to suggest the *Empress* herself, seeing as this was not the true *Caliph*. Besides, she had renounced him in any case, due to his first abdication.)

'Women hold no delights for me,' said the *Caliph*. 'For me, to desire is to possess. To possess, then, what but the fearsome weariness of death itself?'

The *Steward* was dumbfounded by sentiments of this nature, that none but the true *Caliph* had ever before expressed, yet the *Chamberlain* stepped forward, saying:

'Truly, O Splendour of the Universe, then might this not be an admirable night to fare forth in disguises, and view the adventures of your citizenry?'

'Can you promise me that I would not see that which I have seen on a thousand and one such previous nights?' demanded he. 'For indeed, I could not bear it.'

'It is clear, O true Inspiration of the Many,' suddenly interjected the *Grand Vizier*, 'that to taste the ever fresh and infinite splendour, the limitless breadth of Life, what your soul craves is the hearing of a *story*.'

To the surprise and relief of the court, the *Caliph* softened at this proposal, and said:

'Well, it might be attempted.'

'Who will tell the tale?' asked the *Chamberlain*. Then *Majid Shair-al-Walahan* said, 'I may undertake it myself, and the Commander of the Faithful approve.'

'Do what you may,' agreed the *Caliph*.

'Hear, then,' began the Vizier, "The Tale of the Prince Camaralzaman and the Princess of China":

'There lie, about twenty days sailing from the coast of *Persia*, the Islands of the Children of Khaledan, where once lived a great *King*, who had an only son named *Prince Camaralzaman*...'

'Always a *Prince*, always a *Princess*,' grumbled the

Caliph audibly at this point, but the *Grand Vizier* politely
ignored the interruption.

'This son was raised with the greatest imaginable care
and propriety, and was appointed the best possible gover-
nors and tutors by his doting father. As he grew he learned
all the knowledge which a prince ought to possess and
acquitted himself so well that he charmed all that saw him,
and particularly the king.

'When the boy had reached the age of fifteen years,
radiant and finely formed, the king summoned him, and
receiving his respectful salutes, said: "Do you know, my
son, for what reason I have sent for you?"

'The Prince modestly replied, "God alone knows the
heart; I shall hear it from your Majesty with great
pleasure."

'"I send for you," said the King, "to inform you that I
have the intention of providing a proper marriage for
you."'

At this moment the *Caliph* seized a tall lamp that stood
beside him and hurled it at the *Vizier* in a rage.

'Let *me* tell it *you*!' he cried. 'The perfect Prince with all
the attributes will not *want* to marry! He will resist and his
father will grow angry and despair. That will be until he
meets the Princess from China who will also have all the
attributes. Then he will be smitten with Love, and she
also. They will marry to the general delight! Is it not ever
so! Is it not ever thus! Everywhere, always, ever and
again, except in actuality!'

'This is one of the great stories!' cried *Majid* in
measureless indignation.

'Admit it! Admit that it shall so occur!' howled back the
Caliph, who had grown purple in wrath. The *Grand Vizier*
then attempted to withdraw in dignity.

'Indeed, O *Caliph*,' said he, 'the story begins, proceeds
and then ends.'

'Admit! Admit!' cried the *Caliph*, who would not be
placated.

'Truly, O insuperable Sovereign,' attested the *Steward*,
'it occurs just as your Majesty has said.'

'You see how wretchedly clever I am!' then cried out the *Caliph*. 'And can you wonder then that I am weary of the earth and that all your entertainments are but as dust to me!'

And with these words he withdrew to his chamber and would not be approached.

Well, the *Chief of the Kazis* knew of another man in *Libya* who was famous for his resemblance to the *Caliph*. He we presently kidnapped, dressed in the Robes of Silence, and brought before the *Diwan*, after being cautioned to speak not and look to the improvement of his fortune. This day passed as well without disturbance, and the Court assumed the *Caliph* to have again forsaken his rash seclusion and were satisfied. We soon were able to train this third *Caliph* to imitate the others to perfection, and none suspected or knew of it but we five.

And thus we abode to this very day. All three *Caliphs* grew to feel that they were truly the Commanders of the Faithful, and as such they became terribly indolent, and were pleased with nothing so much as sleeping. So we set them to sleep in these three rooms you have discovered, one beside the other.

As for the court and populace, they never discovered what had taken place. Not even the *Prince of Stars* knew, nor the Grand Vizier, *Majid Shair-al-Walahan*. For myself, I retired into the obscurity of these upper regions, and it was eventually assumed that I had died.

Each morning I would enter in and inquire of them who would this day be *Caliph*. All three would scornfully say that as it was but one more in an endless succession of days, they cared not who played the part. But one would always agree to do it – for once in three days was the limit of their appetite for any form of exertion – and we would dress him up in the dress of his pleasing and he would, not without a certain delight, go before the *Diwan* and spend the day making meaningless statements and announcing fantastical decrees. Those remaining would sleep.

None, of course, would accord with the others, and their attitudes were so changeable and uncertain that the court was generally able to make little sense of it, and fell into awe of them. As for ourselves, we grew unable, so absent were any signs of character or physical dissimilarity, to tell one from the other, or, indeed, be able to tell who the original, and you may say *true Caliph*, my son, actually was.

And since no *Caliph* would for any period remain himself, the veritable rule and control of the realm fell also to us five. All the decisions were ours, all of the toil of mind and spirit, but in truth, none of the glory. However, until this day our secret has been kept, and we have ever ruled as one *Caliph*, and the realm has been just as it otherwise would.

But I myself grew weary of the deceptions we practised and tormented with the hollowness of our mastery, while my disgust with my son, whoever he might be, multiplied day upon day. At length I decided to seek some means of ending the situation. I had my purple minion hang the *Moderate Man* this past afternoon (it was not, I think a policy unlooked for or undesired by *Salim bin Haubut*), and since then I have sat here and awaited you, or one like you, in whatever form or garb you would come. He who is in the service of Change, so it is said, raises his hand against the stillness as night raises its dark hands against the day. So in the night I expected you, nor have I yet felt sleep.

'So far as they ever may be answered,' concluded the woman, 'this is the tale which must answer all your questions.'

'Can it be so?' marvelled Zardin al-Adigrab. 'That this great inflexible power was so divided? I cannot but doubt it!'

'Yet it was so,' said the Caliph's mother.

'And now,' went on Zardin al-Adigrab, 'I have so further divided it with the sharp edge of my truth that it shall never again reform itself.'

The old woman shuddered bitterly, and raised her eyes to the Ripe Fruit Man, in wonderful dislike. 'Are you prepared to do that service I asked of you and which you promised me?' she asked.

As Zardin began to assure her, however, their conversation was disturbed by a distant echoing uproar of voices and clattering feet, which caused him to leap up, snatching his weapon as he did.

'Yes, O bloody man,' said she, 'your crimes have trickled down and been discovered. Soon the soldiers of revenge shall be upon you, and you shall find yourself covered in unending war. But *I* do not wish to see it. Are you ready now to perform that service I have bound you to?'

'Speak quickly, then,' said Zardin al-Adigrab, as the noises below them increased at every moment, 'for I intend to go to face my foes!'

'Do for me as thou hast done for my son, my servants, and my friends,' said the woman.

'What is this!' cried Zardin al-Adigrab.

'Come, come,' said the Caliph's mother deridingly, 'do you suppose that I wish to *live*? Do you suppose *I* am to be wooed with your bitter fruits? I spit them out! I loathe them ever! Do for me what I require!'

Zardin was thrown into some confusion. 'I do not believe I am the man to slay a mother!' he said. 'Truly, all mothers are of my party, by very nature, so it seems to me. The cutting off of fathers, upon necessity, is a virtuous enough thing, but to kill a mother without need approaches very nearly to impiety!'

'*What is this*?' echoed the woman, with an expression of infinite scorn. 'Does the bold desecrator of every shrine speak now of piety?'

'There is that to which every man shall limit himself,' said Zardin al-Adigrab.

'Well then, I shall tell you that if you imagine you will not slay me, you little know what you are, nor what you are about!' cried she in a terrible fury. 'Tell me what happened to the blue-eyed apes!'

'They appeared,' replied Zardin al-Adigrab coldly, 'to die of their own hands.'

'And what passed when you forced the Master-cook to fry

the fourth fish?' demanded she.

'Well, again,' answered Zardin al-Adigrab, 'he appeared to die of it.'

'And what was the fate of the soldiers and servants once you had taken your scimitar among them?'

'Indeed,' said Zardin al-Adigrab, 'some of them I slayed, and the rest they slayed each other.'

'And what of the Chamberlain watching at the Caliph's door?'

'Well, I slayed him.'

'And the first Caliph?'

'I have slain him, as you know.'

'And the second Caliph?'

'I have slain him also.'

'And the third?'

'Yes, I, also.'

'Well, Zardin al-Adigrab,' said the Caliph's mother, 'do not suppose you are still yourself, for I know of all these slayings only through the sight of you. Do you imagine yourself so powerful that you could have done these things alone? If they were not themselves *eager to be done*? Do you suppose you can limit their doing now, at this late moment?'

'Well,' said Zardin al-Adigrab stubbornly, 'I do not comprehend all this.'

'*Do as I bid thee*!' thundered the woman in a vast, inconceivable voice, that caused Zardin al-Adigrab to stagger with horror and surprise. For moments on end the echoes roared like a gale through the rooms, and seemed to shudder the very walls.

The old woman's eyes flashed with a brilliant, blue radiance, lighting the place and dazzling Zardin's vision hypnotically.

'Directly above me, in the ceiling,' she whispered in a stentorian voice, depthless and unreal, like that of a god or a king, 'is a loosened tile, through which you may, for the moment, escape. Now, *do* as I *bid* thee!'

'More deceptions!' suddenly cried Zardin al-Adigrab, rallying. 'More chimeras and mad dreams!' In a passion he lashed out with his scimitar and the old woman's head fell cleanly off, the light dying instantly from her eyes, like a lamp snuffed. All the sounds of approaching feet and voices fell silent.

Zardin al-Adigrab pulled himself up by his hands and clambered out on to the windy roof of the great Palace. In the east tiny rivulets of light were beginning to trickle along the curving edges of the earth, the only living things in the wide dark sky. Sleeping Bagdad lay before him in a jumble of pale shadows, ghostly minarets and black canals.

Zardin al-Adigrab filled his lungs and threw back his head. Then came the high pure wailing of the new Muezzin's passionate cry:

'I declare that That Which is Within shall come forth! I declare that I am the vengeance, and that the reign and domination of the evil father-dream is over! Arise, awake, O lovely peoples! For I declare that there is but one dawn, and that it is the dawn of the sun! *And I declare that it has come at last*!'

6 Dawn

Peach-lava running behind black islands of cloud in the east.

Echoes in the dark courtyard.

Shadows moving in archways.

Whispers: 'Death to doubters and deniers! Death to the impure and unclean!'

Many feet running. A wild bird captive in a forgotten room calls.

The Grand Vizier leads a crowd of people hurriedly along a narrow corridor.

'Where have the guards gone?' Creaking of hinges. 'Alert the Empress!'

Echoes in stair-wells. Echoes in hallways, through chains of connecting empty chambers.

Voices cry out sharply for torches and scimitars.

A scratching of metal on wood.

Shadows of unseen figures moving.

Crowds of men running in passage-ways.

'Wake! Wake! Arise O people!'

Echoes in deep food cellars. 'Prepare! Prepare!'

'Who's there?' Metal clattering on stone.

'We must move to meet them, should it be them! Are your men in readiness? Are your men loyal?'

A single ring of steel on steel.

'Husbands! *Husbands*!'

A chorus of voices rising together.

A man spits a holy Moullah with a spear. The Moullah cries out.

A man slays a steward crossing the audience hall in a sleeping robe.

'Is that them?'

'Where are they?'

Figures moving, voices subsiding, then rising. Laughter.

A man with a dagger slays Menshallah, the dwarf eunuch.

'Where is the Prince of Stars? Who has word of the Empress?'

A man dances with a knife.

'O heavenly people, protect the Prince of Stars from deadly treason! Let us wash him in the unclean blood!'

Groups of people running on staircases.

A eunuch dashes from chamber to chamber, searching.

A man is cut in half by a trap. Doors are broken down.

A party of men flailing weapons rush upon nameless Ibn in a starlit antechamber, but he slays them all with his scimitar.

'Come, Amina, Ibn!'

A long soulless howling travels through the halls.

'The Caliph is gone! The Caliph is dead! It is said in the rooms! It is said on the street!'

'What will they do?'

A man slays an Imam in his chamber with a scimitar.

A man is slain by two other men in a stair-well.

A man burns another man with a torch.

An encounter of swords and knives by the fountain in the court by the diwan chamber.

Two men and a woman struggle with a wolf.

'Day and Night! Day and Night! O Great and Dreadful God!'

'Where is the Empress? Where is the Prince of Stars? Have they fallen, then?' I do not know.

A man slays a woman lutanist.

A man attacks a group of men with a scimitar and is slain by them.

'My friends, is that you? Have you a scimitar? Have you seen the Grand Vizier?'

A man slays a man leading two women from the Harim.

A man slays a man from behind.

A large trap springs, catching two women, a eunuch, two supporters of Zardin al-Adigrab, and a mastiff-dog. They hang twitching.

'Call my people to me!'

A party of men with spears enter a dark cell and slay seven men who are in chains there.

A man with a scimitar slashes another man who falls back against an arras, ripping it and staining it with blood.

Hamid bin Talal kills three members of the Ripe Fruit Party in single battle, in a deserted chamber.

The heads of a man and a woman bounce down a stairwell, one after the other.

A retainer and an elderly man fight with scimitars.

Men and women run singly across the wide courtyard, their shirts and garments fluttering.

'Who is that? Who is there?' 'Who is that who asks?'

'They will attempt to escape by water!'

A man kills another man with an axe.

Three men beat a eunuch to death with the pommels of their scimitars.

An escaped bird beats frantically back and forth in a small room.

'O my friends arise, the future has begun!'

A man throws a lamp at another man and it breaks and the oil burns him.

'The cavalry have defected!'

A man saves a wounded man from three attackers.

'Where is it? Where *is* it? *Where is That Which is Within*?' This way.

Two men roll on a marble floor, fighting with curved knives.

A man spears a woman through her lattice.

Two members of the Ripe Fruit Party knife each other in a dark foyer.

A man strangles another man with his own shirt.

A party of men with helmets slay the stewardess Umma Musa and four of her women.

A woman strikes down a man from behind with an ebony staff.

A man wounds Hamid bin Talal and runs away.

Two men alone in a vast saloon with a gilt roof circle with daggers.

'Quickly, follow me! They have gone down!'

A man slays the falcon-master, and all the falcons make a loud whistling.

'O respected master, the situation is most unclear. Who am I to take my commandments from?'

'Lead me to my father, then.'

Two slaves duel with spears in an indoor garden.

A man kills a slave with a paving stone.

A trap cuts a concubine in half.

Several men push over a table laden with empty food dishes.

Two men with torches discover a locked room full of newly slain men and women.

Two slaves slay a dervish with fire-pokers.

'I am not he whom you seek! He is in the saloon of parrots!'

'In the name of the Compassionate, the Vengeful, the All-Knowing!'

'This stroke for the poor farming-men of Sawad and Ahway provinces!'

'This stroke for the Secret Society of the Oranges!'

'This stroke for the royal destiny of the Empress!'

'This stroke for the price of wheaten-bread!'

A man is bitten by a poisonous snake escaped from the palace bestiary.

A man drowns a wounded man in a fountain.

Two men force a concubine to do their will in a vestibule.

A troop of men running on a marbled floor slip in something wet and all fall down heavily, cursing and kicking one another.

Seven pet monkeys bite to death a eunuch in a darkened room.

A group of eunuchs and a group of concubines pelt each other with oranges.

A eunuch burns twelve concubines to death in a locked bedchamber.

A man falls from a window.

Two men meet and embrace in joy.

Three men choke another man by forcing an unravelled turband into his mouth.

A man suffocates a woman with a pillow.

'Come forth and be ready with your weapons! They must be hiding here within!'

'O Majid Shair-al-Walahan! No, it is not he.'

'O Zardin al-Adigrab, speak! No, he is not here; he is fighting somewhere near the Diwan.'

'O accursed ones! O vileness incarnate! O scabs and yellow puss and corruptions!'

'If you find them, do thou draw their soft parts upon your blade!'

The youngest wife of the Caliph is slain in the Harim by a party of street boys with daggers. They disrobe her then to view her.

A man is slain by concubines with toe and nail files.

'O leader! O leader!'

Other concubines greet men entering the Harim with embraces and kisses of joy.

Two men fight with scimitars in the royal coffee-room.

A man stumbles back dying and trips over the Prince of Stars' crochinole board.

Kicking and struggling, the Caliph's second wife is hung from a lamp with a silken bodice by a group of concubines. She writhes like a caterpillar.

The Caliph's third wife slays a man with a knife and is slain with a spear by his friend.

The Caliph's second wife dies, hanging. A few concubines watch her.

A group of dogs pull down a screaming errand boy.

Several children of concubines are slain in a room by one man.

'Vengeance!'

People coming across the dim paving, pouring like the tide rushing over pebbles.

A man is slain by an arrow. A man falls wounded with an axe. A man dies with a knife in his heart.

'Courage!'

A man slays a man in a doorway. A man slays a man with an orange turband. A man chokes a man with his hands.

'Mercy!'

Cries and women screaming and singing in chorus. Scimitars against scimitars. The beating deep in the heart of the palace.

A man slays a man.
A concubine weeps.
A man weeps.

Glowing coral and coals in the grey-black sky.

Someone was moving in the shadows of the dripping room.

'Is it you, Grand Vizier? Speak.'

There was a deep sigh.

'*Speak*!'

'Yes mistress. It is I.'

The Empress and Amina in long pink court-costumes emerged from the shade of an alcove in the Imperial bath-house. Bare-chested Ibn came padding across the tiles with his bloody scimitar in his hand.

'Ibn, where is the enemy? Are we secure?'

The muscular little man knelt down before the Empress.

'The enemy is everywhere about, O mistress of wonders,' he murmured. 'We are safe only a moment at once.'

'We must depart, O majesty,' said the Vizier, with another sigh. 'We are most certainly losing this battle.'

'Who is there with you?'

'The Prince of Stars, and two of his eunuchs, and a boy.'

Fhumdullah and Gondrat got up from the obscurity of an empty bath where they were hiding, and Gharib and the Prince of Stars appeared at the edge of the faint circle of dawn light cast by an aperture high in the wall of the vaulted room.

A man came striding quickly through the pillars, skirting the main pool.

'Here is Hamid bin Talal, the Captain of your Guard.'

'How many men remain to you?'

The soldier knelt several paces back.

'Three, O Empress,' he said in a low, ashamed voice. 'They are watching in the garden adjacent.'

The captain's garments were torn, and he had blood on his arm and a scimitar cut across his face.

'Please remember who you are and what you are fighting for,' said the Empress, addressing them all generally. 'It is necessary to suppress this rebellion. Nor is it in any way befitting persons of our grandeur and mission to run away. They in the stars are watching what we do.'

She turned to the Vizier.

'Where is the Caliph, and where is the Chamberlain?'

The Grand Vizier replied nothing, but gave the Empress a searching glance, then looked away.

'*Where* is the *Caliph*!' roared she in her most terrible voice.

'Well,' replied he, but not before still another pause, 'there have been made some very unlikely discoveries. I am told some very improbable reports. Improbable to me, that is, perhaps more probable to you.'

'*Speak*!' commanded the Empress, while the others looked each to each.

Then, however, the Vizier sighed heavily yet again, and lowered his head.

'Well,' he said, 'whatever either of us may have expected, it appears by all accounts that now the *Caliph* has been murdered. Likewise, the Chamberlain apparently is dead.'

'The Commander of the Faithful, *dead*!' exclaimed the Captain and the two eunuchs together.

'The Chamberlain also, *and* the Purple Man!' said the Empress. 'In a single day!'

'Well, yes, O regaled one,' said the Vizier, 'it has not been a particularly auspicious day.'

'And my household . . .'

'The enemy is, wherever he may, massacring us,' reported the Vizier.

'How did they get *in*?'

'The guard,' said the Captain in a low voice, 'were not all . . . trustworthy.'

'Is Bagdad not loyal, then?' asked Amina, as the Empress considered what had been said with a darkening countenance.

'Who is there to be loyal *to*?' replied Majid Shair-al-Walahan. 'The Caliph is gone (although even before today, he has not been, it should be said, entirely himself). As a matter of policy, the Empress has ever been declaimed to the populace as a mere possession of the Caliph's fancy. Her people, let us say, are liable to have no true appreciation of her worth to them. The Prince of Stars has refused to make any overt appearance, and is no doubt finally thought by all to be but a fabricated rumour of the Government. The Purple Man was popular with them, but he too is gone. *I* am a figure of general amusement – regarded (I think quite rightly) as being totally ineffectual.'

'The Ripe Fruit Party rules all,' said Hamid bin Talal in a grim voice.

The Empress suddenly clapped her hands in fury, and seizing the turband from the head of Gondrat, hurled it at the Captain. It struck him in the face and fell to the floor.

'Does Zardin al-Adigrab declare himself *Caliph*, then!' she cried with rage.

The Captain bowed his head, and Ibn laughed aloud at him, coldly.

'He has yet other matters to occupy him,' said the Vizier. 'There are still some of us to be killed, for example. There is still That Which is Within.'

There were suddenly cries and clashings of weapons nearby. The Captain leapt to his feet, gripping his scimitar, and ran from the room.

'It would be best now to go upriver to Mosul,' said the Vizier. 'Such is my advice. The people there may be inclined to support your majesty in this hour of crisis, due to that amelioration in land-duties allowed them this past season.'

'At this hour there is often an old dhow moored by the southern steps,' chirruped the boy Gharib. 'It belongs to the fishermen who bring river-fish to the palace kitchens. They leave it there overnight.'

'I remember allowing no relaxation of taxes for any province,' said the Empress majestically.

'I judged it necessary,' said the Vizier. 'Due the the poor harvests there. The devastating hail storms. The plague of insects.'

'I trust the difference to the Caliphal Treasury has been made up of dinars from your own hoardings, minister.'

'Such hoardings as I might have, O unspeakable fount of light,' replied the Vizier, 'have been (as you well know) ever at the disposal of the Caliph's slightest whim. For that reason, there remains not nearly enough of them to pay out the tithes of Mosul, meagre and pitiful though they might be. Resolve to be assured, however, that assorted extortions and torturing of unsympathisers practised, in my name, by the Purple Man, have more than made up this deficit.'

'It is to these excesses of your Vizierate,' cried the Empress, 'that we most certainly owe our present condition of humiliation!'

The Vizier trembled greatly at these words. '*I* have ever taken *my* commandments from one who had the lips of the life-cherishing stars at her ear!' he cried.

'O dog of a minister!' shrieked the Empress. 'O execrable hound!'

The Grand Vizier, equally incensed, instead of responding, reached abruptly up and snatched the teeth from his mouth.

At that moment the sounds of fighting began to draw nearer and increase in pitch, and a bloodied man rushed from the colonnade with daggers in his hands.

'I will slay you all, then!' he cried.

Ibn leapt quickly forward with his scimitar.

'We shall *never* resign our right and proper realm, come blood or fire!' shouted the Empress at the man's head as it rolled to her feet.

'We cannot hold!' cried the Captain, rushing into the room, with a loud clashing of swords and pounding of feet behind him.

'Ibn!' commanded the Empress. 'You must kill them all!'

The Captain slid to his knees before the Empress, kissing the floor, and crying out:

'We shall die for you, O celestial Queen! We shall die for you!'

'How utterly frightful!' exclaimed the eunuchs Fhumdullah and Gondrat in unison, bursting into tears.

'Which way to the steps! To where the dhow is!' shrilled Amina, seizing the boy Gharib hard by the ear. Now the room was filled with savagely fighting men. The air was wild with shouting and screams of triumph and agony.

'Take me to my true father!' cried the Prince of Stars. 'Let them do with me as they have done with him!'

'Kill them, *kill* them!' howled voices. Ibn whirled among them like a mad scythe, people began to run.

'We shall *never* abandon the Caliphate!' bellowed the Empress for all to hear.

Shafts and shifting bars of brilliant orange radiance.

A group of tiny figures runs like cockroaches down the long ranges of marble steps to the verge of the dark, flowing Tigris. Behind them in uncertain pursuit follows a mass of other figures, milling and skittering, and hurrying backwards and forwards. The first group disappears into a boat that bobs like a chip of wood in the river, and the boat comes clear of the shore. A part of the pursuing swarm rushes to the bank and tiny slivers fly between them and the boat. The boat at first seems to proceed slowly upstream, but then is caught in the current and swings around like a leaf in a puff of breeze and begins placidly to float off the other way, southwards.

Burning fragments floating in a sea of deepest azure.

> '*O Zardin al-Adigrab!*'
> '*O Zardin al-Adigrab!*'
> '*O! ... O! ... O! ... O!*'

The Caliphal diwan saloons were filled with swaying, chanting people, and the sound of their voices shook the thousand lamps and casements and seemed to rattle the very walls.

Zardin al-Adigrab rose above the press of fevered, bloodied faces, held up by the arms of his Party.

'The work has already begun!' cried he in a piercing voice, and waved his scimitar. 'Even now they are demolishing a section of the eastern wall!'

This was greeted with a vast, sharp cry, and,

'*O Zardin al-Adigrab*!!'

The two identically dressed lovers of the Ripe Fruit Party were at their master's feet, and they cried out,

'Let the love of lovers come forth!'

And this too was exalted immensely.

'Let the price of wheaten-cakes fall!' called a voice from another corner of the saloon.

And this was cheered wildly.

'Let there be no more Caliphs!' cried other mouths.

And this was loudly agreed to.

'Let the profits of corn-chandlers increase!' came another voice.

And this was hugely acclaimed.

'Well, well, well!' said a voice from above.

And the room fell silent, and everyone looked up.

The strange, soft visage of the Burned Man was peering down at them from a tiny arched window, high in the tapestried wall of the chamber.

'O Burned Man!' cried a number of people. And as the tumult threatened to rise once more, others cried, 'Let the Burned Man speak!'

'Well, well, well, Victorious People,' said the Burned Man, 'here we all are.'

'Indeed, O Burned Man!' cried everyone.

'Well, well, and it is most certainly a very excellent thing,' said the Burned Man. 'But, of course, you realise that it means nothing until they are *all* dead. *Nothing* has changed until *everything* has changed!'

'O Burned Man!'

'Well, well,' he went on, shaking his odd head at them, 'but don't you imagine, All-Powerful Ones, that if the Caliph can come back he certainly will? And what will prevent him from hurrying That Which is Within back into darkness and seclusion?

'The evil is never destroyed until it is *all* destroyed. It is always ready to return.'

'O Zardin al-Adigrab!' cried the dismayed populace. 'What the Burned Man says is *true*!'

'You must pursue them and do away with them *forever*, O Zardin al-Adigrab!' exhorted the Burned Man.

'Yes, yes! You *must*!' cried many.

'Hear the word of the Burned Man: *forever, forever*!'

'The Burned Man for Vizier!' rose the general opinion.

Other voices called upon Zardin al-Adigrab to pursue the Empress and the Prince of Stars and destroy them.

'O populace!' responded Zardin al-Adigrab. 'I have done much already this day!'

'*O Zardin al-Adigrab*!!' roared the many voices together, like a sudden blast of air from the door of a brick kiln.

Zardin al-Adigrab's will was seemingly swept away in the startling power of this response. 'To hear is to obey!' he cried at once.

'O Zardin al-Adigrab!' cried everyone now in great approval.

'But where are they, what direction have they taken? What is their condition, and what their support?'

A voice shrilled out from near a doorway.

'The word is, they have escaped downriver with a great army in many dhows! They have pillaged and burned most of Rusafah and al-Kharkh districts as they passed!'

'Well, well, well,' said the Burned Man from above, 'you must go quickly, O Zardin al-Adigrab! You must procure your own boats and chase them!'

'Indeed!' cried the generality of voices. 'You must! You must!' also adding again, 'The Burned Man for Vizier!'

Zardin prepared at once to go. But then he appeared to hesitate, and turned towards the populace again, as one overcome with feeling.

'Praise be to All of You!' he cried in tones of deep seriousness. 'For it is *you* who are my strength!'

'Tell us, Zardin al-Adigrab!' called the voices. 'When you capture them, will you torture them?'

'Will you enjoy the women?'

'Will you bring them back living, or dead?'

'What will you do to the Empress?'

'What will you do to the Prince of Stars?'

'Do you believe there *is* a "Prince of Stars"?' asked Zardin al-Adigrab.

'Certainly!'

'We do not know!'

'Tell us there is not!'

'*Well, there is none!*' responded he.

The populace cheered loudly.

'The stars are spots of dead light, the frozen "souls" of those who once breathed!' cried the leader of the Ripe Fruit Party. 'There *are* no Princes, for we are all as one!'

'No more Prince of Stars!' cheered the voices of the people.

'Nor ever *was*!' cried Zardin al-Adigrab.

'We never really believed in him!' replied the voices.

'Now,' said the Burned Man impressively, 'Zardin al-Adigrab shall catch him and cut off his members, so there will never be any more Caliphs either!'

'Indeed, O Zardin al-Adigrab, indeed!' cried the voice. The Burned Man for Vizier!'

'O Ripe Fruit Party!' cried then Zardin, unexpectedly lunging forward into the crowd. 'Follow me!'

And so they did, except somehow in the surging, enthusiastic press, the young woman member of the two identically dressed lovers was separated from her young man beloved, and, quite by accident, was left behind.

Vast sky from east to west the hue of a tropical bird.

Gradually the steps and the people and the palace had faded into the dimness of the early morning mist. They drifted on silently. On either bank slowly passed the long grey residences, the clutter of moored dhows and river-craft, the dark mouths of the canals. Here and there in the mist arose the vague domes and towers of the waterfront mosques.

Hamid bin Talal sat with his chin in his hand on the top of he cabin roof, surrounded by his three men. A bloody cimitar hung loosely in his hand. All three of the soldiers were dead, arrows protruding from them at various points.

Nameless Ibn sat motionless in the stern-sheets, his arm on the steering-oar. His scimitar rested across his knees.

The Grand Vizier Majid Shair-al-Walahan stood in the centre of the boat, leaning his hand against the mast, looking

at the riverbank, his jaw working slowly, as if he were
chewing a piece of gristle. His silken turband was partly
unwound and spotted with blood.

Perched at the bow of the craft was the boy Gharib,
listlessly trailing one toe in the purple-tinted water.

In the obscurity of the cabin sat five people. On one side,
quietly weeping, were the two eunuchs Fhumdullah and
Gondrat (the former with an arrow neatly piercing the top
part of his turband), on the other the girl Amina, and the
Empress, who was peering out of a narrow window-slit.

In the darkest fore-part of the little space, crouched the
Prince of Stars, watching her.

The Empress spoke.

'O my people,' said she. 'O my people, what is this
darkness dawning now in the sky, obscuring all? Where are
the stars now, to show us the way? I look upon you, and it is
as if you are all sleeping. Sleeping, dreaming, lost to your
selves, lost to *me*. O my people, how long will you stray.
How long before you awake and yearn again for *me*?'

Then she turned to the other occupants.

'Avert your eyes!' she commanded fiercely.

The boat drifted on out of Bagdad.

A clear and gleaming light drowns the entire earth.

A thousand sweating brown backs strained and the great
wooden wheels groaned. Massed voices like thunder cried
out O! in amazement and triumph. Shrill pipes thrilled and
screamed and brilliant banners oscillated on spear-tips.
Gongs vibrated and small children and birds shrieked and
danced as, out through a very huge hole in the ancient palace
wall, and into the blinding light of morning, slowly rolled
That Which Truly and Veritably *Was* Within.

7 The Ruins of Ctesiphon

They were drifting through cemeteries and garbage mounds on the outskirts of Bagdad.

With a splash the body of the last of Captain Hamid bin Talal's soldiers fell into the river and sank from sight.

'Be comforted. They fought. They were men,' said the Grand Vizier to the Captain, as they slumped back to the deck. 'On other days, that would have been enough.' The Captain said nothing.

Amina and the boy Gharib stood in the waist of the boat, at the base of the mast, looking upward.

'If this long part were brought *here* . . .' said the boy, pointing, 'and then we attached it somehow along *there* . . .'

'That appears to be sensible,' said Amina. 'Do that first.'

'Me?' said the boy.

'Of course.'

'It's too big.'

'*Ibn*! Come here!' cried she, quite suddenly and authoritatively.

Ibn gave her a faintly curious look, and continued to steer.

'It really *is* much too dismal for words,' said Fhumdullah the eunuch to the silent cabin.

'*That* may certainly be agreed with,' sighed Gondrat, wiping his nose.

The others did not speak.

The plains on either side were brown and dusty. Here and there birds stood in the flats along the shore.

The Grand Vizier and the Captain from the cabin-top, and Ibn from the stern watched Amina direct the two eunuchs and Gharib as they struggled to swing the boom.

'The Caliph,' Hamid bin Talal was saying very slowly, as if to nobody, '. . . *deserved* to die.'

'What did I hear?' said the Grand Vizier, and turned. 'Could it be what I thought?'

'He *deserved* to die,' repeated Hamid bin Talal. 'He did not deserve the men who died for *him*.'

The Empress appeared at the cabin door and stared up at the sky.

The breeze *was* blowing, very faintly, from the north, or at least from the north-west.

'Is that the best angle, then?' said Amina, studying the slight curve of the sail. 'Is that the best place for it?'

'I suppose so,' said Gharib.

The two eunuchs were asleep.

'There will most certainly be a pursuit,' said the Vizier to the Empress. 'It cannot be imagined that we shall be allowed simply to sail away.'

'The people,' said the Empress, 'will overthrow him, and search for us to call us back.'

'Oh assuredly,' replied the Vizier. 'But *when* will they do this? And will not the same fear occur to the Ripe Fruit Party?'

'It is important that we do not go too far from the city,' said the Empress firmly. 'We must be ready when the people call.'

'O great Majesty,' said Hamid bin Talal, 'we must also preserve the Prince of Stars from the dangers of the moment. He is the future, and he is the past.'

'The people will yearn for him,' agreed the Empress.

'But,' interjected the Vizier then, as if to himself, 'will they know it is *him* they are yearning for?'

'They shall throw away the false and come inevitably to the true!' cried the Empress.

No one at all could be seen in the fields along the river. The sky was cloudless and blue, and the water whispered continuously.

Ibn sat in the stern, with his eyes apparently closed. Yet he steered the dhow perfectly.

Gharib had climbed to the top of the mast and was looking about.

'Where are the allies of the Empress to be found?' asked Amina of the Vizier.

Majid Shair-al-Walahan smiled sourly. 'Wherever flourishes Life,' he answered.

The girl's stone-slashed features did not vary, and she continued to peer directly at him.

'Are we liable to find many of them downriver?' she asked.

The Vizier sighed. 'Perhaps more likely there than *up*river,' he replied. 'The people of the countryside are always slower than those of the city to embrace each new heresy.'

The Empress was alone with the Prince of Stars in the cabin.

'Are you hungry?' she said at length.

'No, mother,' he said.

'Are you thirsty?'

'No, mother.'

The river became shallower and wider for a stretch, with sand bars here and there. Bison stood up to their ankles and dully watched the dhow slide by. The voice of a bird crying along a pathway by the water drifted to them.

'Hesitate not,' said the Captain grimly to Majid Shair-al-Walahan. 'Speak what you wish to speak. It is clearly a necessity for you.' He and the Vizier and Gharib sat together in the sun on the roof of the cabin.

'Well, and yet his heart rises up,' muttered the Vizier, 'and he determines to answer him, saying. "*Truly, I am witness that there is only one God, and that all this, and all else, is God's will. All my trust I put in God, also therein is our future and destiny contained.*"'

'Well,' said the Captain, 'for the present it would appear that "God's will" is no more than a matter of flowing downstream with the current.'

The Vizier paused at this remark. Then he clicked his false teeth (which he had long since returned to his mouth).

'Perhaps you have not noticed,' he said, stingingly. 'A sail has been erected.'

'Does God take credit for that?' asked the Captain.

'Do *you*?' asked the Vizier.

'The Grand Vizier Majid Shair-al-Walahan thinks it's all the will of God,' reported Gharib to the Changing World Club.

'That is simply because he is not acquainted with the alterations which have occurred in this matter,' said Gondrat in gloomy tones.

'He is well-meaning, certainly,' said Fhumdullah sadly. 'Only somewhat naïve.'

'Where men once said "God", they are much more likely now to refer to a certain Principle of Justice and Nature which exists primarily in their hearts and minds.'

'Do you suppose,' said Gharib to Amina, 'that the Empress realises that what she calls the Inhabitants of the Stars are really her own desires and hopes made into people?'

'No,' said Amina, continuing to survey the rigging.

'O Principle of Justice and Nature,' sang Fhumdullah and Gondrat in frail mournful voices, 'comfort us in our sore affliction and lack of breakfast,

> Destroy without mercy our many enemies, and trample them beneath your golden hooves,
> Cause them to fall out among themselves and do each other lasting and grievous harm,
> Promote wretchedness among them and break their fingernails and fill their mouths with bad tastes,
> Strike them down with savage bolts of nature,
> And bring us to some warm place where we may rest our wearied bodies and confused souls;
> Let us be in some beautiful situation, free from harrying and spite,
> Let the harriers and spiters be boiled in oil and their descendants sold into slavery!
> Let them choke on fruits, and lose their ways in the dreadful darknesses of their own hearts,

For their folly is myriad and labyrinthine, and sufficient
thereof is the badness for them to perish;
May they perish utterly, and cease to live.
May none of their fears fail to come to pass.
O great Principle, clear and meaningful,
To you we turn our eyes and hearts, for you are our
justification,
You are our only hope, and also without doubt our only
friend, alas,
Bring us by any means to smoother paths!
Cause us to triumph and be acknowledged by all!'

The river in the afternoon was flowing somewhat more
rapidly through a region of trees and low hills. Occasionally
an island was passed.

The eunuchs were cooking two fish they had found in a
basket in the bottom of the boat. They had assembled a small
iron stove. The smell drifted back along the deck and over
the stern.

In the cabin, sitting on rolled-up nets, the Empress and
Amina and the Vizier studied a crude map of the Tigris and
Euphrates.

'Let us go on down as far as the confluence of the rivers,'
said the Empress. 'Then we may return either directly or by
way of Kufah and Al-Anbar.'

'What manner of people live in this region?' asked Amina.

'They are just arabs,' said the Grand Vizier, 'sheep and
goat people, living mostly in tents. The plain is very dry and
unprofitable there. That is how it is as far as Qalat Salah. But
after that it is all marsh, and the inhabitants are of a less
predictable nature. These are the infamous M'dan. They
must be passed through to reach Qurna and the meeting of
rivers.'

'Find another route,' said the Empress flatly.

'O great beacon of the absolute and impossible, if we
continue on the water, we cannot avoid them.'

'Then we shall stop here,' said the Empress, 'and carry the
boat overland to the Euphrates.'

Above them, alone on the deck-house roof, the Captain

leaned on his elbow and stared fiercely and blindly at the blank lands ahead, his eyes glazed with tears, the breeze ruffling his beard and hair.

'O power that fires the sun,' he fervently whispered. 'O flow that drives the rivers. *Burn on in me, flow on through me!*'

Gharib was asleep in a ball on the mid-deck. The wind was freshening.

Late in the day they passed a high stone marker of great age, rippling in the water.

Then a half-broken row of pillars split the beams of setting sunlight on a hilltop to the west.

At dusk they drifted into the ruins of a vast and ancient city. Reeds grew up among marble moorings, and the shells of huge buildings loomed on either side of them. All was silent and shadowy, and their voices echoed across the river as though they were in an underground cavern.

At the end of a short slip, by a cracked and weedy stone embankment, a giant willow tree grew up through the paving and dropped its branches in a wide arc, spreading like the hair of a sleeping jinnyah across the walkways and trailing in the water. Beneath this sheltering web Ibn wordlessly guided their dhow into a dim hall that was sweet with the odour of leaves and thick with gnats and flies. They moored to a rusted iron ring-bolt, and everyone, even the Prince of Stars, disembarked, parting the willow wands and stepping cautiously out into a deserted square.

In the increasingly wan light the great structures around them were melting into vague cliffs of masonry, gaunt, dignified, and impassive. It had evidently been a capital city, dominated by the imposing civil edifices of an imperial administration, with few smaller, habitable buildings to be seen. Here and there among the oblong grey paving stones at their feet were rows of others of yellow, faded blue or pink, forming clearly marked pathways, as if for elaborate rituals or strange, complex games.

'How *peaceful* it is,' said the Vizier. 'The cool white columns and walls, and the dark river, now grown smooth and noiseless, moving steadily by. Although the cornices are everywhere chipped and imperfect, the domes collapsed, the pedestals deserted, the open spaces littered with fallen grandeur, the place has still a cleanliness and calmness and purity about it that deeply moves one, that no living city, nor even busy nature itself, could ever be said to possess.'

'It might be a good place to rest,' said the Captain matter-of-factly, looking around himself. 'Our boat is hidden, and we can conceal ourselves anywhere in this debris. With a few bows and spears, this would be an admirable place to resist a landing.'

'But is there any food?' asked Gharib.

They walked on a little further, climbing a wide range of steps to another broad terrace, that was bordered by an ornamented parapet. The Empress placed both hands on top and surveyed the forests of stone that stretched away on all sides.

'When my people seek me,' she said, 'it might be well for them to find me in such a location as this.'

But Amina was looking back towards the river.

'O friends!' she cried. 'Hide yourselves at once!'

There was a flicker of motion through columns and two long green boats came gliding silently into view, one after another. The Empress and her party scattered in the dusk like an emptied bag of rats, scrambling down below the parapet and dodging behind pedestal bases and crawling under a section of fallen capital. In the first boat, perched on the bow, posed the unmistakable figure of Zardin al-Adigrab!

The Captain and the Vizier peered through a crack in the parapet wall. There was silver glinting everywhere on both boats, as they circled slowly in midstream, their crews staring out into the shadowed obscurity of the ruins.

'There are too many to fight!' whispered the Captain. 'He has brought the whole Party!'

'It was not *I*,' whispered back the Vizier, 'who was advocating fighting them.'

'They are going to *land*,' whispered the eunuchs, 'and do atrocious things to us!'

But the two boats only continued to circle slowly several minutes longer, as if conferring and considering. Then at last they parted, one pulling round and sailing back upstream again and the other, that containing Zardin al-Adigrab, gliding onward with the flow of the river.

'With a good bow I could have killed him,' said the Captain.

'Take care that your action is not *all* that which you *might* do, or should have, and could have, and *would* have done,' replied the Vizier.

The Captain started and looked at him with fury.

'We are helpless,' said the Vizier. 'It is becoming our whole habit and policy.'

'Why didn't they see our dhow?' asked Amina, as she crawled up beside them. 'As I watched them I felt suddenly certain of our doom. Are you sure this is not some sort of trick on their part?'

'If they *had* seen it,' said the Vizier, 'I can think of no reason why they would not come directly up and kill us all.'

Fhumdullah and Gondrat were the last to emerge from cover.

'O mother of fair chances!' exclaimed Fhumdullah.

'How can you *say* that?' demanded Gondrat. 'Do you not see they have closed off the river both ways? Is it not obvious that all is over for us?'

'Nothing is obvious to me,' said Fhumdullah with some pride.

'We will stay here,' the Empress announced.

'Let us remove ourselves from view of the river then,' said the Captain. 'They may return. Apparently, our boat is safe where it is.'

So they advanced, across a wide public space of sorts, and through a long arcade of pillars that no longer held anything aloft. Presently they emerged into an even grander square, surrounded on all sides by the shells of great buildings and temples. Opposite them gaped the cavernous doors of a huge vaulted structure, whose gigantic size they for several moments could hardly grasp. Even Bagdad held nothing to equal it.

Slowly they approached.

The Vizier finally spoke. 'That which stands before them, towering like a dark and limitless thundercloud of stone, must have been nothing other than the *Taq-e-Kisra* itself.'

'The Grand Hall of the Kings!' cried Amina.

'Said to be the vastest of all buildings on earth. Vaster than the vastest of *Persepolis*, or of *Babylon*, of old *Rome* in power, of *Cairo*, or of *Alexandria*, or *Athens*.'

'So this city is *Ctesiphon*!' said Amina.

'Of course,' said the Vizier.

'Across the river is *Selucia*, also ruined,' volunteered Fhumdullah.

'Together, the most magnificent cities men have ever created, or will ever,' the Vizier continued to muse. 'Currently deserted. Currently used as a quarry of stone for hovels built in the bezesteins and dockyards of Bagdad.'

'This should never have been allowed,' said the Empress.

'It was the wish of the Caliph,' said the Vizier. 'Communicated to me personally by the Chamberlain and the Purple Man. They were concerned, as you may imagine, with building up the glory of Bagdad.'

'Bagdad is a vile and faithless place,' said the Empress.

'Well,' remarked the Vizier, sighing to himself, 'perhaps they *will* yet recall us.'

'It's getting dark,' complained Gondrat.

'The True Consort of the Commander of the Faithful has never, in this capacity, passed a night outside the sacred walls of the round city,' the Empress announced. 'Nor is it by any means proper or fitting that she *should*. Nonetheless, were it by some mischance, or the ineptitude of her closest advisers, to become a necessity, it is probable that no place on earth would be so suitable for her domicile as the great hall *Taq-e-Kisra*, the shelter and pride of innumerable kings and other figures of her approximate magnitude.'

Amina had wandered off to the open doorways of the huge building, and called back to them.

'Here they *are* enumerated!'

'Gather up somewhat to burn,' said the Vizier to Gharib

and the eunuchs, while the others went to look at the list of
kings. Only Gharib obeyed.

'*Kings of Kings of All Iran and also all that is Not Iran!*'
translated Amina.

They were carved up and down the marble mouldings of
the doors, many repeated, a few obliterated, either by age or
by the deliberate resentment of those who followed. It was
the Captain who was most impressed.

'*Darius*,' said he, 'Xerxes,

> Cambyses
> Artaxerxes
> Eratosthenes
> Antiochus
> Demetrius
> Phraates
> Himerus,'

'Ah, Himerus,' said Gondrat, and then sighed heavily.

> 'Mithradates
> Sontruces
> Artabonus
> Gotarzes
> Volageses
> Orodes
> Tiridates
> Ardashir
> Shapur the Great
> Shapur the Lesser
> Hormizd
> Bahram
> Yazdegard
> Balash
> Kavedgh
> Khosrau ...'

'What do *you* know of Himerus?' asked Fhumdullah.

'He was also known as Chimerus,' said Gondrat. 'There
are many tales of him.'

'Where are they gone? Where is there glory now?' cried the Captain.

'Evaporated!' cried Gondrat.

'Perform an elegaic ode!' commanded the Empress sternly.

> *O now must we sing* (suddenly sang Fhumdullah) *of Kings below the earth,*
>> *The Slain minstrels of State*
>> *Dancing on the ebon stages of their final mandate.*
>> *Did they deserve to die? – poor things –*
>> *Poor Kings of over-weaning desire!*
>> *We shall never tire of tales of you,*
>> *Of the rising and the falling of your stars,*
>> *You poor lost noble things!*
>> *... Wherever you are.*

'They are *here*!' shouted the Empress at him. 'They have not left! They have returned! I am of them! So is the Prince of Stars!'

The eunuchs scurried away to help Gharib look for firewood.

'Grand Vizier,' said the Empress, 'I have had an idea!'

'O mistress of innumerable parts,' replied he, 'an idea!'

'We shall establish our new capital *here*, in Ctesiphon! It shall once again be the centre of the earth. When my people come to me to beg me to return, I shall command them instead to come *here*, to *me*! This city will again be brilliant and majestic and beautiful!'

The Vizier looked around himself.

'I suspect I shall always prefer it as a ruin,' he sighed.

'What caused its decay in the first place?' asked Amina.

'The *Vizier* remarks to himself that the girl has a very noticeable talent for questions,' said Majid Shair-al-Walahan, 'and replies that this grand city had fallen (as usual) because of a certain fatal flaw in ambition. It sought, so legend has it, to become its own sun, to renounce the rising and the setting of the natural day. It kept strange and unnatural hours and seasons, waking at night, sowing in autumn and so forth.'

'Actually, it was overrun by arabs,' said the Captain.

'It was the only light in a darkened and helpless world,' said the Empress. 'It shall be so again!'

'*Arabs*!' exclaimed Gharib, whose arms were full of old wooden bowls and utensils and carvings.

The eunuchs appeared behind him, pulling a large broken piece of furniture of some sort.

'It was a place of eternal summer,' panted Fhumdullah. 'When the women of the king came down to the water to bathe, the river itself would cease to flow, but instead lie still and placid as glass to receive their tender white bodies.'

'So they say,' said Gondrat, 'but you have to admit, it does not sound very probable.'

'Things were not then as they are now!' Fhumdullah reminded him. 'The earth was much more flexible!'

'Well, this I know,' admitted Gondrat. 'Much *has* changed since then, it is obvious. Perhaps even the tales of Himerus may be credited.'

'*Heresy*!' thundered the Empress, and the eunuchs dropped their wood with a crash while everyone else looked at her curiously. '*All that has been may always be*, O you sceptical inadequates! To say *was* is but to confess the failure of *is*, and this may by no means be tolerated! I *am* (and so is my son) and we *will not* allow your failure to see this destroy our *being*!'

'O magnificent one,' said the Vizier after a pause, 'I believe you have quite confused the Changing World Club.'

The Empress answered nothing but walked a few paces away into the night, with Ibn following.

'Take them inside and kindle a fire,' said the Vizier to Amina and Hamid bin Talal. Then he walked out into the square after the Empress.

She was staring straight up at the sky, which was blank, and rapidly darkening.

'Perhaps,' said he, in his most tactful manner, 'the night is too obscure, too misty. Perhaps they simply cannot see us.'

'I am asking them to come down to me,' said the Empress, without looking at him.

The old man sighed and wandered on a few more steps.

'Strange it is to the Vizier, that another's delusions have

such power over him that he has forgotten to speak in any way to his own object of faith. But such is the case. He cannot call Him to mind, he cannot remember the words to use. The place they are in has a certain darkening effect on the mind. The Empress, so-called, and her ambitions amaze him and humble him. How can anyone believe that power will return? It is absurd, but it gives her a remarkable advantage. Otherwise, why tolerate her at all? Thus reduced, are we not all miserable equals? She seems to fail to see this.'

The Empress was addressing him.

'Prepare the necessities of our comfort in the *Taq-e-Kisra*,' she said. 'We shall keep a vigil. My relatives *will* come. They will come in the later hours.'

'All is ready for your Imperialness, or for any of your stature,' replied the Vizier. 'All that there *is* to be ready. That is to say, I believe a fire is being lit.'

'We shall go in,' said the Empress. 'Ibn shall guard the doorway.'

When they entered, the red light from a small blaze was casting an unsteady pink glow about the cavernous ceilings and arches of the hall, which, unlike most of Ctesiphon, had not yet collapsed. The air smelled delicately of must, and of the mosses growing on the floor tiles, and every sound they made produced a faint, booming echo.

The eunuchs had recovered themselves. Gondrat was telling tales of the great king Himerus, to an audience partly rapt and partly resentful.

The soldiers of *King Himerus* were assuredly the bravest that ever have existed, just as even the serving women at his table were veritable goddesses and paragons of delicate and sensible female beauty. *King Himerus* had an excellent appetite, and would gorge himself on dishes and wines that were brought to him from every part of the wide earth. After gorging, he would retire to his harims (burping magnificently) in order to choose the concubines he wanted for his bed. Here too, everything was exquisite for him, so that some nights he would take as many as twenty-three delicious and alluring innocents and enjoy them all in succession, while on others he could delight throughout the dark hours with the company of a single, wise, beautiful and well-experienced woman. It was difficult for *King Himerus* to imagine anything more that he might want.

Then one day, however, a certain *dervish* appeared at his diwan, begging an audience.

'Oh, now the bad part begins!' interrupted Fhumdullah. 'We don't want to hear it, whatever it is! Couldn't we just have the beginnings of stories?'

'Are you not at all curious to hear what the dervish had to say?' asked Gondrat.

'I know better,' said Fhumdullah. 'You can't drag me along forever just because I don't know what's going to happen next. I'd rather be happy than know.'

'Well, this is precisely where King Himerus was unable to agree with you. This was to be his whole problem, in fact.'

'Do there *have* to be *problems*?' said Fhumdullah.

'Tell us!' cried Gharib, happily.

'O great *King Himerus*,' said the *dervish*, 'do you imagine yourself to be happy, and content? Do you imagine yourself to have all that you could possibly want?'

'Indeed,' replied *King Himerus*, 'do you know anyone happier than I?'

'In fact, great king, I do!' replied that unkempt and bizarre man. 'And I shall tell you why this is. He has in his possession the greatest *marvel* of all existence.'

'Who is this vile *man*, and what is this *marvel*!' demanded the *King*.

'The *man*, or so I believe,' responded the *dervish*, 'is called the *Emperor of Rome*. And the *marvel* is a tiny *mechanical bird*, which can tell every tale ever told, or sing any song ever sung, and do so in every language men have ever spoken, and with a grace and fascination that surpasses any human singer or storyteller.'

'I will have this bird,' said *King Himerus*.

'So I imagined you would desire it,' said the *dervish*.

The *King* immediately summoned the best of his soldiers and the fleetest and fiercest of his horses and set out for *Rome*, with lust for the marvellous *bird* in his heart. When he came to the sea he called to his *engineers* to find something faster than ships, for his vast impatience could not tolerate the slightest delay.

His *engineers*, who indeed were as wonderful as his soldiers and his women and his palaces, were not at all unprepared for this command, and lo! they instantly called from the sea a large herd of trained *whales*, each surmounted with a driver, as would be a trained elephant.

The *King* and his army rode their horses on to the broad backs of these beasts (and so fine was the mettle of the horses, and so eager were they for war and adventure, that not one of them shied from the means of conveyance) and instantly they set off across the water faster than the sleekest fleet of an ordinary king. Soon they arrived, completely without warning, at the shores of Italy, where the people, seeing the *whales* and the *army* rushing towards them in a glory of spume and pennons and battle horns, like a tidal wave of destruction, threw up a great cry of despair and rushed for the sanctuary of *Rome*. *King Himerus* and his men leapt from their *whales* and charged through the shallows and up across the sand and, without pausing a moment, rushed on over the fields and plains towards the city.

The *Legions of Rome*, seeing the dire peril, issued out from the walls and assembled before the gate in lines orderly and gallant, shield to shield, spear beside spear, and indeed they were a fearsome army, fully a hundredfold as large as that of the Parthian *Himerus*. The great *general* of the *Romans* drew himself up before his troops, and prepared to make a speech to spirit them and stir them to resistance, saying, '*O gallant Romans, Sons of Mars* . . .' But at that moment *King Himerus* and his wildly avid men, who had not hesitated an instant to consider, came careering into their ranks with scimitars savagely swinging and cries of fury in their throats and horse-hooves pummelling, just as a knife would cut through a melon or a hurled stone shatter a pane of glass, so that the *Romans* fell back routed and disorganised. But the Parthians gave them no respite but drove them fiercely on all sides, their robes flying, their horses red-eyed and terrible, their scimitars flashing brightly as they swooped and whirled, till the *Romans* had no choice but to despair and cry out in frustration and throw down their arms. Like a gust of bitter wind through a grain field the army of *King Himerus* blew through the gate and along the streets and, like the hungry sea rising, charged up the famous *Roman* hill.

At the top they could not be resisted and they struck down all who tried, until there emerged the *Emperor of Rome* himself, all dishevelled and dismayed, so suddenly had this visitation come upon him.

'O great *King!*' cried he to *Himerus*. 'Let us parley on this matter!' But *King Himerus* seized him and threw him savagely to the ground and put his foot to his throat and the tip of his scimitar to his brow and shouted,

'*Death*, death is all you may expect O *Roman*, and you deny me!'

'What is it you need?' asked the *Emperor*, with difficulty.

'Thy *bird!*' cried *King Himerus*. 'Thy marvellous speaking bird!'

'Ah,' said the *Emperor*. 'As it happens, only last month I gave that bird to the *King of the Franks*, in return for his daughter and the largest part of his realm.'

'Where is this *King of the Franks!*' demanded the *Parthian* monarch.

'In *Frankland*,' replied the *Roman*, 'hidden away in an impregnable castle, listening to the bird.'

'Let us hope this is the truth,' was all *King Himerus* would say.

Immediately he took his foot from the throat of the *Emperor* and remounted his pacing horse, crying, 'Ahead to Frankland!' and thundered away down the steps on the other side of the hill, scattering a curious throng of street merchants and fasces-sellers. Eagerly and obediently his army followed him, not pausing even to ravage the *Roman wealth* or mistreat any *Roman Women*, but leaving the city almost exactly as they found it, with the exception of a great bronze statue of the *Emperor* mounted on his horse, which one of the *Parthians*, the sun glinting in his eyes, took to be real and charged, knocking it headlong from its base into the river *Tiber*.

Instead of re-boarding their *whales*, the *Parthians* brought their peril the quicker way by land, hardly stopping to take breath till, like a small, icy gale, they swept over the mountains and rushed down into the land of the *Franks*. The *Frankish* peasants could not have been more cast down in mind and heart, yet they were safe, for the army of *King Himerus* was eager for rarer game and richer than were they. Soon they arrived at the castle of the *King of the Franks*, that was said to be impregnable. Indeed, strong it was, and stalwart, built high of stones, surrounded by ditches, locked up everywhere with iron, while all about it lay signs of a recent siege which had tried, travailed and failed. But the great *King* was thrown into a terrible rage at the very slightest delay.

Calling once more on his *engineers*, he demanded the finest and fiercest and most efficient creation of their imaginations, and he demanded it at once. Nor did they fail him, building with awesome speed an immense *catapult* whose strength and purpose were unlike any before or after it. The *Franks* from their walls watched aghast as its mighty sinews were tightened, and prepared themselves for the worst and most terrific in bombardments. But whatever they prepared was not enough, for when the great machine wound up to fire it was not passive objects but the soldiers of *King Himerus* themselves that it sent in long swooping arcs through the sky, even all mounted on their horses as they were. On the hooves of these magnificent steeds were tied bales of hay and straw for cushioning, which they kicked quickly away as soon as they landed. The *Franks* were so amazed and dismayed by this feat of the *Parthians* that their weapons fell from their hands and they could offer little resistance to their ferocious and daring enemies. Soon they were all overcome and *King Himerus* burst through the door of the *King of the Franks* in his tower, himself in a towering passion, his eyes aflame and his scimitar in hand. The *King of the Franks* knelt to offer the *Parthian* fealty but the great *King* kicked him over and put his boot to his chest and threatened to divest him utterly of his head did he not instantly turn over to him the fabled *bird*.

'O unparalleled conqueror,' gasped out the oppressed *Frank*, 'this is a thing that I may by no means do!'

'Why is this!' cried out *King Himerus*. 'Consider that without your head you are nothing!'

'It is no lack in fear of your sincere ferocity that inhibits me,' replied the King. 'It is only that I have given the bird to a savage band of *Mongols*, who were recently besieging my walls. It was in return for the life and happiness of my country and people, whom they were prepared to ravage, though they could do no harm to me.'

Thus to be thwarted a second way caused *Himerus* the most excruciating frustration, so that he instantly raised his weapon to put an end and conclusion to the career of the *Frank*.

But he was interrupted in this business by the *dervish* (who had accompanied him everywhere on his quest).

'O magnificent majesty,' said he, 'consider that this was a generous act on the part of a ruler towards his people, and remember as well, that wanton bloodshed here will in no way help you towards the bird.'

Though entirely contemptuous of such motives, *King Himerus* relented, and instead demanded of the *King of the Franks* the whereabouts of the *Mongols*.

'They have gone east,' replied he, 'from whence they came, riding at great speed, uttering uncouth cries of joy about the bird.'

So *Himerus* and his army burst out through the still unopened gates of the castle and set out eastwards in determined pursuit, leaving the *Franks* much as they had found them.

Fleet as the *Parthians* were, however, just as fast were

the fleeing *Mongols*, and their dust drifted ever on the horizon, themselves just beyond the view of their pursuers. Through *Burgundy* they tore, one after the other, and *Bavaria*, then startling the *Lombards* around their fires and now leaving the tents of the *Gepids* flapping in their breeze. They terrified the *Avars* and confused the *Alans* and the *Huns*, while the *Khazars* and *Kushans* were convinced that some natural disaster was overtaking them as final retribution for their barbaric and lawless ways. The *Volga Bulgars* peering off into the plains saw them pass as they wheeled north around the *Caspian Sea*, marvelling at the speed of the two armies of horsemen that burned like fires of dust across the steppes.

On and on they raced, through vast stretches of waste and broken land, over mountains and plunging through icy rivers, rushing across breathless deserts, and splashing through endless swamps. Then finally, all bespattered with mud, bronzed and burned by the sun, the pursuers' hearts more wild and eager than ever for the bird, and the pursued just as determined to keep it, they both arrived at *China*, which even then was surrounded by a substantial wall. As the *Parthians* strove at last to narrow the distance between them and their quarry, lo! a gateway opened and the *Mongols* were ushered in, but it clanged loudly closed at the very noses of the *King*'s horses and within a moment their *enemies* appeared at the wall above to shower them with abuse and arrows and rocks and taunts.

Drawing back, the *King Himerus* called once more upon his marvellous *engineers*, but they at first, even they, were to a degree discouraged, for they lacked all materials, standing as they did in the vastest, emptiest and driest of deserts. But soon enough an idea was devised. During their long ride across all *Asia*, the *engineers* had had leisure to observe little whirling spouts of wind that capered here and there upon the sand. Occasionally these became veritable *tornadoes* of true power and destruction, for which qualities the *engineers* had greatly admired them. Now they recalled them to mind, and began to set their masterly plan in motion. The *soldiers* were made to withdraw a mile

or so from the wall, and unfurl every pennon and banner
they possessed, and let them flow out freely. Then the
great horses of *King Himerus* were set to work, their
riders regaled in full splendour, and began to race with
their utmost speed in a tiny circle on the barren plain.
The pennons flapping in their wake raised up the air so
that, while the *Mongols* watched uncomprehending, a
tall spouting tornado arose, which, with cries of war and
determination, the *soldiers* started to direct, like the
sling of a slinger spinning round his head, in ever-
widening circles. Then suddenly the *army* burst free, all
foaming and panting, and the tornado, travelling on its
own, was sent whirling and sucking straight for the wall,
a section of which it instantly blew into a million separate bricks scattering across the plain.

The horrified *Mongols* hardly had a chance to mount
their mounts before the *Parthians* were upon them, with
savage cries and richly harvesting scimitars. Ferocious
though they were, even the *Easterners* could not resist
the wrath of *King Himerus* and his men and soon they
were routed and broken, and the great *King* was howling
aloud for the fabled bird. Just at that moment a single
rider on an orange horse was seen to break free from the
fighting and melée and race off eastwards again at
scarcely believable speeds. A collective groan from the
Mongols convinced the *Parthians* that this was what they
sought and in an instant they were hotly in pursuit. But
a horse had never been born that could out-horse the
horse of their *quarry* and so he led them, flying like chaff
in a gale, across the length and breadth of *China*, and
never did they lose him but never did they gain him
either.

Then at length he bent his steps northward to *Mon-
golia*, and the hopes of the pursuers began almost to rise
as they saw him at last begin to slacken and even to
weaken. Presently they all came to a mountain the
highest of imaginable mountains, jagged and savage,
snowy and howling, and the *rider* of the *orange horse*
charged up this, higher and higher. The *King Himerus*

led his men unflinching after him, though it might be towards doom and very destruction!

Finally, even their magnificent horses had to be left behind, as their *game* took to foot, staggering through the snow, clambering over the icy rocks, gasping for air. Upwards slowly into white obscurity they struggled and struggled, and the world below faded away and nothing above was visible.

At last, teetering on a towering pinnacle, scraping the dense roof of the clouds, they came up to him, and he screamed in a mad voice for them to keep their distance.

'Here sit I, O famous *King Himerus*,' cried he, 'with the greatest mystery in the world in one hand and a gross, material *rock* in the other! And you approach me the least part and I shall bring them together and all your dreams shall be ended and all your riding be in vain!'

King Himerus peered through the whipping snow at him and saw that it was true, for there in his left hand was the beautiful shimmering bird, and there in his right was an ugly black rock!

'O mad monk of the *Mongols*,' cried back he (for this is what the other seemed to be), 'hear what I may offer you for that bird of yours! All the riches of my realm are at your disposal, gold, jewels, land, people, and all your labour to have them is but to imagine what they are! Of women, if they please you, I can give you a limitless supply, of foods and sensuous joys you may bathe in veritable rainbows! Of libraries and wisdom unthought of quantities, of power, an infinite and irresistible absolute dominion!'

'Yes, yes! Women, riches, power!' cried out the *Mongol* in a cracked and hysterical voice. 'Nothing may you deny me!'

'Indeed! Indeed!' replied *King Himerus*. 'All this is yours, if only you accept!'

'I do! I accept! I want *all, all* of them! That is why I'm here!' wildly cried the *Monk*. 'I *want* them, I want to *have* them ... *and keep them forever!*' But then, to their unbelieving horror, he clapped his hands ferociously together, smashing the bird to shreds and shards, and, at the same moment, uttering a terrible scream, hurled himself from the pinnacle out into the sickening void of driving snow.

'Where is my fault!' shouted *King Himerus* in a great voice. 'Where is my flaw! What have I failed to do!'

'Nothing! Nothing!' cried the frantic *dervish* at his side. 'It *should have been* yours! It *should have been* yours!'

At these very words, so it is said, the *Great King of the Parthians* simply died, unable to bear the universe. The *army*, without his leadership, could not make its way back to *Ctesiphon*, but perished in the wilderness, and the throne was soon occupied by the outsider *Mithradates*. Although much was still to occur, most compilers of history are in agreement that this marked the beginning of the long slide downward to dissolution and obscurity for the *Parthians*.

Gondrat's audience now sat deep in thought, or melancholy indifference.

'Why *did* the Mongol break the bird?' asked Gharib presently.

'People are always wrecking things,' sighed Fhumdullah.

'The military elements in this story are very untrue to life,' commented Hamid bin Talal.

'Please remember,' said Gondrat with dignity, 'that this was long ago. It is the very question we have been considering, whether such things may *once* have been possible.'

'Life *was* brighter, fiercer, stronger,' breathed Fhumdullah.

'It was simply that they were more *absolute*,' said the Empress.

'More excessive,' added Gondrat.

'More like a story!' said Gharib.

'*Just so*,' said the Vizier bitterly.

'But things now make much more sense!' Fhumdullah protested.

'Only it never ended! It *is* now as it ever *has* been!' ruled the Empress, trying to silence them all.

'It only *seems* less so,' agreed Gondrat with a sad nod.

'It *is* so!' cried the Empress.

'It's nice to think,' said Fhumdullah nostalgically, 'but of course, we know so much more than they did.'

'*Enough!*' shouted the Empress.

There was an unpleasant silence, in which the echoes of her voice could be heard rebounding repeatedly about the hollow vault. Then the Captain threw a piece of carved wood on the fire, sending up a gust of sparks.

'Tell another tale,' said the Prince of Stars presently to the eunuchs. Everyone turned in surprise at his voice.

'Tell another splendid tale of the past days!' added Gharib. 'Tell a tale from the world of marvels!'

'*Well*,' said Gondrat with a quaver in his voice, 'I do not know that, conditions being what they are, we can still tell tales as we have before.'

'No indeed,' chimed in Fhumdullah, glancing uneasily at the Empress, 'it is clearly not the world it once was.'

'You still *know* them, don't you?' demanded Gharib.

'There is no point now, not any more,' sulked Gondrat.

'Isn't there a marvellous tale about a poor man and a jinni?' asked Amina.

'Well,' said Fhumdullah, quickly relenting, 'I believe I know something of a *tax official* of some sort, and a jinni.'

'No! No!' exclaimed Gharib. 'A *fisherman*, and he found a bottle!'

'Fishermen *no longer* find bottles!' asserted Gondrat with force. 'Such things are considered ridiculous!'

The others looked at him in dismay.

'Evidently,' observed the Vizier, 'change has struck deeper than any of us were prepared for.'

'What about the tax official, then?' asked Amina.

'What did *he* find?' demanded the boy.

'*He* didn't find anything!' shot back Gondrat.

'I think it was the other way around,' hurriedly interposed Fhumdullah.

'In the name of the merciful and compassionate!' suddenly cried the Prince of Stars again. '*Tell* the tale!'

This cowed Gondrat, and Fhumdullah began quickly to recite, in a singsong voice:

The *Jinni* and the *Civil Servant*

Once there was a certain starving *jinni* fishing on a distant shore.

Instead of a fish, however, he drew from his nets a small brass bottle, still carefully sealed. On the seal was written, 'Closed by order of *Ali bin Isa*, vizier to the great and gracious *Caliph*'.

'How remarkable,' said the *jinni*. 'The Caliphs have all been dead these thousand years. Nonetheless, I cannot eat it, so it is of no real use to me.'

So saying, he tossed it down and reached again for his nets, preparing all the while to give himself over to despair. However, the bottle popped open and out of it crawled a small civil servant named *Ahmad*, like a cockroach crawling from a hollow bread-loaf.

'Greetings, O *citizen*!' announced he. 'You are indeed a most fortunate mortal!'

'I am not a citizen, nor fortunate,' said the *jinni*, 'nor mortal.'

'Nonetheless,' said *Ahmad*, 'I am authorised to grant you five wishes of your own choosing.'

'Are you indeed?' said the *jinni*.

'Most certainly,' replied the *civil servant*. 'Due to the wide beneficence of the greatest and most gracious of *Caliphs*.'

'Very well,' said the *jinni* indifferently, 'I want a fish.'

'Only a fish?' said the *civil servant*. 'Nothing more elaborate?'

'When you are as old as I,' replied the *jinni*, 'all desire subsides to simple appetite.' And he continued to heave his nets.

'As you wish, of course,' said *Ahmad*. 'What kind of fish?'

'A large one,' answered the *jinni*, 'and blue.'

'I mean, what *name* of fish?' said the *civil servant*.

The jinni thought a moment.

'It is called a *grouper*,' he said.

'Very good,' was the reply, 'the wish is granted. Four wishes remain.'

The *jinni* waited for a space. Then presently he asked, 'Where is the fish?'

'Ah,' replied *Ahmad*. 'Allow me to inquire.' And he disappeared briefly back into the bottle, while the *jinni* looked thoughtfully around for the stopper. But he quickly re-emerged and said, 'Ah. You have specified a fish, but I fear you have not said *when* or *where*. We cannot say with certainty what has become of your fish, but you may be sure that there is one and that we are working on it.'

The *jinni* sighed. 'Very well,' he said. 'I want a large blue grouper, *here*, and *now*.'

'Much better,' said the *official*. 'Three wishes remain.'

Out of the small brass bottle there miraculously issued a contingent of *civil servants* carrying a sizeable blue fish on a ceramic plate.

The *jinni* regarded the fish.

Then he said, calmly:

'It is entirely rotten.'

'*Is* it?' said *Ahmad*, looking closely. 'Well, this is not quite as one would expect. But it is likely a necessity to specify such matters. I don't recall your having mentioned the *condition* of the object desired. What I would recommend you do, in this fish matter, is list as many of its characteristics as you can think of in your next wish.'

'Never mind,' said the *jinni*, 'for my next wish I would like something entirely different. I would like to die.'

'O surely not!' cried back the *civil servant*. 'With three wishes remaining? Is there nothing else in life that might tempt you? What about a beautiful *jinniyah* of some sort? Or what about perpetual happiness? That is very popular.'

The *jinni* considered.

'Very well,' he said. 'If it may be done, I would like to possess a certain faery, *Maimoune* by name, with whom I have been in love for seventeen hundred years. She has always scorned me and my advances, so if she is going to be any good to me she must be made as desirous of me as I am of her.'

'Is that your wish?' asked *Ahmad*.

'Yes,' said the *jinni*. '*Here*, and *now*.'

'Wish granted!' cried the *civil servant*.

Out of the brass bottle there began to flow a delicately scented purple mist, which presently condensed into the most lovely faery imaginable. She had a smile on her face.

'O *Danhasch*!' cried she, 'Is it you?'

'Certainly,' said the *jinni*.

'My sweet little toad!' she exclaimed, approaching him. 'They have told me what you have harboured in your heart all these centuries, and I am moved beyond all expressions by the news. Why did you never speak, O bashful one!'

'I *did*,' said the *jinni*.

'But it does not matter,' went on *Maimoune*, 'for at the end we have discovered each other, and I have the chance finally to tell you that I too am afflicted by the famous old malady. The strength of my passion makes me so bold as to say that no being beneath or above the sun pleases me so much as yourself!'

The *jinni* smiled a horrible smile.

'Are you *sure*?' he asked.

'As sure I am,' said the *faery*, 'as the sun is sure to set and the moon is sure to rise! As sure as the beating of my heart, or the agitation of the sea!'

'Then you will yield yourself to me?' asked the *jinni*.

'Nothing would give me more delight and satisfaction,' promptly replied the *faery*.

'But I find this difficult to believe,' said the *jinni*.

'Yet here I am!' said she with a radiant smile that flashed out over the toiling sea and along the empty beaches.

'Truly,' said the *jinni* morosely, regarding her, 'I am too old for this kind of thing.'

'Is one ever too old?' asked the *faery* beseechingly, and drew herself up before the *jinni*.

'Either that, or too young,' said he, but still he hesitatingly reached out a large horny hand to touch her. Instead of doing so, however, his claws passed unresistingly through her breast, for she was entirely ethereal.

The two looked at each other in dismay.

'And is this really you?' asked the *jinni*.

'Alas!' was all the *faery* could cry. 'I had no idea I was so insubstantial!'

'Well, never mind,' replied he with another sigh. 'It is the emotion involved which is of significance. Even though that, too, is hardly to be trusted, considering the present situation.'

'It does not matter!' cried out *Maimoune*. 'We may still live together! We shall travel the world in company and amuse ourselves tormenting mortal lovers!'

'Well, this is a very generous offer,' said the *jinni*, 'but I think it would be better if you went by yourself.'

'Is this what you would prefer?' asked the *faery*, heart-broken.

'Yes,' said the *jinni*.

At the very word the *jinniyah* disappeared, like a man's breath into freezing air.

'Well now,' said the *civil servant*, 'this is what you get for being *too* specific. If you would let us choose, we could I'm sure find you a mistress with something more *to* her.'

'That I can do for myself,' said the *jinni*. 'For my next wish, I would like to die.'

'O don't give *up*!' cried the *benefactor*. 'How can you be sure that life doesn't hold some further delights, even for you? Why not ask for happiness? That's what everybody else asks for.'

'What if it turns out to be rotten, like the grouper?' said the *jinni*.

'*Happiness*!' exclaimed the *civil servant*. 'Now this truly *is* boundless cynicism! How can you go wrong with happiness!'

The *jinni* sighed yet again, and seemed to contemplate the grouper lying on the sand.

Then presently he said, 'Very well, I wish to be as happy as it is possible to be.'

'Wish granted!' responded the *official* cheerfully. The *jinni* waited a moment and then said, in a mild voice:

'Well?'

'Well?' replied *Ahmad*, slightly confused.

The *jinni* regarded him steadily.

'Hasn't it *worked*?' asked the *civil servant* in surprise.

At this the *jinni* said nothing but only smiled such a grotesque and horrible smile that *Ahmad* and the other *civil servants* (who had brought the grouper) shrank back involuntarily towards the mouth of their bottle.

Then the *jinni* said, 'For my last wish, I wish to *die*.'

'I'm very sorry,' said *Ahmad* in a courteous manner, not unaffected by trepidation, 'but there are no wishes left.'

The red eye of the *jinni* seemed to grow a little larger and a little redder, and his tail began to flick restlessly back and forth behind him.

'No wishes left!' he said. 'But I have taken four, and I was promised *five*.'

'I'm sorry,' said the *civil servant*, somewhat more aggressively, 'I said *four* wishes. It is clearly written in the statutes of *Ali bin Isa*.'

'He *did* say four,' verified the other *civil servants* in unison. 'We were there.'

At last the voice of the *jinni* betrayed a certain suggestion of wrath.

'You know, this *is* monstrous. You have come and disturbed me at my fishing, and caused my peace of mind to be damaged. You have done *nothing* for me. You really have no *right* to do such things!'

'So put me back in the bottle!' sneered the *civil servant* unexpectedly. 'Or learn to take what we offer you, like everybody else!'

At these provoking words the *jinni* stamped his foot so that the earth shook, and made to seize *Ahmad*. But all the *civil servants* ran off rapidly down the beach like sandpiper birds.

In anger the *jinni* snatched up the bottle, and the rotten grouper and the ceramic dish, and hurled them all far out into the water.

But then his fury quickly subsided, and bending slowly to pull in his nets, he began to sing:

The day begins
The day ends
Beneath the dreary sky
The sea towards the shore forever tends.

'They *used* to tell better tales than this,' said Gharib in a
puzzled voice.

'What kind of tales did they tell?' asked Amina.

'Well, anyway,' replied the boy, 'some of them had happy
endings.'

'But are there ever *happy endings*?' mourned Fhumdullah
and Gondrat together. 'Are there ever *endings*?'

'There are endings,' said the Captain grimly.

There was quite suddenly a single loud creak from above.

'What was *that*!' cried the eunuchs.

'The sky is falling,' explained the Vizier.

'They have come,' said the Empress in hollow tones, and
everyone looked at her.

She was sitting upright with a strange glaze reflecting from
her eyes, and two bright tear-drops glistening on her cheeks.
With one hand she had gripped the shoulder of Amina, and
with the other she clutched the brawny forearm of the
ever-impassive Ibn, whose lids were closed.

'Her form radiates emanations of great majesty and self-
importance,' said the Grand Vizier. 'Vibrations from the
cosmos seem to flood and gurgle about her being, as is
customary when this condition comes upon her. As is also
quite usual, the effect, for those around her, is a mixture of
the awesome, and the somehow terribly tedious.'

'They have a tale for us,' whispered the Empress. 'A tale of
the stars and spaces.'

'Will it guide us in our present confusion?' asked Amina.

'Yes, yes,' replied the Empress, 'that is *just* what it is
meant to do.'

'We are all in the most perfect state of attention, O
Majesty,' then said Amina, although the Vizier was making a
show of looking at his fingernails, and at the underwater
gleams of firelight reflected on the ceiling of the vault.

'The story is called . . .' whispered the Empress.

The Children of the Stars

There was once a noble *king* of *kings*, *scion* of a noble land,
majestic *ruler* of a magnificent patrimony, blessed
defender of a gentle and productive people; a noble *king*
who possessed every bounty he dared desire, except one
single boon; he had no heir.

When every wife and every concubine had failed him,
the aging king at last sent word throughout his realm,
commanding all his women subjects of child-bearing age,
who had not lawful husbands, to come at once to him. To
serve, upon pain of death, the great need of his bed.

And this they did, in great numbers, in solemn pilgrim-
ages, some weeping, some rejoicing, and all of them he
knew, but none could supply him with what he craved,
and so he gave them gifts and sent them out again.

And the realm grew pale and empty and grey, and the
crops blew dry and the rivers shrank, for there was no
fullness or fecundity in the king, and no harvest in him,
and no happiness in his coupling.

Then one day arrived from the farthest mountains a
lovely *maiden* of perhaps fourteen winters aged, who
desired audience with the troubled *monarch*. 'O Grace,'
said she, 'I am no man's, nor ever will be, yet I believe I
can bring thee all thy desire.'

'Then come in with me,' said the *King* at once, rising,
for somewhat in the bearing and beauty of the *girl* had
awakened all his hopes anew.

'Nay, but first you must grant certain conditions I set
down. Otherwise, you shall have nothing of me,' replied
she.

'What are these conditions?'

'That you put away all your concubines, and divorce all
your other wives, and have nothing more ever to do with
them. That I be your only wife, living here in this palace,
alone, just as I choose. That you shall come in with me but
one single night, so it may be provided you what you
desire.'

The *King* was amazed at these stringent demands, yet to

the surprise of all around him, he immediately acceded to them. 'This *damsel* has that about her which fills me with expectation,' said he. 'All my other women are nothing to me, and I despair of them. I shall do as she insists.'

So he provided the *concubines* with new owners, and his *wives* with generous dowries so that they might marry again, and invited the *maid* of the mountains to enter his chamber.

'Nay, I shall have my own chamber, in another part of the palace,' said she.

This was immediately provided for her, and then also the *King* asked her if she would recite the words of marriage with him.

'Nay, nor this as well,' replied she. 'Nor shall you be my owner, but you shall share all you have with me in perfect division.'

'Gladly it is done,' replied the *King*, and as he had the deeds for this laid down he was filled with a lightness of heart which had not been his for innumerable days.

'And you shall have no other women after me,' hotly insisted the *maid*. The *King* laughed happily and replied, 'This have I sworn in my heart already.'

'Allow me some days to quiet myself, and prepare my soul for this thing. Then come to me unannounced, so that I may not know previously of it,' said the *girl*, and left him.

So he went in to her some nights hence, and in the adjoining chambers his *bodyguards* heard her cry out repeatedly in joyless pain.

But when several months had passed, the *girl of the mountains* came to the *King* in his chess-room and said, 'Observe me then, O Grace.' And he cried out with astonished delight at the smooth and fruitful rounding of her belly.

And he lavished upon her every imaginable care and kindness, which she with dignity accepted, and while they waited for birth they sat and conversed together on a thousand topics, so that gradually each began to know intimately the other's heart and mind.

Then on a certain day as they sat thus in conversation,

she interrupted him and said, 'The moment is at hand.'
And they carried her in to her chamber, and the anguish of
her work began, and lasted deep into the night.

But when at last she birthed, it was to still-born twins,
small and perfect, but dead before they breathed.

The *King* went out on to the terrace at his Palace, where
it overlooked the river, with a heart gone cold and black,
like a morning's cinder. He purposed at once to drown
himself and be done with the failures and misery of his life.

'How can it be that such perfect desire and devotion as
mine has been should be so grossly rewarded?' he asked.
'How can it be that so lovely and pure a woman as this *girl
of the mountains* should be denied the gift that scullions
and whores and fishwives everywhere receive?'

But even as he stood and prepared himself for the
ending of all things there appeared in the darkness of the
sky two streaks of brilliant silver light, like meteors. They
did not vanish at the horizon but continued to fall, plunging finally into the waters of the river at the *King's* feet,
throwing up a mist of spray that rained across the terrace.

The *King*, upon a strange and ungoverned impulse, ran
quickly to secure a boat, and all alone set out into the dark,
swift-flowing river, poling forward with all his strength.
Soon in the murk he discerned a faintly glowing radiance
ahead of him, and towards this he directed all his efforts.
As he drew closer, he saw that the source was two lights
close together, and when he arrived, he found them to be
cast by two glittering twin babies newborn, floating in
silver cradles on the surface of the water!

He pulled them into his boat and made his way with
difficulty to the shore.

When he arrived in safety at the palace, he hid them in
the folds of his gown and brought them quietly into the
chamber where the *girl* lay with the attendant women
around her. In astonishment they gazed upon them,
shining as bright as they were the full moon, and so
delicately and beautifully formed that all who saw them
were entranced. And they were given the *mountain girl*'s
small breasts and, lo, they fed and were contented.

The *King* ordered that the smooth and breathless bodies of those still-born be buried in secret, and enjoined all present that no one should know of the true origin of the children he quickly had determined would be his heirs.

All of the realm greeted the news of the birth of children to the *King* with great gladness and celebration. At once the green plants began to sprout, and the springs to gush from the earth and the sweet rains to fall.

And so the *King* and the *Damsel of the Mountains* brought up the *twins* as their own, naming one, a boy, *Perdva*, and the other, a girl, *Peravaze*. And together, they formed the most happy and harmonious of families. The *King* and the *damsel*, in the months of her confinement, had made a fair friendship which the strange events of their *children*'s birth did not diminish. On every subject concerning the care of their infants, or the government of the realm, they consulted each other and had full discussion, and each tempered the wisdom and experience of the other with their own. And in all this, the *King* followed to exactness the conditions laid down by his *partner* on the day of her arrival, and was in no way discontented with them.

And if there was felicity between the *parents*, so there was a perfect joy of companionship between the sibling *children*. Throughout the Palace and the gardens they played together, bringing the light of their shining faces wherever they went. And the people of the city would catch glimpses of them above the wall as they ran across the terrace, or at a distance as they sailed in a little boat on the river, and they were enchanted with their beauty and whiteness, and loved them even as their *parents* did. And it was said, and truly, that to *Perdva* was *Peravaze* devoted and to *Peravaze* likewise was *Perdva*, and both were desirability itself in loving and obeying their *parents*.

When they came to the age of dressing differently and yearning for different occupations, the affection the *twins* held for each other in no part slackened. They slept still in the same chamber, and kissed each other when they rose and went to their various amusements, *Perdva* to his horses and friends and dogs for hunting, *Peravaze* to her gardens and lutes and ladies-in-waiting for the making of music and songs of love.

Their lives flowed on with delights and pleasures, but not without certain events as well. One day as *Perdva* was hunting with his companions, they came all unawares upon a savage *lioness* in a cane patch. A shower of shots from their bows would not stop her as she crashed out upon them, thirsty for blood and destruction. Veering uncannily she at once selected the *Prince* from the crowd of youths and lunged ferociously at *him*. Her fangs bit into the shoulder of *Perdva* as he tried to escape, and certainly his neck and his death would quickly have followed had not a *slave* leapt upon the back of the beast, and drawn away her wrath. On this poor *retainer* she turned, and disembowelled him in an instant, but the instant was his *master*'s salvation. With his knife, *Perdva* rushed upon the *lioness*, even wounded as he was, and aided by another *slave* with a spear, he succeeded in destroying her at last, while the rest of the *boys* ran screaming to the Palace.

The court and people all were most distraught at the nearness of this peril to the *Prince*'s life, but he himself spoke more of the nobility of the *slave* whose life had been given for his own. Many a day the matter cast him into deep thoughts which his childhood had never before known. Where the teeth of the *lioness* had entered his smooth skin there rose a bright red scar, that remained undimmed when he was whole again.

To *Peravaze* a quite different adventure was allotted. One sultry late spring afternoon she chanced to fall into a light slumber in the inner garden of the Palace, her perfumed ladies likewise spread out around her, their instruments scattered casually on the lawn. Into this pleasant scene crept the *youngest son* of a certain *merchant*, who once had glimpsed the *Princess* and whose eyes had ever watered with yearning for her since. Too young was he to know the peril of such desires, as he trod the forbidden grass, cast into a trance of love at the near sight of the *girl* herself! He knelt beside her, all unknown,

all but overcome, and bent his lips to kiss, not *her* lips –
that even he could not imagine – but the tender place on
the inside of her elbow, where her delicate arm lay bare
and loose upon the sward. She woke as though a burning
iron had touched her, crying out aloud, wakening her
companions and bringing *eunuchs* running from
everywhere.

The *King* said it could not be but that the *young man*
must die, and die he did, though *Peravaze* sought to save
him, for she thought, in her innocence, the offence light.
True tears fell from her eyes when she saw him strangled,
and on her arm, where the lips of the hapless *man* had
touched her, there arose a scarlet welt which did not fade,
and remained the only mark on her smooth and perfect
body.

When *Perdva* and *Peravaze* reached their sixteenth
year, they began to conceive a great longing to make a
journey, though they did not know for what reason, nor
where. Neither the *King* nor the *Maid of the Mountains*
could understand this desire, and it caused them much
distress. 'We must leave,' their *children* told them. And
they asked, 'But why is this?' Yet the *children* knew not,
and could not answer. The *King* denied them his permission, and even forbade them to stray from the precincts
of the Palace.

And this situation continued for many months, but the
yearning in the hearts of the *twins* did not diminish. Then
it became winter, and an uncommonly cold winter as well,
quite unlike most that ever visited their climes. At first in
the mornings the slightest silver glistening could be seen
on the leaves of the orange trees in the orange tree court,
and at night the air was sharp and the breath of the soldiers
on the walls burned white like ghosts of life escaping their
mouths. But day by day it grew more and more intense, so
that flowers in window-boxes shrivelled, and the earth
grew hard and cracked, and finally, worst of all, the river
itself froze over, something that never before had happened. And still it grew colder and colder, so that the *King*
and *people* waxed fearful, and then truly alarmed.

On the chillest of these chill nights *Perdva* and *Pera-vaze* were awakened in their chamber by a very strange sound. They both sat up shivering and listened in wonder, for in the unnaturally deep silence they could hear a steady, delicate tinkling, like thousands of glass wind chimes blowing in an unwavering breeze. They also felt at once that the air in their room was colder than ever, colder even than the ice of the frozen river, terribly cold and still.

Rising in their nightshirts they stepped out of the chamber and mounted quickly to the open terrace of the Palace. Here, when they raised their eyes, they saw the most marvellous of imaginable sights. The very sky above had crystallised, frozen into a vast, delicate web of geometric stars, like one huge spreading snowflake, brilliantly gleaming inside with light reflected through a million facets from the unseen moon! This intricate and glowing canopy of hollow crystal hung down in uneven clusters almost to the very palace, so that in places one could actually reach up and touch it. The soldiers on the walls around were still and frozen, and the dark city below was smokeless and motionless and utterly quiet. The tinkling sound they had heard in their chamber was louder here, and continuous, and all-pervading, like an enchanting music.

'O sister *Peravaze*,' whispered the *prince*, 'how lovely it is, how clean and peaceful!'

'But my brother *Perdva*,' replied she in the same way, 'have we not heard these beckoning harmonies before?'

And they listened and gazed upon the awesome sight, and gradually the conviction grew up in their hearts that they were in truth being called.

'Come, O *sister*!' suddenly cried the *prince*. 'Before it is gone! This is the way for us to make our journey!'

And he reached up to the nearest descending spur of latticework stars, like a boy climbing into the lowest branches of some great tree, and raised himself into the glimmering mass. In an instant his lithe *sister* had joined him, and together they began to climb upwards through it.

Soon the palace below could no longer be seen, and the icy maze surrounded them on all sides, dense and gleaming and perfect.

For many hours they ascended in this way, yet instead of growing weary their strength freshened with every step they rose, and even as the air grew colder and colder their hearts grew more and more joyous and their eyes brighter and clearer. And below their feet, all unknown to them, out of view, the crystal began to evaporate, receding from the earth as they left it behind.

Finally the tinkling music became louder, and the dazzling light of the moon much brighter, until at once the *twins* emerged from the surface of the honeycombed air into a place of brilliant blackness, where the moon and stars floated in magic and the atmosphere was thick with beautiful sound.

Shining *people* were flying everywhere, singing in glory, laughing with joy, weeping with passions, trailing beautiful glittering robes behind them, that flashed and scintillated and confused the eye with their brightness and clarity, just as their voices filled the ear with a harmonious disorder in which words could not be discerned. It was intensely cold, but no clouds of breath came from their mouths, nor did they seem to shiver or be in any way bothered by the frigid temperature.

Near *Perdva* and *Peravaze* there suddenly swooped three lovely *women*, dressed in fluttering shirts of silvery emerald, mauve and sapphire. In ringing voices they cried aloud to them, saying,

> 'Your father was not your father!
> Your home was not your home!
> You were not who you thought you were!'

'Wait!' cried out *Perdva*, as the *women* began to recede. 'Explain these mysteries to us!'

At his call the three curved gracefully and turned and floated near once more.

'Your father was not your father!' sang they,
'Your home was not your home!
You were not who you thought you were!'

'But who are we then?' asked *Peravaze*. 'And who *is* our father?'

This they answered at once, singing fervently:

'Fly to him! Fly to him!
Cry to him! Sigh to him!
Lift up your eyes to him!'

So *Peravaze* and *Perdva* looked up, desiring very much to see their father, and even as they did they found themselves flying free like the others.

'Let us find our father!' cried *Perdva* in joy.

'Let us go to our father!' cried his *sister* in the same way.

As quickly as they wished they went, not knowing where, but rising steadily from the earth and heading directly out towards the deeps beyond the wide silver moon.

In this black expanse they sped, till presently they saw gleaming objects far ahead of them. When they approached they found these to be a string of glittering cobweb tents, hovering as if pitched in the dark sea and giving off a pure white light.

Without hesitating the two *children* were drawn towards the largest and the brightest of these strange tents, that floated in the centre of the others. Its flaps were closed, and nothing bid them enter, yet they were filled with expectancy and the certain feeling that there was someone within.

'Here it must be!' whispered *Peravaze* to *Perdva*.

'Yes, O *sister*, here!' replied *Perdva*.

'Yes, *here*, *here* and *now*!' cried out a chorus of voices from behind, for many of the other flying *people* had accompanied them unannounced.

Slowly and almost fearfully *Perdva* approached the tent, and taking its soft stuff in his hand – it burned with

cold and crackled as he moved it! – he drew back one flap.
Then together they bent and entered.

Once inside, their eyes were dazzled by such incredible
brilliance that it was as if they were in a perfectly *dark*
closet and could see nothing. Beneath them they felt some
manner of rug, so they sat, just inside the door, and
suddenly they could feel cups being placed in their hands.
Of these they drank, tasting a strange bitter liquid, colder
than ice-water, that seemed to penetrate to their very
bones and sear the insides of their eyes.

Then presently a very loud and echoing masculine
voice, close at hand, began to speak, saying:

> 'Your father is not your father!
> Your home is not your home!
> You are not who you think you are!'

'But who are we!' cried out *Perdva* and *Peravaze* as
one. The voice began again.

> 'Like spark from fire you fall,
> And burn upon earth until you fade;
> But it is not *you*
> And it is not *all*,
> It is not by chance that you are made!'

'Then who are we truly?' asked *Perdva*.
'And what is it then our purpose to do?' asked *Peravaze*.

> 'You were born never to be born,
> You were *there* in order to be *here*;
> You have returned in order to return!'

'Is that what we should do?' asked *Perdva*.
'May we not stay here with you?' asked *Peravaze*.

> 'With me you are with them,
> But your father is not your father;
> You are here when you are there,

But your home is not your home;
You end because you never end,
You are not who you think you are!'

'O but we are confused!' cried both *twins* together.
'What are we to *do*?' asked *Perdva*.

'You have returned in order to return,
You were born in order *not* to be,
You have seen because you cannot see,
You are there when you are here,
You have returned in order to return!'

'It seems we must go back, O my *brother*,' said *Pera-vaze* then, but at the instant that she thought to speak the tent and voice and all vanished from around them.

In the Palace in the morning, the *King* awoke to hear the insects and birds singing in the garden near his chamber. The sun was shining and the halls of the Palace were filled with a delightful warmth. He arose at once, and gloried in the day, and went to wake his friend the *Damsel of the Mountains*, to show her that the cold spell had gone, that the fields lay in a moist and fruitful mist, the river was flowing, and the realm was quick with life again. They went up together to the terrace, where the *guards* were yawning and stretching and starlings and blackbirds were twittering in the minarets. The sky above was clear and cloudless and bright blue, and fragrant breezes blew in their faces.

'Let us wake our *children*,' said the *damsel* to the *King*. 'Let us have them join us in this pleasant hour!'

So they went down and entered the bedchamber of *Perdva* and *Peravaze*. They called out to them to arise and enjoy the sweetness of the day.

But in their beds the forms made no sounds or movement. The *parents* approached in horror to find that each lay still and cold and dead.

'It cannot *be*!' cried the *King*, ripping away the covers of

first *Perdva*'s and then *Peravaze*'s bed, to find them lying
all unclothed and breathless there.

But the *maiden* leapt forward from her grieving and
disbelief at the sight, seizing first the boy's shoulder and
then the dead girl's arm. The red marks, scars of the lion's
teeth and the interloper's lips, were *gone*, and the skin was
as smooth and white as if they'd never been! Yet in every
other way they were exactly as *Perdva* and *Peravaze*!

'*Who are they*?' whispered the *Damsel of the Mountains*
in terror. '*Whose are these bodies*?'

At this juncture the Empress fell silent, and her audience
looked up from the fire into which they had been gazing. Her
face was distorted, red with rage. Like the bursting of a
damned-up torrent, she released a powerful cry.

'*This is not the tale I intended to tell*!'

They all looked at her, saying nothing.

'*This is not the tale I intended to tell*!' she roared once more
in a great accusing voice.

'This is hardly *our* fault, mistress,' muttered the Grand
Vizier.

The Empress looked furiously around at them. 'Yes but it
is!' she cried. 'It *must* be!'

'No great Queen, it is the fault of this *place*!' then said
Amina with fervour. 'All the stories end bitterly here, and all
our mouths are ever full of death and defeat!'

'It's true,' said Fhumdullah to Gondrat, 'I do feel uncommonly low.'

'Each of them realises that this has indeed been the
tendency of their mind,' said the Vizier, looking from face to
face. 'It has crept upon them, this dark mood, all unexpectedly, penetrating all their thoughts and appraisals.'

'Well,' replied Gondrat. 'It's not as if we *had* a great deal to
be thankful for. I think it a perfectly reasonable mood,
considering, and the fact that it's unanimous only recom-
mends it more, really.'

'Stop!' shouted Hamid bin Talal. 'We may always resist,
while we draw breath! We may fight! We may die trying, if
we must die!'

The eunuchs looked very uneager but said nothing.

Amina snatched up the corner of the Empress's robe and kissed it. 'O Queen of Life,' she whispered urgently, 'we cannot stay in Ctesiphon, for it defeats us and destroys our will! We must return to Bagdad, whatever the risk!'

'*It* defeats us too,' remarked Gondrat.

'Bagdad is a vile and faithless city,' said the Empress, 'Ctesiphon is pure, clean and constant.'

'But it is the *past*, O Celestial One, that is why it may remain so,' continued Amina. 'It does not serve us well in this present instant, and we must think also of the future. Bagdad at least contains life, and therefore hope!'

'The future and the past are one,' said the Empress slowly. 'Why do we need hope, when we *have* triumph? In the *present*!'

'But, O Surpassing Woman,' said the Vizier, 'perhaps, for purely tactical reasons, we might allow ourselves to imagine them temporarily separate. Matters being, in this nether tense, not entirely satisfactory, as I believe we all agree. We would not want discredit to come to the past, nor limitation to the future.'

'Indeed, O mistress,' added Amina, 'consider the future towards which your needy realm even now is rushing!'

'I *am* the future,' proclaimed the Empress, starting to shout again, '*already*!'

The rebounding echoes of her voice, however, were caught up imperceptibly by another sound, a weird creaking, groaning and screeching, which, instead of dying away began steadily to grow.

The eunuchs burst shrieking from the door, followed by the boy Gharib, who ran and stopped, and turned and ran again. The Captain and Ibn staggered after, carrying the Empress, as the rumblings increased. Then finally came the Prince of Stars passively hurried along by Amina, and the Vizier, sighing and walking slowly with his hands behind his back.

As they reached the middle of the square the noise rose sharply, and, with a thunderous roar, the entire roof of the great *Taq-e-Kisra* collapsed.

8 An Evening with Zardin al-Adigrab

The distant mysterious booming sound slowly died away.

Under a starry sky the southern detachment of the Ripe Fruit Party sat listening by their fire. The river rippled by quietly beside them, rocking their war-boat, making a faint sucking noise, while the song of the crickets pulsed on steadily.

'O Zardin al-Adigrab,' then presently asked a voice as they turned back to their conversation, 'can it ever be wrong to be happy?'

Arm in arm they sat, their serious young faces warmed by the orange light, their eyes fixed now on their leader. Plumes of sparks rose curling from the blaze and vanished into the darkness. The rinds and scraps of a meal lay all about.

Zardin al-Adigrab stared pensively, saying nothing.

So a pretty youth with a large two-bladed scimitar through his belt suggested, 'It were wrong, if you were *hiding*, or dishonest, or denying That Which is Within.'

'Nay, but if you were doing *that*,' said another, 'you would not *truly* be happy!'

'O Zardin al-Adigrab,' asked several, 'how do you rule?'

'When the fire is fanned,' Zardin al-Adigrab said slowly, with a dream-like gesture, 'air and earth and wood – the flames rise like cedars of gold.'

The Party turned and stared at the fire. Then someone said:

'And yet, by far the majority of sons and daughters of the earth are *not* possessed of happiness!'

'No, indeed,' said a large, ruddy-faced young woman, 'and yet they would all have it if they could!'

'But they *can*!' cried a number of voices at once.

'Then why do they not?' asked the young woman eagerly.

'O Zardin al-Adigrab!' But Zardin al-Adigrab was gazing

wordlessly off into the darkness beyond the lamp of the lookout who was watching the river for the Court Party.

'Perhaps they do not *know* they could have it!' suggested someone else.

'They had it, you see, and then lost it – they think forever!'

'But how could they lose it?'

'Because they tried to *keep* it!'

'But how – But when – O Zardin al-Adigrab!'

'Once there was a man . . .' said Zardin al-Adigrab finally, and the tongues hushed.

'Is it a *tale*?' whispered someone breathlessly. 'And That Which is Within is without . . . ?'

Zardin looked around, grimly smiling. 'And once there was *not*-a-man,' he went on. 'And yet they were, and were *not*, one and the same man, to whom happened, and yet *failed* to happen, the adventure of –'

The Never Harvested Field

'*O Zardin al-Adigrab!*' cried the dismayed yet eager Party.

Once there was, and was *not* (as I have explained) a man in whose life there was no joy – and who wondered why. He gazed around him at his neighbours and his friends, and he saw that they lived, ate fish and bread and sweetmeats, they married, shared beds, and produced children, they were born and grew old and died, yet none were ever completely happy, and most were quite generally miserable.

'How did I ever get the idea one *could* be happy?' he asked himself, and yet the matter continued to trouble him. His anxiety grew; he could not stay calm, and all his peace of mind deserted him.

So he divorced his wife and signed over all his goods to his children, and decided to go about the earth seeking for a people who were happy, in order that he might try to become one of them.

Thus he journeyed for nine years and nine months about the wearisome world, inspecting melancholies and boredoms, sampling griefs and discouragements, hearing the tales of anguish and emptiness from a thousand voices and seeing them in a thousand eyes, in places of misery and opulence, in rude houses and great. And when he asked, he heard:

'Ah happiness! Some part of that we have – that is to say – we had it once, but somehow, we know not how, it slipped away!'

For to none was the idea of joy remote, all had once beheld it – but *hold* it, that they could not!

So the *traveller* travelled on, until at last he came one day into a little farming village in the *Georgian Caucasus*, surrounded by blowing fields of golden grain, hard by towering mountains, from which the deep blue *Kuban* flows swift and cold. Here the air was clear and fresh, and even to breathe it gave the *searcher for happiness* a sense of promise. The unclouded sun shone brightly, making the waters glitter, and deepening the greens and indigoes and yellows and browns to the rich hue of a delightful dream. The cool wind from the highlands pulled at the roots of his hair, and caused all the growing things on every side to dance in constant motion, as if in ecstasy.

The *people* of the village welcomed him courteously, and the *traveller* at once saw in their eyes and faces the lightness and pleasure which had become but a phantasm to him.

'Are you happy?' he cried.

'Of course,' replied they modestly, 'but we are also busy, for it is the harvest season. Come and help us bring in the grain, and we will gladly offer you what we can of hospitality and cheer.'

The *traveller* quickly tossed aside his jacket and went out with the harvesters to reap the golden food. And no one could complain that he did not do his share, and no one could say that he worked with less joyous a heart than those around him, though to do *more* so no heart could attain. For the *peasants* every one were of so radiant a disposition, and so brimming of soul with happiness, that the *traveller* marvelled, and watched as they laboured the

hard labour as though it were the sport most pleasing in
life to all of them.

Soon he was handing his last bundle to the smiling *old
woman* who was carrying them back to the rick for him,
and turned to survey what had been done. All the fields
were down, but for a single plot that nestled in a bend of
the *Kuban*, shaded here and there by tall green trees. The
traveller looked at this small field in wonder that it had
been neglected, for it seemed more perfect even than all
the rest, and its grain shone even more sweet and pleasing
than the others. And yet the *villagers*, arm in arm, had
turned to return to their homes and refreshments, so the
traveller called out to them, saying:

'My new friends! Is there not something more to do
before we rest? Have we not forgotten this one fine field,
yonder, in the bend of the river, blowing delightfully
among the trees?'

They turned, and it seemed to him that some smiled
shyly, and others murmured together the same expression, which he could but uncertainly catch: '*A year of life
and an instant of desire.*'

'But what do you mean?' he cried. Finally one tall
peasant spoke out clearly, saying:

'This is the field we never harvest, though it, like the
others, is a source of the good fortune we enjoy. Each year
it seeds itself and grows, and each year we let it be, and yet,
as you see, it does not become tangled or base, nor does the
quality of its fruit decline.'

And then, speaking no further, nor seeming inclined to
accept any further questions, they went on, so the *traveller* satisfied himself with the answer he had received and
accompanied them.

Back in the village, light spirits and merriment everywhere ruled as the harvest festival was begun, and beers
and grain wines, pies and stews and melons and delicate
roasted birds were heaped up on trestles on the common.
Rude music squawked from strings and droned from bags,
and the rough boots of the *peasants* and their *women*
stamped in the clay, the sweaty sun-reddened faces

whirled around, and coarse shouts of laughter, a laughter which itself could not have been purer, rang out in the air.

The *traveller* did not hold back, but joined and danced with everyone, young and old, drank deeply of the bitter brown beer, and ate his fill of every kind of food.

But after a while, weary and contented, he sat down on a barrow by the wall of a cottage and watched the others, marvelling once again to himself.

'Indeed,' he said, 'these *are* the people I have sought! Happiness is their very being! But how have they done it? *Why* are they so happy? For in my travels I have seen many another harvest and many another village such as this, yet they, though often slightly less miserable than the cities, were never like *this* in joy and blessedness!'

And as he had leisure he observed the *villagers*, trying to discern somewhat in their bearing or their behaviour that might unwrap the matter for him. He saw at once that they were a very proper people, who even now, on the most boisterous day of their year, never once became lewd or licentious even in suggestion. Modest were the women and mild were the men, very nearly all of whom seemed to be married to one another, and utterly without flirtation observed the sanctity of their couples, each man to one woman. (For this was no Islamic land, where men may have more than a single wife, and slaves as well!) No crime, even of the most petty sort, sullied their deportment, and every spirit was temperate, placid, and (as he watched them queue up in an orderly fashion before the food and drink) so *patient* as to cause the *traveller*'s pulse to quicken with admiration. For this above all was a quality so terribly absent among the broken-hearted peoples of the world at large!

'Where is the unrestrainable eagerness and despair of other lands?' he asked himself. 'Where are the fervid expectations, the searing regrets?'

At a very moderate hour the *villagers* bade each other a friendly good evening and prepared to retire to their homes, which caused the *traveller* to wonder about accommodation for himself. He was soon relieved of this concern, however, when a broad-backed *farmer* and his *wife* offered him hospitality for the night, and he followed them to a comfortable cottage on the edge of the town.

'We have no proper bed, as you see,' said the *host* when they entered, 'but you may be happy enough sleeping on these mats here in the storeroom.'

The *traveller* made his thanks, and the *peasants* retired to the other room. In a very short interval all became silent, betokening they had taken their earnestly earned rest.

But the *traveller*, though his bed was everything he could desire, was so perplexed and delighted by the happiness he had seen, and indeed, could feel still like the air on all sides of him, that his mind would not stop working, and slumber was denied him.

After a while, seeing it purposeless to try, he rose and went out and sat on the cottage door-stone, breathing the air and looking out on the harvest moon that rose slowly over the stubble. Still, however, he was restless, and felt a gentle and insistent urging, that seemed to seep from the marrow of his very bones. An intoxicating delight breathed in through his nostrils, and soft fingers of year-ning probed his flesh, so that presently he could hardly bear to stay where he was and leapt to his feet.

Impulse carried him wandering out into the freshly harvested fields, and the strange joy in his heart doubled with every step he took.

'Why are the nights elsewhere in the world not as this?' he whispered. 'What causes this purity and loveliness here, that even denies me sleep and drives me willy-nilly forth to walk the plain alone? What is this fine and overpowering will-lessness inspiring me?'

No answer came from the lovely night, so he wandered on, until all at once he found himself at the edge of that one field the *villagers* chose not to harvest. It shone silver now in the moonshine, and rustled like a living thing in the breezes which seemed never to cease blowing from the mountains. The fine grain rose above the level of his shoulders, thick and even, yet as he stood in admiration before it, he noticed, just a short way away from him, what seemed to be the narrow opening of a little path.

'Now this is a curious thing,' he said to himself, 'for it can hardly lead anywhere, such a path. The field is bounded on all sides by the swift river *Kuban*, and the route to the next field or back to the last village would never pass this way.'

Nonetheless, he found himself drawn by the path, which he entered and followed inwards, like a small fragrant hallway through the shadows. Here and there other passageways branched off through the rustling grain, and one of these he eventually took, creeping quietly now, though he knew not why.

Presently he came to the edge of a small flattened-out place, where he discovered a sight which quickly made him feel he had solved the field's secret. A young man and a young woman here sat arm in arm alone, with their backs to him, and all oblivious in the obscurity, fused their mouths in a passionate and unceasing kiss, their heads nodding slowly.

The *traveller* smiled a smile then, and cautiously withdrew. At another turning he indistinctly observed two young people surrounded by wine jugs and food, gazing steadfastly into one another's eyes, hand clasping hand.

At another place he glimpsed two people in the last stages of undress embracing among the corn.

Soon he came to the trunk of a tree rising from the grain, and sitting down on a root there, allowed himself a subtle laugh.

'So,' said he, 'mystery shall be made clear! In many another town and village have I seen such a place as this. All unknown to the greedy eyes of propriety the lovers come, breathing love and sighs, fluttering like moths in the moonlight. Once, perhaps twice in the brief days of affection's freedom they adventure, then onward to the life of the world, the homes, the children, the passing of the coffee cups! Fondly they will remember this night and place, when all there was was love and themselves!

'Indeed, how quaint and delightful a tradition this is, to

make the field itself a constant – "unharvested" in fact! –
openly admitted by all! How humane and fine, and yet
how modest a convention! And indeed, rather unlike the
outward firmness and decorum of this splendid folk.'

While he was musing thus to himself, he suddenly felt
the light touch of a hand upon his right arm. Recovering
from the alarm he was at first afflicted with, he quickly
looked around to his right. But, most surprisingly, he saw
nothing at all.

'How curious!' he said. 'And yet I must be imagining it.'

And so, leaning back against the tree, he fell once more
to considering the happy *villagers*.

'It does indicate,' he ruminated, 'the finest degree of
self-knowledge in this primitive society, that they should
so carefully set aside a lovely location of this sort for their
youth. But simply to have such a field of play cannot in itself be the source of their joy, for, as I have said, it is not by
any means unique in the world.'

Just then, however, a hand quickly and lightly stroked
his *left* arm, causing the *traveller* to jump up and peer
around to his left, his heart beating. But once again there
was nothing to be seen.

'However,' he muttered to himself, 'I am certainly not
mistaken that it occurred, so I will see what I may see.'

So resolved, he crept around the back of the tree, where
he found the entrance to yet another pathway, this one
partly blocked by a low-reaching bough. Getting down on
his hands and knees, he crawled under the obstacle and
found himself in a little smoothed-out place, even darker
than the others he had seen. Hardly had he arrived when
his lips were tenderly kissed, and two arms wrapped
around him. The warm and unmistakable bosom of a
woman brushed against his chest.

His senses drowning in a delight entirely strange and
unknown, yet somehow anticipated, the *traveller* could by
no means resist these blandishments, and shortly began
himself to return them. Still embracing, they drew their
faces slightly back to look at each other. Gradually, he
could see that the *maiden* in his arms had round and

pleasant features and a smile upon her lips, while her eyes sparkled brightly with excitement. She drew him in further to her little place and arranged the growing grain to curtain them off by themselves completely. Then they fell to kissing once again, and for a longer period.

Finally she drew her lips away and brought forth a skin of wine and offered it him. He swallowed some of the strong green drink, and it burned his throat, and filled his limbs with fire, and ran from the corners of his mouth and down his neck. Then he passed it to her and she raised it to drink also, and the wine ran from the corner of her mouth and down her neck and into her hidden bosom, and they both laughed, and clasped each other and drank again.

They lay in the flattened grain soon after and embraced, and the *traveller* could smell the body of the *maiden* and the rich dusty grain all at once. She wrapped herself around him and kissed his ear and whispered,

'I saw you in the fields, you were working very hard. Your limbs were strong and golden like a mountain-lion, and your skin shone with the glistening moisture of your toil. You were beautiful. I admired your dark beard, and the whiteness of your teeth when you laughed – any woman would have. I wanted you. You were beautiful.'

The *traveller* did not know what to say, so he seized the *maiden* and kissed her with the greatest intensity imaginable.

Then, when her mouth was free, she asked him:

'But you, passionate *traveller*, did *you* want *me*?'

'O assuredly!' he replied at once, still pushing forward his hungry mouth.

'But did I please you!' she eagerly went on, kissing him and pushing him back. 'What did I do that you liked? How did I seem? Did you see my own special magic – did you sense it within? Or did I simply move graciously and well? Did I appear strange and desirable and foreign? Or did you feel you had always known me?'

'You are the only woman in the world!' cried the confused but enthusiastic *traveller*.

She seemed surprised and tried to draw away and look at

him again in inquiry but he forcibly drew her forward, drowning her hesitations in caresses and smothering her questions in kisses. As if overcome with his amazing ardour she began presently to reach, almost in resignation, for her fastenings. Before long she had removed all clothing, and he had followed her example, and it was spread out beneath them in the grain.

In the *traveller*'s ears while they embraced was the soft sifting of the grain, its crackling when they moved, and beyond that the sweeping sound of the wind in the high tassels above them, and beyond that the lovely silence of the night. The faint moonlight filtered down into their dark place, and fell on their pale skin. He sensed the cool, mountain air strangely on his unclothed body, and how wonderfully it contrasted with the delicious warmth of the maiden beneath him. He tasted her with his mouth and felt her with his hands, and she reciprocated in every particular, and at length they denied each other nothing.

Many sweet hours thus were passed, and yet the darkness showed no sign of abating. They sat hand in hand, eye peering into eye, and then again and again sank down to embrace in the shivering golden grass. It seemed to the *traveller* that no delight had ever been, or could ever be so sweet as this.

Yet finally, as the night went on and on, weariness beset them both, and sleep closed the eyelids of the *maiden*. For some short while the *traveller* admired her peacefulness and the rising and falling of her breast, before he too settled himself beside her and fell into a slumber that was warm and dreamless.

When he awoke – he knew not after how long – it was still dark, but the *maiden* and her clothes were gone. Quickly the *traveller* also dressed himself and rose and left the little place and made his way rapidly out of the grain field. Just as he was entering the village the sun began to rise, and light began to fill the clear air.

He arrived quietly on his bed of mats as his *hosts* were rising, so that they did not notice his absence. This was as he wished, for already he was concerned about the reputation of his *lover*.

'This town is the happiest abode of men or women,' said he to himself. 'Though I know not the reason, nonetheless, I am certain that no better place can be found. I shall stay here and work as a farmer, if they will have me, and I shall find out the beautiful *maiden* and marry her and live with her here.'

He proposed to his hosts that he stay and work for them and they readily agreed to the idea. Not only were they glad of him, but he soon found himself freely accepted by all the folk, who were untroubled by jealousy, hostility or any sort of selfishness. Their lives were consumed in joyful toil, their eyes were filled with light, their mouths with laughter and their hearts with kindness and warmth. No hardship could disturb them, with the single exception of the death of one of their fellows. Then, the *traveller* observed, were their funerals animated with a strong grief and distress far in excess of any he had seen elsewhere in the suffering world. Nor was this strange, he thought, considering the happiness and plenty they were able to live in!

'Lucky are they,' said he, 'that the whole hungry, evil world has seemingly not found them here!'

With discretion, he set out to discover the identity of his *companion* in the grain field, taking the greatest possible care not to imply that he had known one of her description before. He dreamed of her daily and nightly, and marriage with her was his only vision. He did not return to the field, but spent his extra hours in town, conversing with the old women, asking about the maiden girls, and keeping his eyes about him. At last, one old *grandmother*, she in fact, who had carried grain for him on the harvest day, told him of a certain *girl*, daughter of the *ox-keeper*, who lived nearby. The *traveller* at once concluded that this was she whom he sought.

He haunted the same street, until at length he caught a glimpse of the handsome *girl* at the doorway.

'O 'tis certain!' he cried. 'I can *feel* her, without doubt; it

is *her* motion, the very movement of her walking!'
Keeping back, he observed her until his conviction
became unshakable, and he ran to his friends and urged
them to present him to the *ox-keeper*, her father. When
this was done, he wasted little talk in asking the *man* for
permission to marry his *daughter*.

'Well, likely this would be a profitable enough thing,'
replied he, 'but some consultation should be had first.'

A screen was established in the room, behind which the
daughter sat, unseen to the *traveller*, and she peered at
him carefully through an aperture, whilst the *ox-man* and
his *wife* had words with him about the matter. The *suitor*
was surprised enough about these curious arrangements,
but was joyful in heart, and did not question them.

'Now,' said the *husband*, 'do you intend to stay here and
live in the village? We do not wish our daughter to leave it.'

'This can I understand,' cried the *traveller*, 'for no more
joyful place flourishes above or below the sun! And you
may be sure that my intention is only to remain here and
farm and live among you forever, if you will have me!'

The *ox-keeper* and his *wife* looked at each other with
grave expressions of approval at this speech. Then the
ox-keeper asked:

'Do you, however, yet have a knowledge of our customs
and practices, and are you fully versed in the duties a
husband owes and is due from a wife?'

'O yes honoured father,' replied the *traveller* soberly.
'In my sojourn here I have taken particular care to observe
the ways of your folk, and now not only do I know them
perfectly, but I find they are in exact harmony with the
convictions of my heart.'

'Well, this is good,' said the *ox-keeper*, 'but there are
other matters. You see that though we are not miserable,
yet neither are we blessed with riches. No sizeable dowry
can be expected for our daughter.'

But the *traveller* only smiled and said that anything,
indeed, nothing at all would suffice him. 'Truly,' said he,
'I admire your *daughter* so well, that I gladly would *pay* to
have her!'

This remark caused his *interlocuters* both to give him very hard looks, and the *wife* to ask, 'Truly, how do you *know* her, so to "admire" her?'

The *traveller* balked in dismay, seeing where his enthusiasm had carried him.

'I have . . . observed her in your doorway!' he replied in a lame and faltering manner.

'*Do* you know our customs?' then pointedly asked his *beloved*'s *mother*.

'Yes, truly!'

'We know you to be a good worker, and diligent,' said the *husband*, more kindly, 'and this makes us confident you could contribute to our *daughter*'s and our *village*'s prosperity. But we will have none of your foreign notions of marriage, your newfangled fantasies. We are sure you are just as every other man and woman in these matters. The question is – are you equal to the task of being a *husband*, and a *father*, as well as a farmer?'

Desperately, the *suitor* subdued his heart, and took again a stern and sober demeanour.

'I believe I am,' he said.

'Well, then, lastly,' went on the *ox-keeper*, as his *wife* frowned slightly but fell silent, 'there is a practice among us that our daughters as well as our sons must fully and whole-heartedly *comply* with any marriage plans made for them. But, lest this seem unfair to you, I should say that it has proven to have benefits for a husband. A daughter, once freely agreeing to be a wife, is ever expected to behave as one responsible for her own actions. It is not allowed her to say that the man allotted to her is not to her liking, nor that marriage itself is a condition she has no talent for.'

'Well,' laughed the *traveller* inwardly, 'in many a land this also is expected, though no free choice is given! And in many a land, may this and much more be expected, and full unlikely to be received!'

But aloud, he said:

'I am no less proud than any man. But it is my deepest desire that your *daughter* only marry me if she wishes, and, indeed, that she *not* marry me if she wishes it not.'

'That is generally best,' agreed the *ox-keeper*, and he and his *wife* appeared to look upon the *traveller* with somewhat more favour.

Then he turned to the concealed part of the room and said:

'Daughter, you have heard what this prospective partner and aspirer to your person has proposed. To your *mother* and myself we will say that his attributes seem altogether acceptable. But tell us first, are you of a mind to marry in this season of your life?'

A feminine voice replied calmly from behind the screen. It spoke, of course, in different tones and of different matters than before, but the *traveller* was sure he recognised it, and soon cool shivers were infesting his body.

'Indeed, O *father*, I see no particular reason preventing it. It seems entirely right and proper to marry, and I do not feel myself too young to do so now. Truly, I am somewhat weary now of the limitations which govern unmarried women such as myself. I feel I can make a fuller contribution to our village than I presently do, and I believe I would enjoy such duties as children and home.'

The *traveller* left in delight and confusion and set about immediately to build a house. A fine cottage rose, and he worked hard in the village to make his way, so that at the end of half a year he was able to marry the *ox-keeper*'s *daughter*. She came demurely veiled to his house, and that night they engaged in its sheltering darkness. She made no reference to the unharvested field (as indeed, he noticed no one did), and so neither did he, charmed at the extravagent care his *wife* took of her reputation, and quite content with the domesticity of their situation. They began happily to live.

Soon there was a child, and then after that there was a second. The *traveller* came back along the riverside with the other village men, and saw his *wife* among the other village wives washing their pans in the cold running water. The horsemen came back from birding among the mountains, and their horses stooped to drink. The wives tucked up their blowing skirts from the wind and sang, and their pans flashed in the water, their children laughed and splashed around them.

Then they came home together and ate at their table, and he visited her cot in the evenings, often at first, and then less often after a period. They danced together when the village celebrated its harvest festivals, and listened together to the jokes and anecdotes told at winter's gatherings. On occasion they had sharp words over the buying of food, or the treatment of children, but soon their anger would subside. Generally, they lived in great peace.

Gradually, though, a curious sensation overtook the *traveller*. Gradually, he began to weary of the life he was living.

'Everyone around me, including my *wife*, is so utterly, almost unnaturally *happy*!' said he to himself. 'Just exactly as happy as they were when first I saw them. Yet life is here as it is elsewhere, in fact. They marry, they have children, they work, and yet where the rest of the world, and I, are brought to sighs, then tears and numbing woe, they but smile and smile and laugh and laugh, as if only breathing the air was the richest of fortunes. And yet I breathe this air too, just as they do!'

He looked about the village day after day, at the women and the men, living each with the other in perfect contentment. No desires except those dutiful troubled them. No lusts or eagerness for forbidden things darkened their features.

'This life seems all they *can* desire,' said he. 'Yet my *wife* grows heavy about the belly and hips, and only infrequently parts the blinds around her bed and admits me to her body at night. And I do not press, because I am no young panther either, but my body also grows slack, and my once ardent desire is cooled when I see that my *wife* touches our children more fondly than myself. And this will only continue, and doubtless we shall both contentedly enough die. Yet they are all *happy* here!'

These melancholy thoughts at once recalled to mind the first evening he ever spent in the village. With great vividness the memory returned, of the cool air and stars, of the rustle of the blowing wheat, and the taste of the wine and his *lover*'s mouth and body, of how surprising and warm she had been against him then.

'Then truly she was my *lover*, and not but my *wife*!' said he ruefully. And it at once seemed to him that any joys they had had on the curtained bed in his house were inferior to those of their first meeting, and that indeed, from the vast joy of his arrival, his happiness in the village had only steadily ebbed away. Soon the picture of the night in the field by the bend in the river fixed itself in his mind and refused to leave him. Again and again he thought of it, and he wept as every detail was recalled to him. 'O, my *beloved* . . .' he whispered to himself at night.

'Do you not miss the sweetness of our love at first?' he asked her, but she replied very straightforwardly: 'I am as happy now as I was then.'

'Alas,' said the *traveller* to himself, 'but it is not so with me!' And he went apart from her and regretted again the memories life had once been able to bring him. When it became again harvest season such sorrow and restless dissatisfaction came upon him that even sleep began to vanish from his bed, and he grew wan and unwell.

Finally, upon the harvest festival evening, he arose in the darkness, glanced quickly at the closed curtain of his *wife*'s bed, and made his way stealthily out of his cottage and across the land towards the never-harvested field.

'It is the law of the world that all things change and nothing remains the same,' considered he as he went. 'Perhaps if I but look upon the place of my early joy I shall see how alteration has affected it as well as me, and it shall cease to haunt me in recollection.'

Though he had not once gone there in all the intervening years, as he approached the field he could sense again that excitation he had felt before, the passionate sensation of life that seemed to inhabit all its surrounds like a spirit. The harvest moon shone down brightly, the breezes that were never still sifted in the rich grain with a soft, rustling sound, the lovely smell of earth and air and plant rose up in his nostrils as a magic gas, drugging him with love and vigour.

Entering one of the little pathways in the thick maze of growth, his heart began to burn with desire, and he felt a glowing warmth in the flesh of every part of his body. In astonishment, he looked down in the dimness at his frame, and it seemed to him that he had been restored in vitality and form to just the condition he had enjoyed on his first arrival in the village, many years before! With his hands he felt his hard, strong legs and arms, and his bushy beard and thick hair, and marvelled. Filled with trembling and indescribable emotion, he went forward slowly through the passageways, turning here and there without design.

Soon he came to the edge of a little flattened-out space, partially screened with grain, where, peering carefully into the shadows, he saw two young people sitting side by side, partly undressed, with their clothes about them. He watched as they kissed each other tenderly, and took each other's hands, and listened as they spoke.

'I saw you make that wonderful jest beside the winter's fire,' whispered the *young woman*, 'when everyone laughed and laughed until tears actually glistened in their eyes. Your face shone with the spark within you, and you looked like you were ready to make a thousand more just as good. Your body seemed warm and rounded and desirable in the firelight. You were beautiful. I admired your wit and your personality – any woman would have – I admired the gleam in your eyes and the quick skilfulness of how you told the jest, catching everyone by surprise. I admired your cheerful and carefree aspect as you tossed back your head and laughed. I wanted you. You were beautiful.'

And she kissed him, and he grasped her arms and said: 'I saw you standing in the doorway of your husband's house in tranquil thought, on the day in autumn. You were perfectly still, and your eyes looked deep and profound, and your clothes sat gracefully on you. You leaned your shoulder lightly against the door-frame and your hand rested on the post, your fingers motionless but curled in a lovely, listless expression. You were beautiful. I admired the stillness that spread out from you, and the graces of your body like a young cypress tree, as I imagined you beneath your clothes, firm and slim and reposed. And I admired your handsome face – any man would have. I wanted you. You were beautiful.'

And he raised his hands to her shoulders and began kissing her ardently, and then, after a moment, with hands reaching vaguely for each other's remaining garments, the two started to sink down together on to the floor of trembling grain. The *traveller* moved on, his mind all a turmoil.

Presently he turned down another little pathway in the rustling obscurity, and came upon two more people seated, deep in quiet conversation. By their side was bread and a wineskin, but their attention was all for each other, and they seemed not even to notice the arrival of the *stranger*.

But as he gazed at them in their sheltering darkness he was all at once overcome with amazement and dismay. For the *man* resembled a certain man from the village, or perhaps one who would be his younger brother, and the *woman* was without any question his own *wife*! But though it was certainly she – he was much too familiar with her to be mistaken – it was not she as he had left her asleep in the house in the village! Instead she looked just as she had years before, not when he married her perhaps, but in the healthiest bloom of her life, after the birth of their second child.

As he watched aghast, the *man* stroked her hair, saying:

'I saw you on the summer's day, bending with your pans by the river, with your skirts tucked up by your waist, and your sleeves rolled up to your elbows. The river flowed by your ankles and your lovely white legs, shapely and strong, filled my heart with exaltation. I wanted you. My soul trembled with joy at the graceful line your arm and back made when you reached to smooth away the ruffling tendrils of your hair. The sun shone on you and glittered on the rippling water around you. You were beautiful! I admired the glow of your skin, the way you caressed your little children and smiled and sang to them in a pure voice even while you worked. I admired your strong healthy loveliness – any man would have. I wanted you. Your clothes flapped and clung around you in the wind, shaping you like a warm, living statue. You were beautiful.'

All unable to move or speak, the *traveller* continued to watch as his *wife* received the kisses of the *man*, and smiling back at him, said:

'I saw you ride your grey horse across the fields, when you came back that day from birding in the mountains. Your hair blew in the wind and your shirt was dark with sweat and a dozen birds hung at your belt. I admired your impetuous motion and the fierce proud arch of your eyebrows. I admired the way you rode your great horse with such certainty and mastery – any woman would have. The horse was not cowed, nor was he wilful, but your will and your joy were his also. I admired your rough manly clothes, and your bronzed face, and your bold laughing eyes surveying all that you saw. You were beautiful. I admired your strong voice calling out greetings to your neighbours and answers to their questions. I admired your powerful-looking arms and legs, and I wanted them, and I wanted you. You were beautiful.'

Then they took each other in their arms and began to kiss in a fervent manner and make as lovers do. The *traveller* knew not how to act, nor exactly what to feel, for such was the staleness of his marriage that he had not felt jealousy for many a year. But as his suddenly young *wife* gradually unclothed herself he was struck again with unbearable regret and longing, and tears started up in his eyes. Here in the scented, shadowy grain field, she seemed to be her fullest and most lovely self again, and he remembered how she had been, and thought how, despite his supposed love, he had hardly noticed her beauty until the day he realised it had faded. Now she and the *horseman* were having the utmost delight of each other, and he awoke as from a dream, and rushed blindly through the grain as hot weeping obscured his sight.

At length he fell down in another place and sobbed in great confusion. But then he became aware of soft hands stroking his hair and gently soothing his back and shoulders. He wiped his eyes and rolled over, and saw that a *woman* was kneeling beside him and smiling.

'Weep not,' she said, in comforting tones, and he felt that her voice and face were strangely familiar. She bent down and kissed him on the forehead, and said:

'*You* are admirable too. You deserve to have been loved by a thousand lovers! *I* admired you greatly – any woman would have. You were beautiful. I saw you in the fields, on the day you came, you were working very hard. Your limbs were strong and golden, like a mountain-lion, and your skin shone with the glistening moisture of your toil. You were beautiful. I admired your dark beard, and the whiteness of your teeth when you laughed – any woman would have. I wanted you. You were beautiful.'

All at once the *traveller* realised to his stupefaction that *this* was the *woman* who had been his lover on the night of the harvest festival so many years before! It had not been his *wife* at all, for everything had been shadowy and dark, and he had all along mistaken her! What was more, the voice he was listening to was familiar to him both from that first night, and now also because it resembled, though youthful, that of the aged *grandmother*, his neighbour, who had carried sheaves for him in the field on harvest day, and advised him on the young unmarried women!

The *woman* smiled and kissed him again, and offered him wine to drink.

'But you say nothing,' she said, with a certain sadness. 'Do you not admire me? Do you not remember me? Why are you here? Did I not please you?' Then she laughed. 'One said he admired my fiery eye, and the whirling way I danced and stamped my feet. While another said I had sat beside my mother like a dove, white and obedient and true. Yet another loved my wisdom, my knowledge of history and seasons, and my firm counselling of the younger girls, while another one delighted in my giddiness and wildness and laughter.' Then she looked wistfully at him again, and his unbelieving recognition grew, that it *was* an old village *woman*, grown years younger, after all!

'Are you not like the rest of us?' she asked. 'Was there not one moment some fineness *you* saw? Did you never once see me, or another, and say, "I would have *her*, and I could"?'

'I am a *traveller*,' he whispered to her, 'I have not understood.'

'Oh!' she laughed, and opened the bosom of her garments and hugged him to her. 'Oh, poor one, poor one! How much have you missed! How much have you forgotten! Understand *now*, at least! Understand *now*!'

And his arms yearned to hold her, and his heart yearned to love her, but yet he thought also of his *wife* and his mind was in confusion and he knew not what to do, but pushed her back jumped up suddenly to his feet.

'Was I not beautiful?' said the *woman* then, in a voice of regret. 'Would not any man have had me?' And suddenly, horribly, she began to *age*. Wrinkles spread rapidly over her lovely face like parasites, her breasts and haunches began to shrivel, and her hair to run grey like a muddied stream. She became suddenly old again, as old as when he first had known her, and then older and older. She looked up at him and smiled a small, sad smile.

'*A year of life and an instant of desire*,' she said. 'That is our proverb. That is the evened balance of the earth. And now you have wasted one year, one instant; and the supply is not endless.'

'Do all of you . . . *do this*?' gasped out the *traveller*.

'Are there any who have not felt desire?' laughed the *old woman* quietly.

'And it is *allowed*, ignored, made legitimate!' cried out he.

'Upon one single night of the year the moon shines on the harvest of our long silence. All other seed must be sown, tended, stored away and husbanded for fear. On one single night we simply reap and eat; one night – but it is enough. That is the balance of the earth.'

'But your bodies, your beauty? How is it you can be so changed?'

'Poor *traveller*, are you baffled utterly then by the passing of a year; a month; an hour? Can you not imagine me as I was? Others can! Has your memory failed you already? Little wonder you are fruitless in all your searchings!'

'And is this one riotous evening the source of all your happiness?' He was all but overcome. 'To *have* but once what you simply *want*?'

'Does it seem so terrible?' asked she, pitying him. 'Is this barter so frightening? But there is something *else* which is more so! That is *not* ever to taste what you hunger for! Take heart! *You* have years left before you are warm and rotting beneath this earth! What rainbows of delight you may yet see!'

An awful coldness came over the *traveller* at these words, and he began shuddering with horror at their import. '*I* shall *die*!' he cried out weakly, as if only then, and suddenly, realising it was so. '*I shall die*!' he cried again. It was as though, despite the worlds of misery he had viewed, he never before had known of this final and greatest woe. And he shook his head desperately and turned from her and took to his heels. As hard as he could he ran from the never-harvested field and across the stubble to the village, arriving there just as the sun was rising. Everything was as normal, his *wife* was cooking, his *children* were shouting, the village was preparing to work, and yet now to him it was all utterly changed and foreign.

He could stay no longer in the place where people lived in such a manner. Soon he slipped away, deserting his second family, and walking along the road back towards the world he had once left behind, he ruminated aloud.

'To be happy,' he said, 'it seems one must but choose to be. If the people of the world are not, it can only be because they will not reach out their hands to take that which is offered them.' And though discouraged by his experience, his calmness and peace of mind with these words returned to him at last.

There was a long silence. The Ripe Fruit Party was enthralled. The orange light of the now subdued fire glowed on their faces.

Then, as one, they began to sing, slowly, a hymn:

We are not like them, the worried ones,
The wronged ones, the wearied ones;
No, we are not like the weeping mothers, the outraged brothers:
No, truly, we are not like the others!

We are not like the broken shahs, with their broken laws and broken jaws,
We are not like the bloodied ones,
The muddied ones, the accursed ones.
We are not the woeful ones, the tearful, fearful, wretched ones!

No! We are not them, the morbid ones,
The boring, lonely, destroying ones;
We do not need them, ruined daughters, jealous fathers,
We do not want them, heartless husbands, hopeless lovers,
We are not of them, we are not *like* the others!

As the song died away, however, one of their members burst violently into tears. It was the young-man-lover, dressed in red and white.

'What, is it *woe*?' shouted several voices. 'Is it grief? Is it misery?'

'He lacks his beloved,' said someone.

'She was parted from me in the confusion of the audience chamber,' sobbed he. 'And in the haste of our pursuit, she somehow failed to board either of the boats. Now she will miss all!'

'How sad!' cried a number of the audience, enthusiastically. But Zardin al-Adigrab said nothing.

Several others, noticing, began to shout, 'Shame! Shame!'

'In this fine company, this hour of triumph, in this sweet, clear evening, does your mood depend upon *another*?' demanded a bearded youth.

'Yes, truly!' cried a young woman. 'Are you thrall to that which is not here and not now, but in fact is far away, and *past*!'

'*Past*!' cried out the lover in horror.

'Indeed!' came a dozen voices. 'Is this *love* of yours meant to cause gloom and sorrow?'

'Ought you not to love those whom you are *with*, if you are not with she whom you *love*?' demanded one.

'*Loved*!' added another.

'*Used to love*!' amplified a third.

He was pulled closer to the heat of the fire by hands half-caressing, half-rebuking.

'Are these tears for present grief? Or are they not the tears of outmoded sentiment?' cried an angry young woman, much disappointed in him. 'We thought you were one of us!'

'When she was here, he *was*,' said a young man thoughtfully.

'He did not *really* believe!' shouted several.

> 'That which we would be –
> Merely to *be* –
> Is not easily been,
> For it means struggle
> *Not* to be
> That not-being that *is* so easily
> Been.'

said Zardin al-Adigrab gravely.

'Ohhhhhhhhh!' cried the Ripe Fruit Party.

'But he's not trying hard enough!' said someone.

'What is the point of everything we have achieved, if we have unhappiness among us?' asked another.

'I can't be happy without my beloved!' now defiantly shouted the lover.

'O terrible!' cried a number of voices. Everyone appealed to Zardin al-Adigrab. The lover's love had been so fine a thing – before – but now, chance had intervened. ('Is not chance holy?' demanded one rather extreme young woman.'

The lover had suddenly become an open devotee of the other party, worshipping unseen memories, implicitly scorning the actualness and presentness of the young women at this very moment around him. What was to be made of it all?

'The young man is being ridiculous,' said Zardin al-Adigrab, 'but in one hour we are strong, and in another we become weak.'

'When That Which is Within has emerged –' began someone loudly.

'It *has* emerged!' shouted the lover. Cries rose on all sides. Matters appeared to be getting out of hand.

But then Zardin al-Adigrab began to laugh. He laughed gaily, yet bitterly, and giggled, and showed his teeth, and generally discomfited his heated followers.

The young-man-lover, however, snatched up the end of a loaf of bread and flung it at his leader, to the astonishment and scandal of all. It missed, and the miscreant quickly fell to his knees, buried his head in his arms and plugged his ears with his thumbs. Zardin al-Adigrab leapt up, crossed the circle, and kicked the lover hard with his foot, spilling him forward on his chin. The Party hushed at once, seeing his look of passionate anger. Then, oddly, after a pause he smiled, and looked around at them.

'He has rather a nice behind, does he not?' he asked, pointing.

They, somewhat scared, and uncertain whether to laugh, all nodded.

The small and withered young man, the strange and ill-sorted one, seemingly overwrought with the violence and emotion of the moment came scrambling out of his usual place on the peripheries.

'O leader-leader-*leader*!' he whined, scratching and fidgeting. 'There is a *tale* for all this! There is a *tale* to be told!'

'*Back*!' Zardin was stern and magisterial. The strange one whimpered but quickly retired again.

'For *some*,' ruled Zardin, gazing meaningfully about the gathering, 'That Which Was Within has emerged. For *others*, in their ignorance, this has yet to occur.'

'O Zardin al-Adigrab, exactly!' cried the delighted Party in relief.

'O, *leader*!' cried a young woman's voice, muffled, from the darkness. 'O! Ah! *O*!'

Here and there, periodically, from different corners of the camp, there were other cries and gasps.

The young-man-lover, however, sulked by himself among the rushes on the river-bank. Beside him sat the extinguished lookout lamp. He was watching the bodies go by. Drifting downstream in slow but steady succession, of men and women equally, they were generally nude, but on occasion partly or wholly garbed in the court costumes of Bagdad. On most could be glimpsed marks of blood and violence.

A little way away from him two Party members were copulating in the water, making a quiet splashing sound. They seemed to ignore the corpses that now and again almost brushed them as they passed.

The young-man-lover shivered, and wrapped his robes around his shoulders. It was chillier now, and the wind had risen a little. Presently he heard two people creep near, without noticing him. They were conversing. A young man's voice said: 'I piss on my lover and she pisses on me. Someday, I believe, all love will be this way. What do you think?' Another young man's voice answered doubtfully. 'Perhaps we should consult Zardin al-Adigrab.' Then they passed out of hearing.

The young-man-lover paid little attention. He was full of anger and bitterness, and toyed with his curved knife. As he watched, the body of a familiar-looking man went by, nude except for his turband, which was wrapped around his neck. The young man dully recognised him as a former Minister of Protocol.

He began to chant, quietly:

'I curse you, all you generations who came before!
I curse you all, you spoilers of the lovely world, ruiners of the fresh and beautiful!
You desecrators of happiness, staining all you touched

With your cowardice, your despicable weakness,
Your evil stupidity, your underestimating, insensitive conventions!
I curse your sickly smearing of the healthy earth!
I curse you for what you were:
I curse you, I *curse* you!

I curse your legacies also,
Your nightmare past, your adulterings and divorcings, your numberless breakings of faith;
Blemishing the unmarked faces,
Savaging earnest aspirations with the cynicism of your
Impure and stubborn and restless selfishness!
Your all-destroying laziness!
Your sophisticated passivity!
Your ugly little admissions of defeat – you stopped trying!
I curse the way you corrupted us all, would not let us believe!
I curse you for what you were, and what you did!
I curse you, I *curse* you!

He pulled the curved knife from its sheath and plunged it over and over into the soft sand of the bank. Then he let it drop and wept. Then he put it back in its sheath and buried his head in his hands.

Suddenly there was a small, surprised squeak and a heavier splash. The copulating lovers had fallen over into the river. He watched as they quickly parted and swam ashore, drew on their clothes and slipped away in different directions.

Then he stared at the river again. Then he smiled and sighed. Then the smile faded and the sighs deepened. 'O my beloved!' he whispered. Then gradually he fell asleep.

He awoke to find an arm around his waist and warm bodies on both sides of him. The arm belonged to Zardin al-Adigrab, and he had with him two beautiful young women of the Party, who sat dreamily on either hand, their heads on his and Zardin's shoulders.

'O fresh young men and girls,' Zardin was whispering, without further preamble, 'all whirling and impermanent are the world's most lovely fruits! And we too, whirling and fading like flowers, loved and destroyed in a golden delicate hour – never knowing, never suspecting, never staying still nor ceasing to decay!'

'O but Zardin al-Adigrab,' whispered one of the women, 'O Leader, tonight, but the sweetness of the decay!'

'Pinch not up the swelling, blushing lips!' exhorted Zardin. 'Blast not the unborn kisses nor waste the fragrant gasp of breath on sighs! You cannot imagine how little separates you each from each, how much is lost in wanton constancy, like stones lying forever apart in arid plains! True Faithfulness is not to this!'

'Yes it is,' objected the young-man-lover in a small voice.

Zardin al-Adigrab squeezed him warmly.

'Are we so unlike the green and growing,' he asked, 'the dipping, crying, whistling, creeping, flowing, that all around us show us images of ourselves? How fine they are and pure, *how* constant, truly, to themselves and their perishable beauty! Never does the wind lie fallow! Never does the river gather up and wait for its tributary! Nor bird alone along these bird-loud joyous banks pines and wastes its little breathing horde of riches. But sings and is! Its singing *is* its being; it can no more be without singing than sing without being! Nor can it cease to sing, or be, nor slow the flow of its being for some absent cause!

'O *be*, young man, there is nothing else! In the birdless places of imagining and death, none will be there to care for your lost hour of breath and joy! None may return to you the riches burned away in feverish thought, evaporated in sighs, dreamt away in vain exchanges for fretful cold worry and sickening suspicions!'

'I'm not *suspicious*!' objected the young-man-lover. 'She feels exactly the same way I do!'

'But *you* do not feel the way you *think* you do!' tenderly cried out Zardin al-Adigrab, and taking him fully in his arms, kissed him powerfully on the lips.

'Yes I do!' said the young-man-lover in a high voice, as

soon as he could get his mouth free.

'No you don't!' cried the two young women sleepily.

'Yes, but I *do!*' cried the young-man-lover.

'Alas no,' sighed Zardin al-Adigrab, standing and heaving him effortlessly over his shoulder. 'It's obvious you have not the slightest idea what you *actually* feel. It seems you must be shown.'

The young-man-lover tried to struggle and reach for his knife, but Zardin al-Adigrab was much too strong and pinioned his arms. He was carrying him towards his tent, leaving the two young women to fall immediately asleep in one another's arms.

'Flowers, birds, bees, bears, whales, goats, oryx's,' whimsically recited the leader as he strode through the perfumed obscurity of the evening. 'Yes, yes, without exception a forward-looking group. Charter Party members all.'

'O leader,' panted the young man, still straining to escape, 'I think I see now the light of your truth, and a very fine truth it is indeed; however –'

'No, but it is all a matter of perspective,' replied Zardin al-Adigrab. 'You can *say* you understand. But will you *really?*'

'O but yes, yes, certainly –'

'You may be sure,' said Zardin cheerfully, 'that what I do, I do for your own true betterment and well-being, and release from staling grief.'

'No, no, but you mistake my condition entirely!' protested the young man in haste. 'You see, what you have believed to be grief in me is actually only a very refined form of *pleasure!* Most certainly, separation is but a very clever form of enhancement! I lusciously enjoy these sighs and tears you see me give off, because I enjoy *anticipation* almost as much as performance!'

'*Almost* as much,' laughed Zardin al-Adigrab, and he dropped him to his feet and cuffed him soundly across the ears, then kissed him again. 'Why not *as* much?' They had reached the entrance of his green and purple tent.

'No, truly!' squeaked the young-man-lover. '*As* much! Truly!'

'Myself, I find anticipation to have its limits,' said Zardin al-Adigrab. He laughed loudly and propelled his captive through the flaps into the dark interior. A few Party members raised their heads from the grass and watched as their leader went in after him and did up the flaps from inside. Then they lowered their heads again.

No one emerged from the tent until the first light of morning.

What occurred within the tent may perhaps be surmised. What will occur when the Ripe Fruits close, as they surely must, with the Court Party, however, and what their various destinies shall finally be, can only be discovered by reading the sequel, entitled 'The Prince of Stars'.

THE PRINCE OF STARS

Book Two of The Prince of Stars in the Cavern of Time
by award-winning Canadian author Ian Dennis.

With Bagdad in revolt and the Caliphs and Kazis
destroyed, the survivors flee down the river Tigris from
the fanatical Ripe Fruit Party and its crazed and charis-
matic leader Zardin-al-Adigrab.

Across seas and deserts and cities the chase ensues; and as
they go, the characters tell each other stories that weave
into a tapestry full of mystery and romance, of an Arabia
strangely mutated from the medieval world of *The
Thousand and One Nights*.
  But even these tales cannot ward off the final confron-
tation in this vivid and violent land.

Also available from Unwin Paperbacks

All these books are available at your local bookshop or newsagent, or can be ordered direct by post. Just tick the titles you want and fill in the form below.

Name ....

Address ....

....

....

Write to Unwin Cash Sales, PO Box 11, Falmouth, Cornwall TR10 9EN.

Please enclose remittance to the value of the cover price plus:

UK: 60p for the first book plus 25p for the second book, thereafter 15p for each additional book ordered to a maximum charge of £1.90.

BFPO and EIRE: 60p for the first book plus 25p for the second book and 15p for the next 7 books and thereafter 9p per book.

OVERSEAS INCLUDING EIRE: £1.25 for the first book plus 75p for the second book and 28p for each additional book.

Unwin Paperbacks reserve the right to show new retail prices on covers, which may differ from those previously advertised in the text or elsewhere. Postage rates are also subject to revision.